W9-BGA-554

THE HUSBAND HUNT

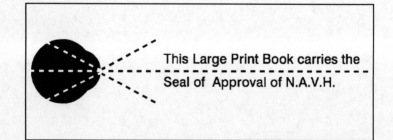

This Large Print Book carries the
Seal of Approval of N.A.V.H.

THE HUSBAND HUNT

LYNSAY SANDS

THORNDIKE PRESS

A part of Gale, Cengage Learning

GALE
CENGAGE Learning·

Detroit • New York • San Francisco • New Haven, Conn • Waterville, Maine • London

GALE
CENGAGE Learning·

LIBRARY OF CONGRESS CATALOGING-IN-PUBLICATION DATA

Sands, Lynsay.
    The husband hunt / by Lynsay Sands. — Large print ed.
      p. cm. — (Thorndike Press large print romance)
    ISBN-13: 978-1-4104-4464-6 (hardcover)
    ISBN-10: 1-4104-4464-3 (hardcover)
    1. Large type books. I. Title.
    PR9199.3.S2195H87 2012
    813'.54—dc23   2012002076

Published in 2012 by arrangement with Avon, an imprint of HarperCollins Publishers.

Printed in the United States of America
1 2 3 4 5 6 7 16 15 14 13 12

THE HUSBAND HUNT

CHAPTER ONE

"How long do you think you will be?" Lisa asked, watching her older sister carefully set a small pillbox hat on the complicated hairstyle in which her maid had arranged her tresses.

"We could be out all afternoon, Lisa. I'm afraid Lady Witherly's teas tend to drag on a bit. She will insist on every one of her grandchildren entertaining us with a musical performance." Christiana scowled and then added dryly, "Whether they have any talent for it or not."

Lisa bit back her amusement at the vexation in her sister's words. "Perhaps they will have improved since you were last there."

"Hmm," Christiana muttered dubiously as she finished with her hat. Then frowning, she turned to peer at her. "I feel awful leaving you here by yourself when you don't feel well. Maybe we should send our apologies and —"

"Don't be silly. Suzette is probably already dressed and waiting for you to collect her," she protested at once. The mention of their sister, the middle of the three Madison girls, made Christiana's frown deepen, and Lisa continued, "Canceling at this late hour would be terribly rude. Besides, it's not like I'm deathly ill. I just have a bit of a headache and a stomach complaint. A little rest and I am sure I'll be fine for this evening's season-opening ball at the Landons'."

"Well, if you're sure," Christiana said uncertainly.

"Very sure," Lisa said, trying not to fidget impatiently or seem too eager to have her gone.

"Very well then." Christiana heaved out a little sigh, gave her a quick hug, admonishing her to rest and feel better, and then headed for the door.

Lisa held on to her smile until the door closed, and then rushed to the window to watch her older sister traverse the front walk to the Radnor carriage. The moment the slender blonde climbed inside and the carriage pulled away, Lisa immediately rushed out into the hall and upstairs.

As expected, she found her maid, Bet, preparing the gown Lisa would wear that night to the Landons' ball.

Forcing a grimace, Lisa placed a hand to her forehead and moved toward the bed with a little sigh. "You can finish that later, Bet. I have a bit of a headache and should like to rest a while. Please be sure no one disturbs me."

Bet paused and stared at Lisa blankly. When her eyes narrowed suspiciously, Lisa feared she'd overplayed it, but much to her relief the maid merely nodded, laid out the gown to prevent wrinkling and headed for the door, saying, "I'll be downstairs if you need me."

Nodding, Lisa settled on the side of the bed to remove her slippers . . . only to quickly slide them back on the moment the door closed behind Bet. She then leapt up, suddenly all excited motion and activity. Bustling to her chest, she dug out the bag she'd hidden at the bottom, checked to ensure that the gift she'd so carefully wrapped for Mrs. Morgan was still inside, and then hurried to the door. She listened briefly and, hearing nothing, opened it to peer up the hall. Finding it empty, she immediately slid out of her room to scurry to the stairs.

Lisa held her breath until she got to the landing. She paused and exhaled slowly, ears straining. But when a steady silence was all that came from below, she took another deep breath and crept quickly down the steps. She was halfway to the parlor when the kitchen door at the end of the hall began to open. Panic rising in her, Lisa quickly ducked into the office to avoid discovery, praying no one saw her as she eased the door closed.

She listened at the door in hopes of hearing when it would be safe to continue on her way, but frowned when silence met her ear. Either whoever had opened the kitchen door had changed their mind and not come out after all, or someone was even now traversing the hall but the door she stood behind muffled the sound. The problem was, Lisa didn't know which would be the case.

Sighing, she shifted on her feet, impatient to be on her way, and then dropped to her knees and pressed her eye to the keyhole. Sadly, she couldn't see much of the hall through the little opening, certainly not enough to assure herself it was empty. But she knelt there long enough that she was sure anyone coming from the kitchens would have passed by now.

Getting back to her feet, she took a breath, crossed her fingers for good luck and eased the door open.

A little sigh of relief slipped from her lips when she found the hall empty. Lisa listened for a moment just to be sure no one was on the stairs and then scampered quickly up the hall to the parlor door and slid inside.

The relief she felt as she closed the parlor door was rather extreme considering she was only halfway out of the house. She still had a long way to go to make a clean getaway. Pushing that thought aside, Lisa hurried across the room and knelt to retrieve her cloak and pelisse from under the settee where she'd hidden it early that morning before the house was awake.

She quickly donned the heavy cape, pulled the hood over her head, and hooked her pelisse over her wrist. Then, clutching the gift to her chest, Lisa hurried to the French doors and peered out. The parlor overlooked the side yard of the house. As far as she could see, there was no one about.

She didn't hesitate, but eased herself through the French doors and moved quickly toward the front, silently praying that no carriages would arrive with unexpected guests, or her brother-in-law, Richard, returning from his tailor's. She was also hoping that there would be no reason for any of the servants to suddenly look out the front door or one of the front windows and spy her escape. Lisa didn't look around to be sure she wasn't seen, half suspicious that by doing so she would draw someone to a window, so hurried forward with her head firmly straight ahead.

When she reached the front gate and slipped out without anyone coming out of the house or arriving to stop her, Lisa thought she was home free. However, when she turned from pulling the front gate closed, and started to bustle up the walk, she came to an abrupt halt as her maid, Bet, suddenly stepped out of the bushes to confront her.

"I knew you were up to something when I saw you sneaking about the house this morning," Bet said with satisfaction. Her freckled face and stance were triumphant, her legs slightly parted, arms crossed over her chest, and one eyebrow arched. "Now, what are you about, my lady?"

"Oh, Bet, you gave me quite a fright," Lisa said placing a hand to her chest. "Whatever are you doing creeping about out here?"

"Never mind that. What are *you* doing creeping about out here?" Bet asked pointedly.

Lisa grimaced at the question and then straightened her shoulders and lifted her head to say sternly, or as sternly as she could ever be with Bet, who was as much a friend as a maid, "It really isn't your place to ask things like that, Bet. I am your mistress." Some of her bravado wilted under Bet's narrowing eyes, but Lisa forced herself to continue firmly. "Now I suggest you return to the house and see to preparing my gown for tonight."

"Certainly," the maid said pertly. "And I'll just mention to Handers that you left the house all by yourself without a maid to accompany you, shall I?"

Lisa's eyes narrowed at the mention of Richard and Christiana's new butler. Handers was a dear, but he would pass the information on to Richard the moment he returned. Scowling, she said, "You wouldn't."

"I would," Bet assured her firmly, and then raised an eyebrow and added persuasively, "Unless of course you want me to accompany you. Then I couldn't tell anyone. And it would be all well and proper."

Lisa sighed with frustration and glanced back toward the gate. She had been almost relieved when Mrs. Morgan had suggested in her letter that she come alone. Christiana had been rather difficult about her friendship with the woman, asking if she was the one who had given her the banned book about Fanny, and suggesting she may not be the kind of friend Lisa should acquaint herself with. Going alone had seemed simpler than trying to convince Christiana to accompany her. But Lisa supposed she shouldn't really go alone altogether. It was more proper to have her maid accompany her anyway. The only reason she hadn't considered it to begin with was . . . well, she supposed she'd been caught up in the whole adventure and simply neglected to consider taking the girl. Now she decided it may be the best way to handle the matter all around. Gentle ladies simply did not travel unescorted in London.

Sighing, she finally nodded. "Very well, you may accompany me."

"Thank you," Bet said dryly and fell into step beside her as soon as Lisa began to move. "Now, where are we going?"

"To visit a friend," Lisa answered, a smile slowly claiming her lips. Now that she was on her way, she was actually looking forward to the visit. She had found Mrs. Morgan's company stimulating and entertaining in the country and expected it would be the same in the city.

"Is it far?" Bet asked with interest.

"No. Mrs. Morgan promised to have her carriage wait around the corner," Lisa

14

admitted, biting her lip.

"Mrs. Morgan?" the maid asked with a sudden frown. "Not that lady what had her carriage break down at Madison Manor back three years ago? The one the men were all goggling over until his lordship had them take her and her carriage into the village to be repaired?"

"Yes," Lisa answered, her chin rising in response to the maid's obvious disapproval.

"Are you sure we should be visiting her?" Bet asked with a frown. "Mrs. Simms said Mrs. Morgan wasn't proper company for young ladies when she was at the house. She said —"

"I'm not interested in Mrs. Simms's gossip," Lisa said with a frown, wondering why the housekeeper would disapprove. She didn't know the woman had given her the banned book. In fact, Mrs. Simms had barely met Mrs. Morgan in passing when her carriage had broken down on Madison land and been brought to the house.

"But —" the maid said with a frown.

"Hush. There is the carriage," Lisa murmured as they reached the corner and she spotted the black carriage with the dark drapes at the windows. "Come."

Leaving the maid to hurry behind her, Lisa rushed to the carriage.

"Lady Madison?" the driver asked, moving to open the door even as he asked the question.

Lisa smiled and nodded, then quickly climbed into the carriage.

"Say, I was told to expect just the one lady today," the driver said, blocking the way when Bet made to follow her in.

"She is with me," Lisa said with a frown, half rising from the bench seat she'd just settled on. "It isn't proper for a lady to travel without her maid."

The man hesitated, but then moved out of the way with a sigh, and muttered, "All right, but Mrs. Morgan isn't going to like it."

Lisa frowned at the claim, then smiled encouragingly at her maid as she climbed in to claim the bench seat opposite her, "I'm sure she wouldn't expect me to come completely alone."

The man merely shook his head and closed the door.

Lisa and Bet exchanged an uncertain glance at that reaction and then the coach rocked as the driver reclaimed his perch. When the carriage began to move, they could do little but settle back in their seats. However, Lisa was suddenly a tad nervous, worried that Mrs. Morgan would be an-

16

noyed with her for bringing Bet along on this visit. Though, she couldn't imagine why.

While Lisa had often left Bet to shop in the village while she'd visited Mrs. Morgan at the inn during the five days the woman had been stranded there waiting for her carriage to be repaired, she had taken her with her a time or two as well. And what was proper, or at least ignored, in the country was different from what was allowed in London. Surely her friend wouldn't expect her to come unescorted in the city? While it had been her original intention, now that Bet had made her comments about what was proper here, Lisa had to agree her first plan of going alone had been rather foolish and thoughtless. That sort of thing could ruin a girl's reputation, and really, the family had narrowly escaped several scandals now as it was.

The ride to Mrs. Morgan's took a surprisingly long time. At least it seemed a long time to Lisa, who sat fretting in the back of the carriage with an obviously worried Bet. It didn't help that the drapes were closed and they had nothing to look at to pass the time. But they didn't dare pull them open and look out for fear of being recognized and the news of this excursion somehow making its way back to her sister and brother-in-law.

Lisa grimaced at the very idea, her hands tightening around the gift she'd brought for Mrs. Morgan. It was a small thing really, a book she thought the woman might enjoy. Nothing as risqué as the volumes Mrs. Morgan had given her during their visits in the country inn. Those had been . . . well, frankly, they had been rather shocking . . . and titillating all at the same time. Lisa had found herself fascinated by the tale of the prostitute Fanny and her adventures. The descriptions of what had occurred had quite taken her breath away and left her imagining what it would be like if Robert were to do some of the things to her that Fanny's lover had done to her.

Lisa scowled unhappily at the thought of Robert. Their nearest neighbor at Madison and Lord of Langley. He was a dear family friend as well. And Lisa had been in love with the man since she was knee high. He was beautiful and strong and smart and . . . thought of her as nothing more than a little sister. Seeing Christiana and Richard so happy, and Daniel and Suzette so happy had made Lisa long for a husband and happy home too, and it had galvanized her to make Robert realize she was not a child and was perfect for him. She'd done everything she could think of the last two years to achieve that end, but the idiot man appeared to be blind and stupid and still persisted in treating her like an annoying, if adorable, little sister. And frankly, she was quite sick of it. Lisa had determined that she wouldn't love him anymore and intended to find someone else to be interested in at tonight's ball. Or at least try. Surely there would be someone there she would find attractive and could distract her from her interest in Robert?

Perhaps Lord Findlay, she thought, recalling the one man she had danced with when she'd come to London for the first time two years ago. She and Suzette had come in search of their father, who hadn't yet returned home from a business trip. They had attended a ball with their sister, Christiana, the night they had arrived. It had been in the hopes of finding Suzette a husband. To achieve that end, Suzette had danced nearly every dance with nearly every single male in attendance. With all but one, actually — Charles Findlay. He had not asked Suzette to dance; instead he had asked Lisa.

Lisa smiled at the memory of the man. Tall, with aquiline features and ice blond hair, Findlay had been very attractive. Unfortunately, Lisa had been so busy trying to watch Robert at the ball that she'd hardly paid any attention to the man other than to take note at the fine figure he cut. But perhaps he would be there again tonight and again ask her to dance. If so, she would pay more attention. She would force herself to if she had to, Lisa thought grimly.

She might even let him take her out on the terrace for air and allow him to kiss her so that she could see if he could stir any of those warm feelings Fanny had written about in her book. If he did . . . well, then, Robert could go hang for all she cared. She was no longer interested in showering her love and adoration on someone who didn't appreciate it.

The slowing of the carriage drew Lisa's attention then. She glanced to Bet. The other girl was suddenly sitting a little straighter on her bench, her expression more alert as the coach came to a halt. Lisa managed a reassuring smile for the girl, despite her own uncertainty that the maid's presence would be welcomed by their host, and moved quickly to disembark when the driver opened the door.

She glanced around nervously as she waited for Bet to join her. Lisa was anxious over the possibility of being spotted and recognized, but needn't have worried. The carriage wasn't stopped in front of a house with a long walk, but had pulled up mere feet from a door in what appeared to be a back alley behind a building.

"In ye get," the driver ordered gruffly, slamming the carriage door behind Bet and gesturing to the house before them. "Mrs. Morgan won't be pleased does someone see you entering."

Lisa bit her lip, but led Bet to the door and then quickly knocked.

"Just go in," the man ordered grimly. "You're expected."

Lisa hesitated, but then sighed and reached for the knob, relieved when the door suddenly opened before her. Some of that relief was replaced with surprise when she was suddenly caught by the arm and dragged inside.

"Get in here, girl. Mrs. Morgan wouldn't want you seen," a large, older woman in the uniform of a cook said breathlessly as she drew her into the hot, dim kitchen. She started to close the door then, but paused as Bet scurried inside. "Well, what have we here?"

"My maid," Lisa said quietly, beginning to think perhaps this visit hadn't been a good idea after all.

The cook eyed Bet up and down, but then

21

seemed to recall herself and quickly closed the door, saying, "Well ye'd best both go on through. I sent Gilly up to fetch Mrs. Morgan. She'll be down in a minute no doubt. Yer to wait in the . . . er . . . parlor." Turning back, she eyed the pair of them briefly again, and then gestured across the steamy room. "Through there and up the hall, last door on the right."

Lisa hesitated, a frown catching at her lips, but caught it back when she saw that Bet too was frowning. This wasn't at all the way visits for tea generally went in her experience, but then Mrs. Morgan wasn't a member of the gentry. No doubt it was hard to get good servants when you couldn't pay as well as members of the nobility did, and all of this was probably a very kind attempt on Mrs. Morgan's part to prevent her from getting in trouble for coming. The older woman had proven to be very intelligent during their previous encounters and might realize Lisa's visiting might be frowned on by her family.

Forcing a serene expression to her face, Lisa caught Bet's arm and urged her across the room to the door the cook had gestured to.

"This ain't right," Bet hissed the moment they were out of the kitchen and moving up a long, dimly lit hall. "Ladies don't have to be snuck in the back door of the homes of respected people. And they aren't greeted by a surly, fat old woman in dirty clothes either. And —"

"Hush," Lisa warned, but otherwise could hardly argue the point. This *was* highly unusual . . . and really, the cook *had* been surly and her clothes *were* filthy. Unsanitary, Lisa thought, and decided she would avoid eating any pastries or such that might be served with tea. Catching the rebellion growing in Bet's expression, she whispered, "I'm sure Mrs. Morgan is just trying to protect me by slipping me through the back door."

"If she was a decent woman there'd be no need to protect you," Bet growled sharply.

Lisa frowned at the truth behind those words and felt a niggle of concern, but then sighed and said, "Well, we are here now. One tea and we shall leave, I promise. But we can hardly —"

"Ah, there you are. Gilly said you'd arrived. I had intended to be in the kitchen to greet you, but got held up."

Lisa paused in the hall and glanced to the curving stairway and the dark-haired woman descending it. Some of her worry and nervousness eased just at the sight of Mrs.

23

Morgan as she recalled the lovely visits they'd enjoyed in the country. Lisa smiled widely as the older woman reached the bottom of the steps and moved up the hall toward them.

"I was worried you wouldn't be able to get away," Mrs. Morgan said with a smile that faded as she spotted Bet. Slowing, she raised an eyebrow. "You brought a friend."

"You remember Bet, my maid," Lisa said and grimaced at the apology in her voice. "It seemed best to bring her along. Ladies don't travel alone or —"

"Yes, of course." Mrs. Morgan's smile reappeared, wide and unconcerned. "Well, come along, the two of you then. We shall have tea and a nice long chat. It's been ages since we last met, my dear."

"Yes, it has," Lisa agreed with a smile. All would be well.

CHAPTER TWO

"You do realize she's in love with you?"

Robert grimaced at Daniel Woodrow's words and tossed back his whiskey. Which merely made his grimace deepen. Sighing, he set his glass on the table and then glanced from the Earl of Woodrow to Richard Fairgrave, the Earl of Radnor, and asked with feigned ignorance, "Who?"

"Who?" Richard echoed dryly. "The young lady I just mentioned had come to town for the season. Lisa. Surely you recall her?" he added dryly. "The youngest sister to my wife, Christiana, and Daniel's wife, Suzette. You grew up next door to them. Played with them when young. Are like a big brother to Christiana and Suzette, but are a hero to Lisa."

Robert glanced around in search of one of the club servants, thereby avoiding the eyes of both of his companions. While he'd been in school with both men, he'd been a year or so behind them and hadn't really known either of them well until Christiana and Suzette had got mixed up with the two men.

Although, he supposed, *mixed up* wasn't quite the right term. Christiana had married Richard's brother George while he was impersonating the Earl of Radnor. The man had hired scaliwags to murder his brother so he could take his place. Fortunately, the hired men had failed at their task and Richard had upheld the marriage when he'd managed to return to his life. The Earl and Christiana had fallen in love and theirs was a happy union.

As for Daniel and Suzette, Daniel was a close friend of Richard's who, along with Robert, had stood by the pair and helped sort out the mess that George Fairgrave had created. That sorting had included uncovering a plot where George and two other lords were to marry the three sisters and thereby gain control of the rather large inheritance the Madison sisters had been left by their grandfather. Once the marriages had taken place, of course, the three sisters would have been expendable. Fortunately, they'd discovered the plot and put an end to it. Two of the three sisters had settled with husbands during the ordeal; Christiana with the real Richard Fairgrave, Earl of Radnor, and Suzette with his best friend, Daniel Woodrow, the Earl of Woodrow.

Daniel had been as helpless in the face of Suzette's charms as Richard had been with Christiana, and Robert wasn't at all surprised that the two couples were so blissfully happy together. He was glad for his old friends the sisters, and equally glad to make new friends in their husbands. Both Daniel and Richard had quickly become very good friends this last two years . . . and at times, friends could be a pain in the arse.

This was one of those times, he decided and merely muttered, "A silly schoolroom crush is all it is."

Daniel gave a bark of disbelieving laughter. "A schoolroom crush? Lisa's twenty-one, long out of the schoolroom."

"Twenty-one?" he asked with surprise. It seemed like just days ago the chit had been chasing after him in pigtails, her skirts flying and adoring eyes on him with a serious case of hero worship. Where did the time go? he wondered, and then glanced to Richard when he spoke.

"Yes, she's twenty-one and has finally consented to a coming out. You'd best be careful else you shall lose her. I think Lisa's lost hope for her longstanding devotion to you and decided to be sensible and find a

27

husband among the available bachelors in town this year."

"Hmm." Robert frowned at the suggestion. His feelings for Lisa had always been more filial than anything else so the sudden outrage he felt at the very suggestion that she might give up on him to seek another was rather startling. Pride, Robert excused himself. He had probably enjoyed her silent adoration on some level and was just miffed at the possibility of losing it. Shifting uncomfortably, he muttered, "Well, good for her. I wish her luck. I, myself, am not ready to settle down. I am quite happy with my mistress and my life as it is."

"Of course you are," Daniel said dryly, and then grinned and added, "But then why should you be happy while the rest of us suffer in matrimonial hell? As a good friend, you should really join us there."

Robert chuckled at the suggestion. "Matrimonial hell, my foot. It's been two years since you married Suzette and you still can't keep your hands off each other. Dear God, I caught you in the broom closet at the Handly tea just last week. And you and Christiana are no better," he added dryly when Richard burst out laughing. "It wasn't the stars you were showing Christiana when I caught you out in the gardens at that dinner at the Witherspoons' the week before."

When the two men just grinned unrepentantly, he shook his head. "I don't know why I willingly spend any time with the four of you. You're always billing and cooing, or slipping away to dark corners or empty rooms. It's really rather nauseating."

"Perhaps what you think is nausea is really envy," Daniel suggested with a grin.

"Hmm." Robert didn't deny it, but merely said, "Envy or nausea, it matters little. The men in my family have no luck with marriage. My father, his father, and his father's father before him all married faithless, adulterous women. Hell, it's only getting worse. Not only was my mother unfaithful, there's a possibility that she helped my father on his way into death's sweet sleep so she could openly be with her lover, Lord Gower." Robert shook his head. "No thank you. I shall wait until I am old and decrepit before marrying and do it only then to fulfill my duty and produce an heir to the dukedom before I toddle off to the grave. Until then, I am perfectly happy with my mistress."

He glanced around again for a servant to refill his drink. Not spying one, he turned back to find both men now solemn faced and silent.

"What?" he asked dryly. "Surely you'd heard the rumors?"

Daniel and Richard exchanged a glance and then Daniel sighed and admitted, "Aye, but we weren't sure you had."

"Of course, I did," he said grimly. "She hasn't exactly been discreet. She didn't bother with mourning at all, has attended London ever since and is often seen in Gower's company."

Richard nodded and then asked solemnly, "Do you really think she had something to do with your father's death?"

Robert sighed and once more looked around for a server. Failing to see anyone, he glanced back and shrugged. "What does it matter? He was dying, and it was a slow and torturous wasting away for him. But . . ." He grimaced and shook his head. "I was sure he'd last another day or so. I had gone out for my morning ride, got back and went up to sit with him only to discover she'd arrived on one of her infrequent visits from town while I was gone." His mouth tightened. "She was crying prettily into a hanky when I entered the room, but paused to announce with a sad moue that he was dead."

He looked away and then muttered, "If she did help him on his way, it may have been a favor to him. He was suffering a great deal." Silence reigned for a moment and then he shifted impatiently. "How the devil did we get on this depressing subject?" When Richard and Daniel merely shook their heads silently, pity in their expressions, he stood abruptly. "I'm heading back to the townhouse. At least there I can get a drink when I want it. Good day, gentlemen."

"Are you a virgin, dear Bet?"

Lisa blinked her eyes open and frowned, both at the fact that she was dozing off in the middle of tea — which was surely about the rudest thing she could do — but also because Mrs. Morgan's question was completely inappropriate. Good Lord, one simply didn't ask a lady's maid things like that. Or anyone, really.

Realizing she'd somehow slumped in her seat, she sat up and found herself swaying alarmingly. Good Lord, what was the matter with her? Lisa wondered and gave her head a shake.

A confused mumble from Bet drew her gaze and she found the maid peering at her with the same dismay she was now experiencing.

"Well, never mind," Mrs. Morgan said with unconcern. "I suspect you are, but we shall have the doctor verify it. He has to anyway for the auction. Otherwise, no one will bid on you. They don't simply take these things on word alone when paying such high prices."

None of that made the least bit of sense to Lisa, but it did send a frisson of alarm through her.

"Mishes Mor—" she began, but paused abruptly as she heard the slur to her words.

"Oh my, I do believe the tincture is starting to take effect," Mrs. Morgan said pleasantly and picked up the small bell on the table beside her to ring it twice. "Time for bed I think. It will keep you out of trouble until they arrive."

"They?" Lisa asked with bewilderment, some part of her brain — a very confused and slow-working part — trying to tell her she needed to get herself and Bet out of there . . . now.

"The doctor who examines all my girls before I sell them to the highest bidder," she explained. "And your suitor, of course. I sent word to him that you're here. However, he does like to sleep most of the day away and it will no doubt be well after dinner before he arrives. Of course, we shall have to get you bathed and properly attired for his visit. He does like his girls presented just so. Quite fussy about it, actually," she added with a grimace and then glanced around. "Oh, good, here are Cook and Gilly. They'll put you both to bed. I have things to do, but trust they'll take good care of you."

Lisa stared blankly as the woman stood and moved toward the door. She was vaguely aware that others had entered the room, but didn't seem to be able to stop staring at Mrs. Morgan. Her friend. Who had apparently put something in her tea? Drugged her? And Bet? What had that been about a suitor?

The thought was the last she had before her eyes drifted closed.

CHAPTER THREE

A great loud snoring woke Lisa from sleep. Scowling at the annoying sound, she turned over in bed and then scowled again as she bumped into something hard. Bet's elbow she saw, opening her eyes. What the devil was Bet doing in her bed? She had her own room in the servant's quarters. She —

Stiffening as memory flooded back, Lisa sat up abruptly and peered around the room. It was small and mean looking with little more than the bed in it and four bare walls. One wall held a window covered with dark drapes and one had a large, solid door.

Sucking in a breath, Lisa slipped her feet to the floor and stood up, alarmed to find the room doing a slow spin around her. When it stopped, she let out the breath she hadn't realized she'd been holding, and moved slowly around the bed toward the door. Reaching it, she grasped the handle and twisted it, disappointed, but not terribly surprised when it turned but the door didn't open. They were locked in.

Swinging back to the room, she crossed to the window and dragged the heavy drapes aside. Sunlight poured in through the opening, splashing the room with stark light and bringing an end to Bet's loud snoring. There was the rustle of material and a muttering from the bed, but Lisa ignored it for now and considered the view out the window. They were on the second floor, overlooking the alley along the back of Mrs. Morgan's terraced house. Reaching out, she pushed upward on the window, relieved when it slid up with just a whisper of sound.

So, the window wasn't bolted shut or anything. That was good, Lisa thought as she eased it closed again. Probably because they were on the second floor. Climbing out and getting down to the ground wouldn't be easy if it was even possible. One or both of them could fall and be badly hurt. But they could hardly stay here and just await whatever fate Mrs. Morgan had in store for them either.

Lisa sighed unhappily. She'd thought Mrs. Morgan was her friend, had liked the woman a great deal. *Had* being the key word. At that moment, she thought she could snatch the woman bald. How dare the old cow drug the tea and lock them in this room for . . . well, whatever it was she had planned. Lisa had some vague recollection of the mention of a suitor. And a doctor to examine Bet before she was sold. But it was all rather fuzzy and hard to recall exactly what had been said.

"What the bloody hell?"

Lisa turned back to the room to see Bet sitting up on the bed and gaping around with confusion. That confusion was quickly replaced with a scowl that she turned on Lisa.

"I told you the old bitch wasn't a proper lady. What have ye got us into here?"

Lisa ignored the maid's cuss. Bet never cussed, and she supposed her doing so now was a result of the dire situation they found themselves in, so she merely said, "Come. You may berate me later if you wish, but right now we have to get out of here."

Bet scowled, but climbed off the bed and flounced toward her, muttering, "Well, ye'd do better to try the door then. We aren't climbing out no window."

"The door is locked," Lisa said quietly.

"Brilliant," Bet proclaimed and paused beside her to peer out the window. Her scowl immediately turned to dismay as she took in their situation. "We can't go out this way. There's naught to hold onto but brick and nothing to break our fall."

Lisa frowned. Bet had just verbalized her own worries, but after a moment, she turned to survey the room. "We shall have to make a rope."

"With what exactly?" Bet asked dryly.

She hesitated, but then brightened and said, "Do you remember that story I read to you about the dastardly Lord Haroway who kidnapped Lady Laticia to have his wicked way with her?"

"Oh, aye, that was a good one," Bet said with a small smile. "He done some wicked things to her, all right. Ravished her good and proper."

"Yes, but then she escaped out the window using a rope she made from —"

"Bedsheets," Bet interrupted with a grin and turned to hurry to the bed. By the time Lisa caught up to her, the maid had pulled away the heavy comforter and begun dragging off the linens. "Dear Lord, these are filthy."

"Yes, well, perhaps the filth will make them stronger," Lisa said with a grimace, bending to help her.

"Gor! We were actually laying on these," Bet said with dismay. "We'll be crawling with fleas now . . . or worse."

"Yes," Lisa said with a sigh and took the top sheet to begin rending it into strips.

"Gad . . . the trouble you get me into with your shenanigans," the maid muttered, rending the bottom sheet.

"Don't blame me for this," Lisa protested at once. "You were the one who blackmailed me into bringing you along. If not for that, you'd be safely at home now."

"And where would ye be if I hadn't?" Bet asked sharply, continuing her work. "Kidnapped and forced into prostitution."

"Well, I still am. It's just now we're both — prostitution?" she squawked as the word sank in.

"Well, what did you think she meant about suitors and a doctor examining us?" Bet asked dryly. "It's like that other book ye read to me. The one with the youngest daughter of that Baron who was kidnapped by a madam and forced to . . ." She paused, her eyes wide. "Dear God! We're living that book right now, we are. Kidnapped and locked in a room, awaiting a man's pleasure to come ravish us. Oh, Lord save us," she breathed. "It's like she read the book too."

"She probably did. She is the one who gave it to me," Lisa said unhappily, her mind on the ravishing part. A suitor to ravish her . . . and she *was* the youngest daughter of a Baron. Dear Lord, it *was* like the writer was writing about her before it had happened. Seeing the alarm on Bet's face, she forced her own disturbing thoughts away and straightened her shoulders. "We will escape."

"Aye," Bet muttered and both of them began to work more quickly. Within moments they'd finished tearing their respective sheets into strips and started weaving and knotting the strips together to make one long slightly knobby makeshift rope.

"The window," Lisa said as soon as they tied on the last strip. She started to lead the way holding half the rope while Bet carried the other, but nearly fell flat on her face on the first step. Muttering under her breath, she shifted her part of the rope to one hand and bent to scoop up the heavy comforter with the other and toss it back onto the bed. Straightening, she then hurried to the window. Bet trailed her with the rest of the rope.

"What'll we tie it to?" Bet asked with concern.

Lisa hesitated, but then glanced around the room. The only thing available was the bed. Mouth tightening, she hurried back to it, grateful it was close as she quickly knelt to tie one end around one foot of the bed.

"Will it hold?" Bet asked uncertainly.

"It shall have to." Lisa straightened grimly and slowly unfurled the rope as she moved back to the window. Once there, she handed off the remainder of the rope to Bet. "Right, tie the end around your waist."

She waited just long enough to see Bet nod and begin to do as she'd ordered, and then turned to quickly open the window. Much to her relief, it slid silently up and stayed in place. By the time she turned back, Bet had finished tying the rope around herself.

Lisa smiled encouragingly. "Now, sit on the ledge and swing your feet out, and then use the rope to lower yourself out the window. When you reach the ground, untie yourself and I shall pull the rope up to use myself."

Nodding, Bet settled on the ledge, but then frowned and said, "Maybe you should go first. Yer —"

"You wouldn't be here if not for me, Bet. Now just go. Quickly," Lisa insisted, pushing on her arm gently.

Bet didn't look happy, but did shift her legs out the window and then ease herself out to hang from the ledge. Pausing there, she glanced to the ground below and muttered, "I hope there is enough rope."

So do I, Lisa thought, but didn't say as much as she quickly threw the rest of the rope out the window. She then smiled encouragingly and waved at the maid to lower herself.

Sighing, Bet removed one hand from the ledge to grasp the rope and then did the same with the other. There was immediately a loud scraping sounded behind Lisa as the bed began to slide across the floor under the sudden weight. She instinctively grabbed at the rope to keep the bed from moving further, then gasped, "Go, quickly."

"But what about you? How will you —"

"I shall have to wait here while you fetch help," Lisa interrupted, in a panic to get the girl going. If anyone had heard the shifting bed and came to investigate . . . "Just hurry, Bet."

"But who do I fetch?" Bet asked, eyes wide with horror. "Lady Christiana and Lady Suzette are out to tea, and —"

"Go to Lord Langley's. Bring him, just be quick," she hissed, and groaned as her arms began to strain. "Please, go, Bet. I cannot hold this much longer."

The maid looked like she wanted to argue, but nodded grimly and began to lower herself out of sight. Lisa immediately closed her eyes and tried to ignore the ache begin-

41

ning in her arms as she waited. It seemed to take forever before the weight she was holding suddenly eased. Lisa had begun to lean back, using her weight to help her hold on, and nearly fell back when the rope suddenly went slack. However, she managed to keep her feet.

Dropping the makeshift rope with relief, she moved to the window to lean out and watch silently as Bet hurried away up the alley. She then quickly dragged the rope back into the room and closed the window.

Lisa gathered up the rope as she moved back across the room. She untied it from the foot of the bed and then glanced around uncertainly before just stuffing it under the comforter. She started to straighten, but then had a thought and quickly bent to spread the thick, knobby rope about, fluffing the comforter around it as she did. Once satisfied with her effort to make it look like Bet was still asleep in the bed, she then began to pace, counting off in her head how far along Bet might be in her efforts to get to the Langley townhouse and Robert.

The problem was she didn't know how long it would take. She hadn't even thought to look around for her reticule to give Bet money to hire a hack, but didn't see it now anyway. The girl would be on foot. Would she have the sense to hire a hack with the promise of payment on arrival at Robert's? Or would she try to get there on foot? Dear God, if the girl didn't hire a hack . . . well, Robert might not get here in time, Lisa realized with dismay and turned to move back to the window, debating the merits of tying the rope to the bed again and climbing out herself.

Perhaps if she moved the bed up against the window . . . But that might make a lot of racket and bring people to investigate. She could always just tie the rope around her waist, hold on near the top and slide out the window. That way if the bed scraped across the floor it would only lower her halfway down the wall and then she could climb down the rest of the way. Surely she'd be on the ground and free before anyone was drawn by the racket the moving bed would make? She —

Lisa paused, her gaze shooting to the door as she heard approaching footsteps. For one moment, she froze, but when she heard a key rattle in the lock, she moved toward the door, hoping to block the view of the bed with her own body. Lisa had nearly reached the door when it opened, but paused a few steps away when Mrs. Morgan appeared in the opening.

"Oh, good, you're awake. It's time."

Alarm clutched Lisa at that greeting, and her mouth was dry as she squeaked, "Time for what?"

Mrs. Morgan merely tilted her head to glance around her toward the bed. "Bet's still sleeping I see."

"Aye," Lisa murmured, struggling not to move to the side to block her view.

Mrs. Morgan shrugged. "I suppose I shouldn't be surprised. She drank that tea rather greedily. Ah well, the doctor isn't here to examine her yet anyway. Now, come along. We have to get you ready."

"Ready for what?" Lisa immediately asked as Mrs. Morgan caught her arm and urged her to the door.

"For your suitor." Mrs. Morgan smiled and for the first time Lisa noticed that it was rather toothy, almost wolfish.

"I don't wish to . . ." Lisa's voice faded to silence, her eyes going wide as she was pushed out into the hall. She found herself facing a rather tall, huge bald man with quite the most unpleasant face she'd ever seen.

"This is Gilly," Mrs. Morgan announced cheerfully as she pulled the bedroom door closed behind them and locked it once again. "If you give us trouble, he will have to help bathe and dress you."

"Oh," Lisa breathed, wide-eyed, and then swallowed any further protest and allowed herself to be led up the hall, very aware that Gilly was directly on their heels.

"My lord?"

Robert lifted his head off the back of the chair and opened his eyes to peer at the man addressing him from the door of his office. Mosby, his butler. Raising one eyebrow in enquiry, he asked, "Yes?"

"There is a . . . lady, and a gentleman enquiring to see you," the man said with an air of doubt that suggested perhaps the lady wasn't a lady at all, the gentleman not a gentleman, and Robert wouldn't wish to see either of them. "They are still on the front step if you'd care to look out and decide if you wish to be 'in' or not."

Robert allowed his second eyebrow to rise at the suggestion, but then stood and moved to the window to peer curiously outside. His office was at the front of the house with a bay window that looked out onto the street. He peered through the gauzy curtain at the figures on the step and frowned. Robert hadn't a clue who the great, round fellow was on his front step, but the female looked vaguely familiar. It looked like Lisa

45

Madison's maid, Bet, he thought, and then tugged the curtain aside to get a better look at the woman.

The much clearer view simply made his frown deepen. The young woman was so pale her freckles stood out in relief. She was also wringing her hands almost desperately, and shifting nervously from foot to foot despite the obviously tight hold the man had on her arm.

"Show them in," Robert said letting the curtain drop back into place.

"As you wish," Mosby said calmly, though there was an undertone that suggested he thought this a very bad idea indeed. But then he often disapproved of the things Robert did since he'd moved to town. He suspected the butler felt he should be finding a wife and producing an heir to continue the Langley line. It's what everyone seemed to think he should do. But Robert just had no intention of doing that, so they could all just continue to disapprove all they liked.

Sighing, he moved to his desk and settled in the chair to await the arrival of his guests, his mind puzzling over what Lisa Madison's maid could be doing there. He supposed she had some message from Lisa and Christiana, though the presence of the man holding her so tightly was rather puzzling.

"Oh, my lord!"

Robert glanced up in time to see Bet try to rush across the room, only to be drawn up short and dragged back to the side of the man holding her arm. The wince that immediately covered her face told him that the fellow's grip was as clawlike as it looked. Scowling at the rough treatment, Robert stood up. "Unhand her."

"Just as soon as I get the money I was promised," the man growled, though he did appear to ease his hold somewhat.

"Money?" Robert frowned and then peered to Bet in enquiry.

"I'm sorry, my lord," Bet babbled in a rush. "My lady sent me to fetch you to save her, but I had no idea where I was and no money for a hack. I promised him you would pay when we reached here."

"Your lady sent you to fetch me to save her?" Robert echoed with amazement.

"Aye, she — we —" Bet paused, eyes sliding worriedly to the man holding her and then back to him unhappily.

Realizing she didn't wish to speak in front of what was obviously a hack driver, Robert glanced to his butler. "See the man paid and show him out."

"Aye, my lord," Mosby said calmly and then arched an eyebrow in the driver's

47

direction. After the briefest hesitation, the man released his hold on Bet, nodded at Robert, and then turned to allow the butler to lead him from the room.

Noting that the butler had left the door open, no doubt so he could hear what would follow, Robert moved around his desk and quickly crossed the room to close the door.

Turning back then, he peered at Bet. "Now, why did your lady send you to me?"

"I told you. To save her. We must hurry, my lord. She's in dire straits," Bet said anxiously.

Robert frowned. "To save her from what, exactly, Bet?"

"Oh," she moaned with something like despair. "It's awful, my lord. The tea was drugged and we was locked up and I escaped out the window, but Miss Lisa had to remain behind because the bed wasn't heavy enough and we must get to her and get her out of there!" Bet cried.

Robert blinked at the rush of words, not really understanding. Lisa had had to remain behind because the bed wasn't heavy enough? Heavy enough for what? It didn't make any sense, but was sounding a good deal like one of those melodramas Lisa so enjoyed reading, and he was beginning to suspect that's all it was. It seemed Lisa hadn't completely given up on him after all, but in some last ditch effort to gain his attention, had come up with this wild tale to —

"Please!" Bet moaned, rushing forward to clutch at his arm and urge him toward the door. "I'll never forgive meself if Miss Lisa is ravished and ruined because I went out the window first. I should have made her go first. I should have —"

"Ravished and ruined?" Robert interrupted with amusement. Good Lord, she'd gone all out this time. Lisa was usually the sweetest, most biddable of females, dreamy eyed and seeming only to half live in the real world while the other half of her mind was stuck off in the wild machinations of the latest story she was reading. But every once in a while she got swept up in her stories and —

"Why are you smiling?" Bet asked with horror. "This is not amusing, my lord. She will be ruined if that suitor fellow has his way with her. She —"

"Suitor fellow?" Robert asked with interest.

"That's what Mrs. Morgan called him. Her suitor," Bet explained unhappily. "She —"

"Mrs. Morgan?" Robert barked, his

49

amusement dying abruptly and concern beginning to take its place. "What the devil has Mrs. Morgan to do with this?"

"We was there for tea, and —"

"At Mrs. Morgan's!" he bellowed and Bet flinched as if he'd struck her. She also looked suddenly terrified. Forcing himself to calm down, Robert asked more gently, "What on earth would make Lisa go to tea at Mrs. Morgan's? How does she even know a woman like that?"

"Mrs. Morgan's carriage broke down just outside Madison more than two years ago and Lord Madison invited Mrs. Morgan in to tea while the stable master took a look to see if a new wheel could be put on or the undercarriage was damaged. Miss Lisa and Suzette kept her company while she waited. It turned out there was much to repair and Mrs. Morgan took a room at the inn while waiting for it to be ready for the road again. She was in the village for near a week and Miss Lisa visited her nearly every day. They became friends and Mrs. Morgan gave her a couple of books and they've been writing ever since."

"Dear God," Robert breathed with dismay. "Doesn't she know what kind of woman —" Pausing, he shook his head. Of course she didn't know. How could she?

Lisa spent very little time in the city. The girl was as naïve as a babe. "Does Richard know Lisa planned to tea with Mrs. Morgan?"

"Nay," she said on a sigh. " 'Twas a secret. In fact, even I wasn't to know. Miss Lisa tried to sneak out on her own, but I knew she was up to something and caught her and so she let me come with her, but the carriage dropped us at the back of the house. The kitchens, if you can imagine," she added with outrage. "I knew that wasn't right, but Miss Lisa insisted on going in for tea and we did, but the tea was drugged and Mrs. Morgan was asking the oddest questions. Was I a virgin, and —" She paused, her face now flushing so that the freckles were nearly invisible as she whispered, "And that the doctor would examine me to see."

She shuddered at the thought, but continued, "The last thing I remember before the drugged tea overtook me is her saying as how we would be taken to a room to rest until the doctor and Miss Lisa's suitor came." Her mouth firmed. "And sure enough, we woke up locked in this room on the second floor. But we made a rope from the bed linens like in that book about that Lord Haroway what ravished Lady Laticia,

51

and Miss Lisa said as I should go first, so I climbed out the window, but the bed couldn't take the weight and started to move and Miss Lisa had to help hold the rope which she couldn't do for herself and she said I should come find you to go get her."

Robert stared blankly as her long, rushed explanation soaked through his mind and then he gave his head a shake, and stepped around her to head for the door. "Wait here. I shall fetch her back."

"Oh but —"

"Wait here," he repeated firmly.

"But ye don't know which window to go to," she protested in a wail.

Robert paused, a frown curving his lips as he turned back. "Which window?"

"I should come with ye. I —"

"You're not coming with me, Bet. I've enough to worry about without worrying over you. Now which window?"

"There," Mrs. Morgan said and took a step back to look her over with satisfaction.

Nodding, she pronounced, "You look perfect. He should be very pleased."

"Who?" Lisa asked and frowned at the garbled sound to the word. Mrs. Morgan had been pushing some sort of beverage on her the entire time while seeing her bathed, powdered and dressed in . . . well, what was really the most comfortable gown. It felt feather light and airy, allowing the smallest draft to make its way through and caress her skin. It was as close to wearing nothing at all as she'd ever experienced and left her feeling rather . . . well . . . odd, really.

"You'll see soon enough," Mrs. Morgan said with a laugh and led her to the bed. "I'm surprised he feels he needs this to get your attention. Most girls would throw themselves at him. Although, my girls say he can be a bit rough, but you may come to enjoy it. A little rough can sometimes be a pleasure."

Lisa grunted for answer. She wasn't really sure what the woman was talking about. Attractive sounded nice to her fuzzy mind, but the being a bit rough part . . . well, she suspected she should be a bit alarmed, but her mind didn't appear capable of it at the moment. Instead, she was struggling with a rather odd desire to giggle.

What the devil had been in those drinks they'd been pushing on her?

"Now you sit here. He should be here soon to see you and then your new life will start."

"Why are you doing this? I thought you

were my friend," Lisa said plaintively, or hoped she did. It didn't sound quite right coming out of her mouth. It felt like she was talking around a mouthful of marbles. But Mrs. Morgan seemed to understand her words.

"Now, now," the woman said on a little sigh and patted her hand as she settled on the bed beside her. "I know it may seem awful of me to hand you over to him like this. But he plans to marry you, my dear. So no harm done. And he's paying me a very large sum of money to help him woo you like this." She paused and then grimaced and added, "Of course, Bet is something else. But really, do you think she wants to be a lady's maid the rest of her life? She's a beautiful girl despite those unfortunate freckles of hers. She'll wear the finest silks and drink the finest wine and enjoy many fine men rather than putting up with the callous rutting of stable boys and the like. Really, I'm doing you both a good turn here today . . . and making a great deal of money as well. If the girl's a virgin, I'll get top dollar for her." She stood and moved toward the door, adding, "I really must send word to find out what's holding up the doctor. I've already sent out a notice to every possibly interested party that a fresh girl is to be auctioned off tonight. I need his certification that Bet's pure before then."

Lisa watched her go, and remained where she was as Cook and the big man named Gilly carried the tub out, then waited for the door to close before standing up. She was a little alarmed when the room spun wildly around her and for a moment she had to brace herself with a hand on the bed and take deep breaths to keep her stomach from rebelling as she waited for the spinning to stop. When it finally did, Lisa straightened more cautiously and peered dully around.

Her mind was screaming at her to do something. The problem was that the message was as garbled in her head as her words had been when she'd spoken and Lisa couldn't figure out what exactly it was her mind was trying to tell her she should be doing. She suspected it was important though.

CHAPTER FOUR

Robert perched on the window ledge and peered cautiously inside, then frowned and peered more closely. The room at first appeared empty, but then he spotted the lump under the comforter. Lisa. How could she sleep at a time like this? Good Lord. Muttering under his breath, he lowered himself to sit on the outer ledge and then tapped softly on the window. The sound was very faint. He didn't want to attract attention, but it was surely loud enough for Lisa to hear. The bed wasn't that far away. However, she didn't stir at all. He knocked again, a little louder, but when that still brought no result, he eased the window open, and climbed inside.

It was only as he reached the side of the bed that Robert realized the shape under the comforter wasn't quite right. He pulled back the thick blanket and then straightened with a curse when he saw the ripped and knotted sheets beneath. Returning the comforter, he straightened and moved quickly to the door. It was only when he found the knob wouldn't turn that he recalled Bet's claim that they'd been locked in.

Robert turned on a hissed curse and returned to the window. He was back out on the ledge with the window closed in little more than a moment, but then paused, unsure what to do. He could hardly just leave. He needed to get into the building and look for Lisa.

He'd try another room, Robert decided, and then glanced first right and then left. The window on the left was the closer one. It was also the way he'd come, climbing up the trellis on the other side of it and moving across that ledge and then to this one. But the room had been occupied.

Not wanting to be spotted, Robert hadn't stuck around long enough to see who occupied it on his way by, but had shifted past the window as quickly as he could, barely catching a glimpse of what had appeared to be a woman in the room.

Unfortunately, the next window over on his right was farther away and he didn't think he'd reach it safely. He couldn't get Lisa out of this trouble if he was lying broken on the ground, so it was the first window he'd have to try, Robert acknowledged. He'd just have to hope that room was empty now or that the woman inside was of a friendly nature and wouldn't raise the alarm when he entered through the window . . . or that he could silence her before she did, he thought grimly. Money usually did the trick in such situations. He would have to check things out and decide from there, Robert supposed.

He sucked in a breath and clutched the edge of the window frame with one hand and stretched his other hand and one foot toward the next. It was a tricky business, and he barely reached, but barely was good enough. A moment later he was easing onto the first window ledge again with a little relieved sigh.

Robert took a moment to let his heartbeat slow down, then shifted on the ledge to peer into the room. A grimace covered his face when he saw that it wasn't empty now as he'd hoped. The woman was still there, a petite, blond and very curvaceous prostitute who stood by the bed, all ready for her first client of the evening.

Damn, she was wearing something that . . . well, she might as well not be wearing anything at all, Robert thought wryly as his eyes slid over her curves through the diaphanous gown. Mrs. Morgan had always had the best girls in town. He ought to know. He'd visited often enough over the years. Beautiful, curvaceous and talented women were what Morgan's was known for. He couldn't believe that Lord Madison had let the woman into his home and even served her tea, for God's sake. The fact that the man had let his unwed daughter spend any time with the woman was rather horrifying.

Of course, Lord Madison spent most of his time out in the country too, and probably hadn't had a clue the sort of woman he'd let into his manor. Still . . . Robert had to wonder how he'd missed hearing of the Madisons' acquaintance with this woman before now.

Although, he supposed he shouldn't be surprised. He hadn't seen much of Lord Madison or Lisa since his father's death. In fact, he'd only seen them the once, those few short weeks when Lisa had been in London around the time of Suzette and Daniel's meeting and marrying. Truth be told, he'd been avoiding her to keep from encouraging the silly schoolroom crush he knew she had on him.

Robert cared for Lisa, just as he cared for

Suzette and Christiana. But that was it and he had no desire to break her heart. It would make it uncomfortable to be around her sisters and their husbands and while he had always been close to Suzette and Christiana, he was even closer now. They and Daniel and Richard had become his closest friends these last two years.

His thoughts were distracted when the woman in the room turned slowly, her gaze moving to the window. Sure she couldn't see him through the gauzy curtain, he eyed her with interest. The girl reminded him of Lisa. Well, Lisa as she would look if not properly attired in her frilly pastel gowns and with her hair up in those fancy styles women in the ton tended to wear, he thought, his admiring gaze running over the girl's front now just as it had her back.

She was a ripe little peach, all generous curves and shapely legs. And her hair was a silken mass that framed her face and fell over her shoulders in a golden cascade. And what a face, he thought. It was heart-shaped with huge eyes and full, kissable lips.

Perhaps he should visit this little strumpet later in the evening after finding Lisa and getting her safely home. Well, if he managed to rescue her without getting caught or seen. Mrs. Morgan would hardly welcome his clientele if she found out —

Robert's thoughts died, his eyes locking on the girl's face as she suddenly gave her head a shake as if trying to clear her head and ran her hands through her hair, pushing it back and up from her face.

"Damn," Robert breathed. Dear God, the alluringly dressed little strumpet was no strumpet at all. It was Lisa Madison!

For one moment, he simply stood gaping, his eyes again traveling over generous curves that her damned frilly gowns didn't normally reveal. But then he recalled that he was perched on a ledge outside a window gaping at and — if he were honest with himself — lusting after a damned near nude Lisa Madison . . . who was like a little sister to him.

Cursing, Robert squatted slightly to reach and open the window, and then leaned in, whispering, "Lisa."

The word was a bare hiss of sound, but enough to draw her head around. Her eyes widened when she saw him, and then rushed forward.

Robert couldn't help noticing that her breasts jiggled temptingly with each step, and her generous hips swayed. Damn, who knew she hid such a tempting little body under those voluminous gowns she wore?

Richard and Daniel were right, Lisa was definitely all grown up. When the devil had that happened?

The question was lost to the corners of his mind when she reached the window, threw herself at him with a happy cry, and damned near sent him tumbling backward off the ledge.

Catching at the window frame, Robert managed to save himself, not to mention her, since she would have gone out with him. He then released one hand from the frame to wrap his arm around her.

"Oh, Robert. Thank goodness. I knew you'd come," she mumbled into his neck and he frowned at the slight slur to her words.

"Have you been drinking?" he asked, pulling back slightly to try to see her face.

"Uh-huh." She nodded apologetically. "Mrs. Morgan made me drink this sort of spiced wine. I mean it tasted like wine but I know it had other stuff in it. She said it would relax me for what was to come. I think it was drugged like the tea. But not with a sleeping powder. With something else. It made me feel all soft and floaty."

"Hmmm." He frowned, his gaze dropping down over the gown she wore. It didn't hide a damned thing, not the round globes of her breasts or the dusky pink of her nipples, which were presently erect, he noted and scowled. "What the hell are you wearing?"

"Mrs. Morgan made me wear it. She said my suitor would like me in this. Do you like me in this?" She glanced down at herself. "I like how it feels on my skin. It feels floaty."

He couldn't help noticing that the theme seemed to be floaty, and since she was swaying on her feet and not the least bit self-conscious about standing in front of him damned near naked, he suspected whatever Mrs. Morgan had given her was the culprit.

"Do you?"

Robert blinked and forced his gaze from her nipples to her face. "Do I what?"

"Do you like me in this?" Lisa asked with a frown. "Don't you think it's pretty?"

"I —" Robert found his gaze sliding down over her body again, drifting over and past her breasts, down across the soft swell of her belly to the curves of her hips and the nest of blond curls between them. Too right he thought it was pretty and liked her in it. Far too much, he thought grimly and gave his head a shake. Trying for reason, he said quietly, "Lisa, we have to get out of here."

"Oh, yes. I don't like it here, Robert. Mrs. Morgan made me strip and bathe in front of this man named Gilly, who was very big and scary and I didn't like it at all, but she wouldn't make him leave when I asked and said if I didn't cooperate she'd let him strip and bathe me and I didn't want him touching me and so I had to pretend that he just wasn't there and get on with it, but it was terribly embarrassing and I didn't like it."

He'd kill the bastard, Robert thought grimly. Gilly was Mrs. Morgan's muscle, a massive, moon-faced mute who kept the girls in line and handled troublesome clients. He'd kill the bastard for having looked on Lisa and made her so uncomfortable . . . right after he handled Mrs. Morgan. But not till after he had Lisa safely out of there.

"Okay," he murmured, urging her back a bit. "I want you to climb onto my back."

"Onto your back?" she asked uncertainly.

"Yes, you climb onto my back and I shall climb back down the wall."

"How are you going to climb down the wall, Robert? You're not a spider. Perhaps we should make a rope out of the sheets like Bet and I did and —"

"It's all right. I climbed up, and I can climb down. Just get on my back, Lisa," he said turning sideways on the ledge and urging her around to his side.

She muttered under her breath the whole time, but climbed onto the ledge behind him and then wrapped her arms around his shoulders as instructed.

"Wrap your legs around my waist," he ordered.

Lisa mumbled by his ear, and her legs came around his waist, the feet hooking together against his belly. Robert stared at them blankly, noting that she was barefoot and had the most adorable little toes and a lovely high arch, and —

"Now what?"

Giving his head another shake, Robert was now the one to mutter under his breath. Then heaving a sigh, he said, "Just hold on tight."

He waited to hear her say that she understood and then began to shift them both out of the window. It was a much trickier maneuver with her clinging to his back like a monkey, and Robert began to grit his teeth, his attention divided between what he was doing and her hold on him. He was concerned that she might lose her grip and fall, but couldn't spare a hand to help her hold on.

"Tell me if your grip starts slipping," he hissed, easing along the ledge toward the trellis.

"Yes, Robert," she mumbled against his neck and he felt a shudder run through him as her breath brushed his ear. Damn, he'd never had this reaction to her before. But then she'd never looked quite so . . . well —

"Ow."

Robert paused. He'd just stepped off the ledge and onto the trellis when she'd made the sound of pain. Twisting his head slightly he tried to glance around to see what was wrong. "What is it?"

"Nothing. My foot just hit something," Lisa muttered, digging her heels tighter against him to try to avoid the wall and wood. She'd slid lower once he'd straightened on the ledge, and her feet were no longer against his waist, but now dug into his groin. Pain wasn't the word for the sensation she was unintentionally causing. Robert managed not to groan out loud, and bent slightly to protect her feet, then began to descend the trellis with a little more speed than care. He was somewhat amazed when they made it to the ground without a misstep, and the moment his feet were planted solidly on the ground he urged her off his back.

Relief sped through him when her feet were no longer rubbing him so intimately, but he ignored it and turned to lift her into his arms. It was an attempt to hide some of her nakedness as well as to protect her poor bare feet . . . and had absolutely nothing to do with a desire to hold her in his arms, he assured himself as he strode toward the end of the alley and the carriage waiting there.

Robert moved as quickly as he could, eager to get her inside and away from prying eyes, not to mention any kind of confrontation with Mrs. Morgan or her goon. That would wait until he'd got Lisa safely away. He wouldn't risk her being caught again should Gilly prove more of a problem than he expected, or if the man got in a lucky punch with one of those hammy fists of his.

"Oh, Robert, I knew you would save me," Lisa sighed, nestling into his chest.

Robert grunted and tried to ignore the way her breasts were pressing into his chest.

"You're so brave and clever. And strong and handsome too," she added with a pleased little sigh. "You will make beautiful babies."

Robert blinked, his mind filling with baby making: the act, not the result. Realizing the treacherous road his thoughts were taking, he gave his head a shake and picked up speed, rushing the last few steps to the carriage.

The driver saw him coming and was off his perch, opening the carriage door at once so that Robert was able to simply step inside with his burden. He dropped onto the bench seat as the driver quickly closed the door, but found himself reluctant to set Lisa down on the opposite bench. Staring at her dressed as she was just didn't seem that smart an idea. That, of course, was the only reason he held her pressed tight to his chest, he told himself as the driver climbed back up on his seat, setting the carriage rocking.

"Are you taking me home?" Lisa asked as the carriage set off.

"Good God, no! I can't take you home like this," he gasped, his eyes skating over her revealed body in the see-through gown. Feeling himself begin to harden at just the sight, he forced his eyes away and muttered, "I am taking you to my townhouse. Bet is waiting there. I shall have to send her back to Richard and Christiana's to fetch you something more appropriate to wear."

"I suppose they would realize something was amiss did I show up in someone else's gown," she said agreeably, and wiggled her bottom about on his leg, apparently trying to find a more comfortable position. "I never noticed before that you had such bony legs, Robert."

"It's not my leg," he muttered and then

could have bit his tongue off at the admission.

"Then what is it? Have you something in your pocket?" she asked curiously, shifting about again.

"Aye," he growled, his hands grasping her hips to hold her still. His eyes then wandered of their own accord down her body again before he could catch himself. Robert looked quickly away and gave himself a firm lecture. This was Lisa Madison who was like a little sister to him. A sweet, innocent, dreamy-eyed — Damn, when the hell had she filled out like this?

Tilting her head, Lisa eyed him curiously. "Can I see it?"

"See what?" he asked with a distracted frown, his eyes sliding back to her, but staying firmly on her face this time.

"What you have in your pocket that's so lumpy and hard?" she explained. "What is it? Show it to me."

Robert simply stared for the longest time, aware that his lumpy hardness was growing lumpier and harder at the very thought of showing it to her. But then he regained enough of his senses to catch her by the hips and shift her to sit on the opposite bench.

"It shan't be long before we reach my townhouse," he announced, desperate to

69

change the subject. "I told the driver to use the back alley so that you wouldn't be seen."

"That was kind. I think," she added with uncertainty. "Although I don't see why I can not be seen entering your townhouse. Unless, of course, it's because I'm a single lady. But everyone knows our families are friends and surely wouldn't think anything of it. It is daytime, after all, and Bet will be there."

"Lisa, Bet is already at the townhouse, so she wouldn't be seen accompanying you," he pointed out patiently, and then added with exasperation, "And frankly, it wouldn't matter if it were morning, noon or night. Dressed as you are it would cause a scene should you be seen at all, let alone entering a man's home."

"What is wrong with the way I am dressed?" she asked with surprise.

"Your gown is see-through," he pointed out, unable to believe she would even ask. Of course, pointing that out made his eyes wander over all that lovely revealed flesh again and he was hard pressed to stop devouring her with his eyes this time.

"Is it?" Lisa asked with what appeared to be real surprise, and then squinted down at herself rather owlishly.

Frowning, Robert asked, "Is there something wrong with your eyes?"

"Yes. No. Well, perhaps," she said on a sigh and then admitted, "Everything has been a little blurry since the second drink Mrs. Morgan insisted I down. Things keep going in and out of focus. Mostly out of focus." She sighed and then confessed, "The only way I recognized that it was you at the window was because your scent drifted in on the breeze when you opened it." She heaved out a little breath and squirmed slightly on her bench seat. "You do have a very particularly lovely scent, Robert. It's spicy and a little woodsy and really quite nice. It makes me all tingly."

"Tingly," Robert echoed faintly.

Lisa smiled at him beatifically and nodded. "Yes, tingly. All over. When I was sitting on your lap your smell seemed to envelop me. I liked that, Robert. Can I not sit there again?"

"No," he growled, desperately battling the urge to say yes and pull her back there himself. "It's not proper."

"Oh, of course," she said on a disappointed little sigh, and then leaned back and announced, "But Robert, I love you. Surely that makes it okay?"

"I love you too," he muttered, struggling to keep his eyes above her neck. "You are

71

like a little sister to me."

Lisa scowled. "I am not your little sister."

"You are to me," Robert assured her, his gaze drifting downward and then quickly away. Forcing some firmness into his voice, he added, "You, Suzette and Christiana have always been like the sisters I never had."

"Sisters," she snapped with disgust. "I am not your sister, Robert Langley."

"Well, that is how I see you, Lisa Madison. Like a sweet little sister." Usually, he added silently. Dear God, there was nothing little sisterly about her just then, and neither his thoughts nor his body's reactions were anywhere near filial in nature.

"Well I am not your little sister, Robert. In fact, there is nothing little about me anymore at all. I'm a grown woman, and if you're too dense to see that, then perhaps it's time I found someone more intelligent to give my love to."

Robert's gaze slid to her again and he quickly removed his cape and leaned forward to wrap it around her, muttering. "I wish you would."

Lisa stiffened as the first real emotions she'd experienced since Mrs. Morgan had forced those drinks on her pierced the fog clouding her brain. And those feelings were disappointment and fury. She had loved this man forever, since she was knee high to her father, and Robert valued it about as much as an old pair of shoes thrown out on the dung heap.

"As you wish," she said coldly, gathering his cape around herself. She then leaned to the window to glance out as the carriage slowed. "That is Richard and Christiana's townhouse."

"Aye," Robert muttered, not bothering to look. "We have to pass it on the way to my place. Close the curtain, Lisa. One of the servants might look out and see you riding past."

Lisa scowled, but just shrugged. "I may as well just go home rather than trouble you to take me to your townhouse. Send Bet home when you get there, please."

"You are not — Lisa!" he snapped as she opened the door and leapt from the stopping vehicle. It was only when her feet hit the pavement that she realized she was barefoot. Ignoring that, she glanced to the front of the carriage to see what had made them stop. Richard and Christiana's neighbors, the Wortheys, were returning home from an outing, their carriage blocking the road as the couple disembarked.

"Lisa!" Robert hissed from behind her, but she ignored him and hurried to the gate leading to the walk to Richard and Christiana's front door. She heard his boots hit the pavement behind her, but didn't glance around, merely hurrying to the door and rushing inside.

The entry was empty. Even in her still somewhat muddled state, Lisa thought that could only be a good thing. Pushing the door closed, she slipped quickly up the stairs, and then along the hall to the room she was occupying, neither slowing nor stopping until she was safely inside.

Once there, however, Lisa paused briefly to lean against the door, her eyes closing. She should want to cry. She should want to scream and throw something. She knew with some part of her brain that she really did want to, but the brief, sharp pang of fury and disappointment that had managed to pierce the numbness claiming her had already receded and become a faint memory. She couldn't seem to feel anything again. All she seemed to want to do was lie down.

Pushing herself away from the door, she crossed the room in what she suspected was an unsteady gait and then simply collapsed on the bed.

■ ■ ■ ■

Robert started to follow Lisa, but stopped after just a couple of steps and waited uncertainly. If her arrival was witnessed, his presence might just cause more trouble. Hell, if Richard had returned by now and witnessed her arrival and her state of dress — or undress as the case may be — he'd come out and demand an explanation. However, if she got in without being seen, his approaching the door might draw attention to her arrival and her state.

He hesitated, unsure what to do, but after several moments passed without anyone coming out after him, Robert turned and got back in the carriage, then tapped on the wall to let his driver know to continue. He would return home and send Bet back to help her mistress. Lisa hadn't been in the best shape and could no doubt use assistance getting out of that gauzy creation laughingly called a gown.

Then he'd take himself down to Mrs. Morgan's and release some of the frustration now filling him by raising a little hell. By the time he finished with her, the woman wouldn't ever again think of mixing herself up in anything like this and he'd know exactly who this "suitor" was . . . And then he'd pay that bastard a visit too.

"Miss."

Lisa stirred sleepily and opened one eye to peer at the woman leaning over her. Bet. Pushing the other eye open, she smiled at her a bit woozily. "Oh, good. You're okay."

"Aye. Thank goodness you are too," Bet said, settling on the side of the bed with a crooked smile. "I was ever so worried until Lord Langley returned and said he'd got you safely away."

Lisa grimaced at the name and then closed her eyes on a muttered, "Horrid man."

"Horrid man?" Bet asked with confusion. "Did you meet the suitor then? Lord Langley said he got you out in time."

"Not the suitor," she growled. "Robert."

"Oh." There was a pause and then Bet asked uncertainly, "Did he behave inappropriately?"

"No . . . the deuced fellow was as proper as could be," she growled with exasperation and then rolled onto her back with an unhappy sigh. "I told him I love him, Bet, but he said flat out that he thinks of me as a little sister."

"In that gown?" Bet asked with amazement.

Lisa glanced down with disinterest. It did seem rather revealing and she suspected she should be embarrassed to be wearing it, but couldn't seem to find the emotion within herself. In fact, she felt rather disconnected from all her emotions at the moment . . . even her exasperation and irritation with Robert were a sort of far-off sensation. As if they were standing outside of her somewhere, there but untouchable. It was really quite strange, Lisa thought, and knew she should probably be alarmed by that too, but wasn't.

What the devil had Mrs. Morgan poured down her throat? she wondered, not for the first time, and then glanced to Bet. "Did you just get home from Robert's?"

"Nay. I've been home for hours. Lord Langley said ye'd most like be needing help getting out of that getup, but when I came up here you were dead to the world so I let you sleep. But if you're going to that ball tonight, ye need to be dressing." She frowned uncertainly. "Are ye going to the ball?"

Lisa debated the matter briefly and almost said no, she wanted to sleep, but then reconsidered. Robert wasn't interested. It appeared she'd wasted her love on him all these years. She was twenty-one years old now, an old maid to many, and here she'd sat on the shelf all these years in the vague hope that Robert would finally notice that she was all grown up. But frankly, if seeing her in this gown didn't stop him from looking at her like a "little sister," nothing would. It was time she took herself off the shelf and found a husband.

Sitting up determinedly, Lisa tossed the covers aside. "Aye. I am going to the ball. 'Tis time I found a husband, Bet, and all of the ton will be at the Landons' season-opening ball, which means every single eligible bachelor presently in town will be there as well."

Noting Bet's concerned expression, she smiled and got to her feet. "Mayhap Findlay, that handsome, blond lord who asked me to dance at the Landon ball two years ago will be there again. He was very handsome and seemed to like me the last time we attended. If he's still single, mayhap he'll ask me to dance again." Her mouth firmed out determinedly. "If he does, this time I shall pay him more attention and let him woo me."

"Are ye sure?" Bet asked, looking troubled. Reaching out to steady her mistress, she added, "Lord Robert said ye'd obviously been given some sort of tincture and I don't think it's quite worn off yet."

"I'm sure it will wear off by the time I'm dressed and ready to go," Lisa said with unconcern, but wasn't at all sure it would. She simply felt . . . well, she felt oddly invincible, untouchable . . . or maybe she just couldn't seem to care.

CHAPTER FIVE

"Robert, I'm surprised to see you here. I thought you intended to avoid these things like the plague this year," Richard commented as Robert reached where he and Daniel stood enjoying a drink on the fringes of the ballroom.

"Aye," Daniel agreed. "Thought you were happy in your bachelorhood and completely uninterested in being chased by marriage-minded maidens and their mothers."

"Aye, I am," Robert muttered, his eyes searching the ballroom. "Where's Lisa?"

"Oh ho, don't tell me you've finally deigned to notice she's all grown up?" Daniel teased with amusement.

Robert shook his head with a frown. He'd certainly noticed that today, but that wasn't why he had asked the question. After a hesitation where he briefly and silently debated just how much to reveal of that day's escapades, he sighed and said solemnly, "I would have a word with you two gentlemen. In private."

Richard raised his eyebrows and exchanged a glance with Daniel, but then the two men turned as one to lead him out of the ballroom. Robert hesitated before following, his gaze searching the room for Lisa again. It was only when he spotted her safely between her two sisters in a group of women at the other side of the ballroom that he relaxed and trailed the other two men.

"Lisa Madison!" Suzette said with amusement as the latest would-be suitor moved disappointedly away. "Why are you lying to all these men and claiming your dance card is full? I know darned right well that you have three dances left.

"I am saving them," Lisa said with a shrug.

"For Robert?" Christiana asked gently.

"Not likely," Lisa said dryly. "I wouldn't waste another dance on him if he were the last man on earth."

She didn't miss the raised eyebrows of her sisters or the glance they exchanged, so wasn't surprised when Suzette asked delicately, "Did you and Robert have a falling out we don't know about?"

"Not at all," Lisa assured them airily. "It's just perfectly obvious that his feelings for me don't reach beyond filial and I've decided that neither do mine. He is far too stupid a man for me. Our children would be dunces. So I am turning my attention to more likely, intelligent game."

"Game?" Suzette asked with disbelief, patting Christiana's back when she choked on the punch she was drinking. Mouth quirking with amusement, she asked, "Are we on a hunt, then?"

"A husband hunt," Lisa said with a firm nod. "I am ready to find a husband, have children, and start my life."

"Hmmm," Christiana murmured. "So if it isn't Robert you are saving those dances for, who is it?"

"It's —" Lisa paused, her eyes lighting up and a smile gracing her lips as she recognized the man approaching them. Tall, fair-haired and with a winning smile that he was presently beaming on her, Charles Findlay, the man she had danced with two years ago. "Him."

"Lord Findlay?" Suzette asked, eyeing the approaching man with interest. "You danced with him the last time we were at the Landons' ball, did you not?"

"Aye," Lisa whispered, her eyes skating over the man and wondering what she'd been thinking back then. Mooning after

Robert when someone like Findlay was holding her in his arms. He truly was a beautiful male, with ice blond hair, strong, acquiline features, wide shoulders and slim hips. Really, he was more handsome even than Robert, she admitted with a smile. Truly, he was an Adonis. If a girl had to wake up to the same face every morning, she could do worse than to find his smiling down at her.

"Ladies," Lord Findlay said in greeting, pausing before them and sketching a graceful bow. Straightening as they murmured in greeting, he smiled. "May I say you all look exceptionally lovely this evening?"

"You may," Suzette said with a laugh. "We may even believe you mean it."

Lord Findlay grinned with appreciation, and then turned his gaze to Lisa. "I arrived later than intended this evening and know there is probably no hope, but you would not have at least one dance left on your card that I might put my name to?"

"As it happens, my lord, we were a bit tardy arriving as well," Lisa lied, retrieving her dance card. "And I believe I just happen to have a couple of dances still free." She perused the small card as if she didn't know exactly which dances she had open, and then asked, "Would you prefer a waltz or a quadrille?"

"Both," he said at once, and then grinned and added, "If I may be so bold?"

Lisa ignored the narrowing of her sisters' eyes and then said lightly, "Well, I shall put you down for the waltz. I suspect I shall be quite worn out by the time the quadrille comes around and in need of refreshment."

"Then I shall be pleased to fetch you a beverage and take you out on the terrace for some night air during the quadrille," he assured her with a grin, and then immediately added, "Along with your sisters, of course."

Lisa smiled and wrote his name into her card. She then nodded and murmured appropriately as he excused himself.

"Who are you and what have you done with my sister?" Suzette asked, catching Lisa's arm and pulling her around to face her and Christiana once the man was gone.

"What ever do you mean?" Lisa asked with feigned confusion. But she knew exactly what Suzette meant. She had handled the entire situation with an aplomb she just didn't normally possess and suspected it was the aftereffects of the drinks Mrs. Morgan had poured down her throat. While she was no longer unsteady on her feet, she did still feel slightly disconnected from her feelings. There hadn't been any of the usual hand sweats or fluttery nervousness that she had suffered in the past at country dances. Tonight she'd felt completely unconcerned and confident as each man approached, even with the very handsome Lord Findlay, and that was despite the fact that she'd hoped he would approach.

This unusual confidence and calm had allowed her to arrange things as she wished, however, which she was grateful for. At least one good thing had come out of today's adventures. Well, two, she decided. If Robert was never going to love her as she loved him, it was better she accept it now than to wait on the shelf until she was too old to find a husband.

The thought made her chin lift with determination. Bollocks to Robert. He would die a lonely old man, and it would be all his own fault for turning away the one woman who could love him with all his flaws.

"You —" Suzette began, but then paused as the music started and Rotham, the first fellow on Lisa's dance card came to claim her.

Lisa was a good dancer. Despite being a little disoriented, she managed to follow the steps with grace and ease as she was repeatedly claimed and whirled around the room by admirers. But she was on automatic, her eyes searching the ballroom for two men, Lord Findlay and Robert. She was keeping tabs on Lord Findlay to see who he danced with and who her competition was. She was searching for Robert because . . . well, out of habit, she supposed, and forced her attention back to her dance partner.

Really, she had no further interest in Robert Maitland, Lord Langley, Lisa reminded herself firmly. Besides, he obviously hadn't bothered to come tonight. But then, why would he? When Christiana had asked Richard if Robert planned to come tonight as they'd ridden here in the Radnor carriage, her husband had laughed and said no, Robert intended to avoid being anywhere there might be husband-hunting maids and their mothers.

Well, bully for him. She didn't need him here distracting her anyway, Lisa decided. Though, one small part of her brain wished he was here to see what a success she was. And she *was* a success. Every man who had approached her to request a place on her dance card had complimented her on her beauty, her wit and her grace. It was like balm to her shaken confidence after Robert's "little sister" business. It seemed all men did not see her as still belonging in the schoolroom.

"My dance, I believe."

Lisa came to a halt beside her last partner who had gallantly been leading her off the dance floor, and glanced around to flash a smile at Lord Findlay. "Yes, my lord, it is."

"Ahh," Lord Pembroke murmured, releasing her arm and giving a bow. "Thank you for your charming company, Miss Madison. It was a delight to dance with a lady as lovely and graceful as you."

Lisa turned her beaming smile on Pembroke now. Dark-haired and nearly as attractive as Lord Findlay, Pembroke had been amusing and fun for most of the dance until her mind had begun to wander.

"Thank you, my lord. I enjoyed it," she assured him.

"Then perhaps if you are attending the Hammonds' ball tomorrow night, you would be kind enough to grant me a dance there?" he suggested hopefully.

"Most definitely, my lord. I shall look forward to it," she said with an encouraging grin.

"As will I," he assured her as Lord Findlay led her back onto the dance floor.

"You've won a heart there," Lord Findlay

said with amusement as he took her into his arms for the dance. "But then from what I have seen you have won many hearts tonight. Almost every man who has danced with you has walked away happy to have made your acquaintance."

"Why my lord, one would think you had been watching me all night," she teased lightly.

"I have," he said without apology. "It's impossible not to. You exude an air of confidence and beauty that is hard to look away from."

Lisa blinked at the words and then laughed gaily. Her confidence was a combination of the residual effects of Mrs. Morgan's potion and all the compliments she'd received this evening. She hadn't realized until tonight just how Robert's lack of return interest in her had squashed her self-esteem. She knew it hadn't been deliberate on his part, but that had been the end result anyway — confusion and despair over the fact that he didn't return her feelings, concern that she wasn't pretty enough, witty enough, smart enough. But it was hard to feel that way after being showered with compliments all night by the other men in attendance. It seemed Robert was just a dullard too blind to see how lucky he was to have her affections.

"Are you enjoying your stay in London so far?" Lord Findlay asked, drawing her attention back to him.

"Well, it's definitely been interesting," Lisa said wryly and then to keep him from questioning how, added, "although my maid and I only arrived two days ago. It is lovely to see my sisters again and get caught up on things."

"Aye. You don't come to town to visit them often enough I think." When she raised her eyebrows, wondering how he knew how often she came to town, he added, "I was most disappointed when you disappeared from town after just a couple balls the year before last. And devastated that you didn't return last year."

Lisa found herself chuckling at the claim. While he was offering her a sad moue, it was somewhat ruined by the twitching of his lips and the fact that his eyes were twinkling with merriment. He was obviously teasing and flirting with her. It was fun. Much more fun than mooning after a reluctant Robert.

"I hardly think a handsome fellow like you suffered for lack of company," she said lightly.

"I didn't," he admitted easily. "However,

all the other young women seemed dull and unattractive after holding you in my arms."

Lisa's eyes widened slightly. If she had been feeling quite herself, she suspected she would have blushed madly at the words and got all flustered. At the moment, however, all it did was make her smile. The things he was saying could have come from one of the books she read, spoken by the hero to the heroine. They were quite lovely, not to mention flattering and charming. They made her feel beautiful and wanted. And she liked it.

"I enjoyed our dance that night as well," she said boldly.

Lord Findlay raised one dubious eyebrow. "And here I thought you were distracted during our dance."

Lisa laughed wryly. "I fear I was a little. There was much going on at the time, but I certainly remembered you afterward, my lord."

"Why? Did I step on your toes?" he teased.

Lisa grinned, but shook her head. "You dance beautifully and you know it."

"Then what made you remember me?" Findlay asked, the words almost a challenge.

"Because you are a very attractive man, my lord," she said simply, unconcerned with meeting the challenge. She had no doubt he knew he was handsome. "You are handsome enough that it would make it hard for a girl to forget."

"Really?" he asked with interest. "You find me attractive?"

"Oh very," she assured him with amusement, and then added, "So much so that I deliberately kept a dance free for you in case you were here tonight."

Lord Findlay blinked in surprise at her words and Lisa supposed most women wouldn't have made the admission. They would have played coy and probably teased and flirted while acting like they weren't attracted to him. Such games just seemed silly to her. The man saw right through it anyway if he had half a brain. So, why bother?

"My word, you are the most refreshingly honest female I have met in a good long while," Lord Findlay breathed finally, his arms tightening around her a little more and drawing her almost scandalously close.

"Hmmm," Lisa murmured, noting the way his eyes had darkened. She grinned and eased back from him a bit, making their embrace more proper. "And beautiful, smart and witty according to all the men I have danced with tonight."

"Definitely all of that," he agreed without hesitation. "Your eyes sparkle with intelligence and mischief and your lips . . . they put a man in mind of kissing you."

"Really?" she asked with interest. "Does that mean you want to kiss me, my lord?"

"Definitely," Findlay assured her, all teasing gone and Lisa allowed a burst of laughter to slip from her lips. She felt so . . . well, powerful, she supposed. All these compliments from so many different men after years of nothing from the one she had been interested in . . . Well, it was heady, made her feel good, made her feel lovely and wanted and . . . She liked it. A lot.

"I fear our dance is over," Lord Findlay said with regret, bringing her to a halt as the music ended.

"How sad," she said, her lips curving into a happy smile.

"Yes. It is," he assured her, shifting her to his side and tucking her hand into the crook of his elbow to lead her off the floor. His head dipped to hers as he asked, "When is our quadrille? I would not wish to miss my chance to fetch you a refreshment or escort you out onto the terrace."

"Now," Lisa said, flashing him a smile as the next dance began.

"Then I am a fortunate man, indeed," Lord Findlay said with a grin. "I shall leave you to ask your sisters if they wish to join us on the terrace while I fetch you that drink."

"And you say Mrs. Morgan was gone when you returned to the brothel?" Richard asked grimly, pacing his library.

Robert nodded solemnly. He'd just finished explaining the adventure he'd had to rescue Lisa, ending with how he'd returned to Morgan's directly after stopping to collect and drop off Bet. Only he'd arrived at the brothel to find the woman had packed in a rush and fled.

"It would seem she discovered almost at once that Lisa and Bet were gone and decided a trip to the Continent might be in her best interest." Robert explained what he'd learned that afternoon. "The cook said Morgan packed what she could as quickly as she could and left moments before I arrived."

"I'll say it was in her best interests," Daniel said grimly.

"Hmmm." Richard nodded. "Morgan never was a stupid woman. She must have realized the three of us would not be pleased. We might not have been able to have her arrested without damaging Lisa's reputation and raising a scandal, but drugging and holding the maid could have been used against her. I doubt she'll return anytime soon for fear of landing in shackles." His mouth tightened and he glanced to Robert. "If she left only moments before you arrived —"

"I did have my driver take me around to try to catch up to her. I even went down to the docks, but there was no sign of her at all," he said with displeasure. It still irked him that the woman had got away.

"She could have traveled up the coast to any number of places and caught a boat from there," Daniel pointed out.

"Aye," Robert nodded grimly. "Which is why I didn't bother to search further on my own. I plan to hire a runner tomorrow morning to track the woman and either get her to reveal who the suitor was, or bring her back for charges. I suspect given that choice she'll reveal who hired her to drug and hold Lisa for him."

"No doubt," Richard agreed. "I'm just surprised you didn't hire the runner before coming here tonight."

"I would have if there had been time," Robert assured him. "But it was late when I gave up the search. And I knew Lisa was planning to attend this ball. I thought it best not to leave her on her own until we sort out who this 'suitor' was. He might make another attempt to get her." He frowned and added, "In fact, I don't like that she is out there right now without anyone to watch over her, but I didn't dare speak of this out in the ballroom where someone might hear, and you two needed to be apprised of the situation so you could watch for trouble."

"Christiana and Suzette will keep an eye on her," Daniel said reassuringly, and then asked, "So the cook wouldn't tell you who this supposed suitor was?"

Robert shook his head solemnly. "She didn't know. Neither did any of the women I questioned. It seems it was a well-guarded secret."

"Or the women are loyal," Richard suggested dryly.

Robert gave a dry laugh. "Believe me, none of the women were feeling terribly loyal when I spoke to them. They were all furious with Morgan. It seems she gave them all only until tomorrow morning to get out of the brothel and find themselves a new situation, then someone is coming to close it down and sell it."

"Hmmm," Daniel muttered. "I don't suppose they would feel very loyal then."

Robert shook his head and pointed out to Richard, "You'll have to hire someone to

95

guard Lisa until this is over. She —"

"He can't," Daniel interrupted.

Robert blinked in surprise. "Of course he can."

"No, he can't. Christiana is with child and to hire someone he'll have to explain what's happened and Richard doesn't want Christiana upset right now. We were just talking about that before you arrived," Daniel said easily.

"What?" Robert's eyes widened and swung to Richard. "Christiana's with child?"

Richard didn't respond at first. His gaze was on Daniel, but then he smiled faintly and nodded.

"Well, that's brilliant!" Robert laughed and moved to slap his shoulder. "How far along is she? And why didn't she tell me?" he added with a frown.

"She isn't far along and doesn't want anyone to know until it's a little further on," Daniel answered for Richard. "So, as you can see, he can't hire guards and such and put her through all that stress and worry again."

"Hmmm. No, Christiana tends to be a worrier. We don't want her to lose another child," Robert agreed with a frown. It was the second time Christiana had got with child since their marriage. Losing the first had crushed her, losing a second would devastate her. Glancing to Daniel, he suggested, "Well then perhaps you could have Lisa stay with you and Suzette and hire a guard . . ." His voice died away as Daniel began to shake his head.

"You know Suzette can't keep a secret to save her soul," he pointed out dryly. "We can't possibly tell her either. Christiana would know at once. Besides, how would we explain moving Lisa? Christiana would want to know why."

Robert rubbed his forehead unhappily. "Well, what are we going to do then? We can't just leave her unguarded. This suitor might try to get his hands on her again using another method."

"Yes, he could," Richard agreed grimly, for some reason glaring at Daniel.

"Well, we can't bring in an outsider without the whole situation getting out and Christiana and Suzette knowing," Daniel said resolutely.

"I realize that," Robert said unhappily. "But she needs watching until we can sort out who the suitor is and ensure he won't try again."

"The three of us will have to do the watching then," Daniel said with a shrug.

"How the hell are we supposed to —"

Robert began with frustration.

"You don't mind house guests for a bit, do you, Richard?" Daniel interrupted him.

"House guests?" Richard asked with surprise.

"Robert, Suzette and I," he explained. "You can say Robert is having renovations done to his London home and you offered him a room while it's under way, and . . . Well, actually, I suppose there's really no good excuse for Suzette and I to stay there," he said with a frown. "But if you and Robert are there to watch Lisa at night, we don't need to sleep there too. We shall just visit a lot during the day. That won't be considered unusual at all since Lisa is newly up from the country. The girls spent the first day doing nothing but natter and catch-up and would have done the same today had Christiana and Suzette not already been roped into that tea."

"Aren't you clever," Richard said slowly, and then added, "Of course, Robert is welcome to stay at Radnor and spend all his time looking out for Lisa."

The two men exchanged a strange smile, but Robert hardly noticed; he was more concerned with the logistics of keeping Lisa safe. Nodding, he muttered, "That would work. I can help keep an eye on her and between the three of us we can assure she isn't left alone until this is all done and dusted."

"It's settled then," Daniel said beaming brightly as he slapped Robert on the back. "You can move into Radnor tonight after the ball."

Robert nodded and then frowned. "Speaking of which, we've been in here a while. I'd better go out and check on Lisa. It's not likely someone would try to snatch her away from the ball with so many people around, but it's better to be safe than sorry."

"Yes. It's probably best to stick close to her for the next little while," Daniel said solemnly. "None of us would forgive ourselves if anything happened to her. Not to mention Christiana and Suzette would never forgive us either."

"Hmm." Robert headed for the door with a nod, leaving the men to chatter quietly.

"It's a beautiful night," Lisa said on a sigh, leaning on the terrace rail and peering up at the star-studded sky. The stars somehow didn't seem as bright here as they were in the country, but it was still lovely.

"Is it?" Lord Findlay asked with disinterest.

Lisa glanced sideways with surprise to find

him peering down at her with hooded eyes. Suzette and Christiana hadn't been interested in a walk on the terrace. They were alone. Or as alone as one could get at the busiest ball of the season, where even the terrace tended to be crowded. It wasn't too bad right now though, she noted. There were only two other couples on the terrace besides themselves, and they had spaced themselves out, seeking the shadows and privacy.

"I shall have to take your word for it that it's beautiful. I'm afraid I cannot be bothered to check for myself with you here to look at."

Turning back to Lord Findlay, Lisa grinned at the compliment and shook her head. "Then you're missing out, my lord. The sky really is lovely."

"As are you," he assured her solemnly. "Your beauty challenges the stars."

"Oh." She widened her eyes, fighting an irresistible urge to giggle at his flattery. The drink Mrs. Morgan had given her was obviously still affecting her, she decided, but said, "I suspect you are a dangerous man to innocent young debutantes, Lord Findlay."

"Call me Charles," he suggested, his voice seductive.

"Charles then," she said on a laugh, and

then asked, "How many girls have you charmed with such flowery words?"

Even as the words left her lips, Lisa wondered where they had come from. It was just so unlikely a thing for her to say. She simply wasn't this laissez faire about men and their attentions. On the other hand, she suspected if Robert had said those words to her, she wouldn't be nearly so relaxed and amused.

"I assure you I don't make a habit of saying such things to debutantes," Charles said solemnly, moving closer to take the drink from her hand. He set it carefully on the rail and then caught her by the arms, drawing her forward as he murmured, "In fact, I generally bypass these gatherings to avoid being hunted down and leg shackled."

"Do you?" Lisa asked with mild interest as she watched his head lower toward hers. "Then why are you here tonight?"

"I had heard you were back in town and was hoping to see you again," he whispered, his lips a hair's breadth from hers.

"Why?" she asked. Her eyes sliding from his eyes to his lips and back, her mind wondering what it would be like when he kissed her.

"Because I have been endlessly fascinated by you since this same ball two years ago.

Your smile and beauty have haunted me ever since, and all I've thought about since then was taking you in my arms and kissing —"

"There you are!"

Lisa pulled back with a start, her head swiveling to find Robert bearing down on them like an annoyed parent. Vaguely aware that Charles was releasing her and stepping back, Lisa frowned with annoyance at Robert for interrupting what would have been her first kiss. Not that he noticed, he was too busy giving her a disapproving scowl.

"What are you doing out here alone?" Robert asked, catching her arm and dragging her toward the terrace doors.

"I'm not alone, Robert," Lisa snapped, tugging at her arm. "I am with Lord Findlay."

"But without Christiana or Suzette," Robert countered, not releasing her arm. "Proper young ladies do not step out with strange men to —"

"He is not strange," Lisa hissed, lowering her voice to avoid drawing attention their way as he dragged her through the terrace doors and back inside. "And do stop pulling me about like a recalcitrant child. You are acting like a jealous ass and causing a scene."

Robert eased his hold and slowed so that it looked less like he was dragging her and more like he was walking her. He then paused and turned to eye her solemnly. "I am not jealous, Lisa. But after what happened today, you should not be wandering outside with anyone. For all we know, Lord Findlay is the suitor Mrs. Morgan was procuring you for. Any one of the men here tonight could be. You must be careful."

Lisa blinked in surprise at the reminder of her narrow escape that day. Not that she'd forgotten it, but it hadn't occurred to her that she might still be in danger. She'd just assumed that with that day's plot foiled, it was done. Perhaps that had been naïve, but . . . Grimacing, she nodded reluctantly in understanding. "Very well. I shall be more cautious, Robert."

"Yes, you will. Because I shall ensure it," he said firmly, starting to walk again.

"What do you mean, you shall ensure it?" she asked warily, keeping her voice low as he led her through the ball attendees.

"I had a talk with Richard and Daniel and we have made arrangements to keep you safe until we find this so-called suitor."

"You told Richard and Daniel about today?" Lisa asked in almost a squeal of horror.

"They had to be made aware of the situation to help keep you safe," he said firmly.

"Christ," she muttered with disgust and thought that the last of the drugged drink must be finally wearing off. She was definitely feeling her emotions again, mostly mortification at her sisters' husbands knowing about her ordeal that day.

"Did you just cuss?"

Lisa blinked and noted that Robert had stopped walking and was now staring down at her with shock. Lifting her chin, she glared back at him defiantly. "And what if I did? I am not a child, Robert. I may cuss if I wish. And I will go out on the terrace with who I wish, and — what arrangements?" she interrupted herself to ask suddenly as those words sank through her brain.

"I shall be staying at the Radnor townhouse and watching over you day and night to help keep you safe until this situation is resolved," he announced calmly.

Lisa simply stared at him. It occurred to her that right up until that afternoon in his carriage, this news would have put her over the moon. The very idea of his being so close would have been like a Christmas and birthday gift all rolled into one and would have had her beaming and dancing with excitement. Right now though, after his breaking of her heart in the carriage, it seemed like a nightmare. Robert's presence day and night. Having to be in his presence at all times when he felt nothing for her but filial emotions. She wasn't having that!

"Miss Madison?"

Relieved to have the excuse to do so, Lisa turned away from Robert to face Lord Findlay with a smile that was wider and warmer than it would have normally been. "Aye, my lord?"

"You left your drink behind," he said with a smile, offering her the glass and completely ignoring Robert, who was scowling again.

"Oh, thank you." Lisa beamed and accepted the drink, saying a bit archly, "I do apologize for Lord Langley's rudeness in dragging me off like that."

"Not at all. 'Tis hardly your fault," Lord Findlay said easily, still not acknowledging the other man's presence with even a glance. Smiling, he asked, "Are you attending the Hammonds' ball tomorrow night?"

"No," Robert answered for her, moving closer.

"Yes, I am," Lisa countered, ignoring him just as Lord Findlay was. "My sisters and I spoke about it when I arrived yesterday. We plan to attend and have already sent a reply that we would."

"Then I hope you will agree to another waltz with me there, Miss Madison," Lord Findlay said with a grin.

"I shall save you one," she promised. "And keep another quadrille free as well."

"You are too kind," he murmured taking her hand and bowing to place a kiss on it. His lips never made contact, however, because Robert's patience had apparently run out and Lisa suddenly found herself tugged away and hurried through the crowd once more.

"Really, Robert," Lisa said with exasperation, struggling not to spill her drink. "You are being incredibly rude."

"And you are behaving like an idiot," he growled. "Smiling and fawning all over Findlay like some loose —"

His voice died as she jerked her arm from his hold. He stopped at once and whirled on her with surprise, but that turned to shock when the contents of her glass splashed into his face.

"You —" he began furiously.

"Miss Madison?"

Lisa turned from Robert and glanced in question to the man now at her side. Lord Tibald, she thought was his name. She raised her eyebrows in question. "Yes?"

"I believe this is our dance," he explained and Lisa nodded grimly.

"Oh, yes, Lord Tibald. I believe you're right. This is your dance." She forced a smile for him that withered as she faced Robert and silently slapped her empty glass into his hand. Without another word, she turned back to Lord Tibald and offered her hand.

Smiling, he took it and laid it over his arm to lead her away from Robert and onto the dance floor.

"Are you all right?"

Lisa stopped glaring at Robert, who had moved to the refreshment table to find a napkin to dry himself off with and glanced to Lord Tibald in question. "What?"

"You appear a bit upset," he offered quietly. "Would you prefer to step out for some air rather than dance?"

"Oh, no," she said on a sigh, and then lips quirking, added wryly, "Langley would just drag me back inside anyway."

"Ah." Lord Tibald was briefly silent, and then asked tentatively. "Has Lord Langley a prior claim on your attentions? Should I be —"

"No," Lisa assured him grimly. "He has no claim at all. Robert is . . . Well, he is an old friend of the family, like an annoying older brother. And tonight he's being particularly annoying," she added with displeasure.

"Ahh," Lord Tibald repeated and something of the sound made her glance to him. This time she really looked at him, noting that he was as handsome as Lord Findlay, though in a dark, dashing way rather than the icy beauty of the other man. He also had deep dark eyes and a charming smile.

"I apologize, my lord," she said, forcing herself to relax and allowing a smile to claim her lips. "It's not well done of me to take out my annoyance with Robert on you."

"Oh, you weren't taking it out on me," he assured her gallantly. "You just seemed distracted and distressed.

She smiled slightly and shrugged. "Well, if I was, I am no more. You have managed to distract me from my distraction."

He chuckled at the claim. "You're really quite lovely when you smile, Miss Madison."

"And you're very handsome, Lord Tibald, so we are a match," she said with a grin.

Lord Tibald chuckled at her boldness and drew her a little closer.

"I see she's well and hasn't been snatched away," Richard commented, drawing Robert's scowling attention as he and Daniel approached. Raising one eyebrow, he added, "You, on the other hand, appear a bit vexed . . . and damp."

"She is —" Robert cut himself off and turned to glower at Lisa as her gay laughter sounded. She and Lord Tibald were apparently having a grand time . . . and were dancing entirely too closely. Finally, he muttered, "She is going to be difficult."

"Lisa?" Richard asked with surprise, his gaze going to the couple. "No. She is never difficult. She matches Christiana for sweetness."

"Lisa may even surpass Christiana in sweetness," Daniel suggested, and then added, "Suzette is the difficult one."

Robert noted the man's grin. It seemed to suggest he liked that "difficulty" in his wife. Shaking his head, he glanced back to the woman under discussion and grimaced. "Well, Lisa is being difficult tonight. I found her on the terrace with Findlay. The man was moving in for a kiss as I arrived. And she was letting him," he added with disbelief.

"Well, that is hardly being difficult. Perhaps she likes him," Daniel said.

Robert frowned at the suggestion, not at all pleased by it for some reason. Shifting uncomfortably, he muttered, "Yes, well when I dragged her away and explained that she had to be more careful until we found out who the suitor was, she threw her drink in my face."

There was silence for a moment, and then Daniel cleared his throat and said, "You are sure it was your explanation that had her tossing her drink in your face?"

"Well, it was after that really," he admitted unhappily. "I may have said something that she didn't appreciate."

"Ah," Richard murmured. "And what would that be, pray tell?"

Robert shifted again, and then grimaced and admitted, "She was behaving a bit . . . Well, she was laughing and smiling and flirting with Findlay and I may have said that her behavior was a bit loose."

"Ahhh." It was Daniel who spoke this time, amusement underlining the sound. "And then she threw her drink in your face?"

Robert nodded.

"Well, I think you got off lucky," Daniel said dryly. "Suzette would probably punch me if I suggested her behavior was . . . er . . . loose. In fact, I am surprised you said it. If she was just talking and smiling —"

"As I said, he was about to kiss her when

110

I arrived. And she was going to let him," he protested.

"What do you care?" Richard asked patiently. "You don't want her."

"Or *do* you?" Daniel added.

"No, of course not," Robert muttered, his gaze turning to Lisa again. At least he didn't want her in the way they were speaking of. He didn't want a wife, didn't want his life to turn into the misery of an unhappy marriage. He did, however, want Lisa for other purposes, ones he couldn't possibly carry out or even consider.

It was that damned see-through dress, Robert thought grimly. He couldn't get the vision of her naked body beneath the filmy cloth out of his mind. The luscious curves, the dusky rose of her nipples . . . Damn. He could have happily lived a lifetime never having seen that. Now it had raised a whole passel of completely unbrotherly feelings in him for the girl that he just didn't know what to do with.

He needed to hire that runner and get this whole situation resolved as quickly as possible, Robert decided. He also needed a night with his mistress soon. Hopefully a romp with Giselle would help wipe the vision of Lisa in the brothel from his mind. Perhaps then he could return to seeing her

as sweet, young, dreamy-eyed, silly little
Lisa Madison.

CHAPTER SIX

The slamming of her bedroom door stirred Lisa from sleep and had her blinking her eyes open to see Bet rushing excitedly toward her.

"You'll never believe it," Bet said excitedly, rushing around the bed to her side, her face flushed with excitement. "Lord Langley is here. Cook says he spent the night and is going to stay for days. That he is having some painting done at his townhouse and Lord Radnor invited him to reside here to avoid the smell and noise."

Lisa groaned and pulled her pillow to cover her head with disgust, only to have Bet pull it away.

"Didn't you hear me? Lord Langley is here," she said slowly and loudly as if Lisa may have misheard her.

"I heard," she said with a grimace. "And I already knew. The painting is just an excuse. He's staying here to keep an eye on me until they find out who the suitor was. The men seem to think the fellow might make another attempt to take me."

Bet's eyes had grown wider and larger as Lisa spoke, and now concern covered her face. "Really? I hadn't thought of that. I thought that business was done once he got ye safely away." She bit her lip worriedly. "Ye shall have to be careful then."

Lisa sighed and took her pillow from Bet's hands to put it back under her head. "I shall be. But right now I am going back to sleep."

"Wouldn't ye rather get up and go down to breakfast?" Bet asked with a frown. "Lord Radnor and Lord Langley just went down. Ye can still join them if we hurry."

"Why on earth would I trouble myself to dine with a man who isn't the least bit interested in me?" Lisa asked grimly and turned on her side, eyes closing.

"Are ye sure that's all he feels?" Bet asked with a frown. "His wanting to look out for ye shows he cares. You always said he did and —"

"I was wrong," she interrupted with annoyance. "He made it abundantly clear that he thinks of me as nothing more than a little sister, Bet."

"Oh," she said sadly. "Well . . . what are you going to do then?"

"Find a husband among the available bachelors this season and forget about him," she said firmly. "But to do that I need my rest."

"Right," Bet murmured, getting the point. "I shall let ye sleep then."

"Thank you," Lisa whispered, and listened as the maid left the room. She lay still and tried to relax into sleep, but it wasn't as easy as she'd hoped. She was awake now, and not likely to find sleep again.

Lisa shifted from one side to the other, and then rolled onto her back and stared up at the ceiling, grimacing when her stomach growled. Sighing, she finally just gave up and got out of bed. She was hungry. She may as well get up and go below. The problem was she had sent Bet away.

Lisa shrugged. She could dress herself, and she'd just leave her hair down. It wasn't like she cared to look attractive for Richard or Robert anyway.

Decision made, she walked over to kneel in front of her chest and began to sort through her gowns. After a moment, she sat back on her heels with disgust. Every single gown she owned was awash in frills and ruffles, and for some reason, she was repulsed by the overly feminine creations now. She'd always thought them pretty before, but last night at the ball she'd noticed that they seemed to make the other women look young and sweet. It was no wonder Robert had seen her that way for so long, she'd thought, and now found herself preferring a more simple arrangement with less of the ruffling.

Lisa hesitated for a moment and then lifted out a pale pink gown and eyed the ruffles narrowly. They just had to go, she decided, and grabbing a handful of the material, began to rip.

"Do you plan to go out to see the runner, or is he coming here?"

Robert chewed and swallowed the blood pudding he had just taken a bite of. "I sent my valet with a message for him to come here before I came in to breakfast. I didn't know what your plans were for the day and thought it best not to leave the house in case you had appointments and couldn't be here to watch Lisa."

Richard nodded. "As it happens I do have appointments today, so that's for the best. I — Oh good morning, Lisa."

Robert returned his attention to his plate and raised his toast for a bite, but lifted his head sharply at Richard's greeting . . . and nearly choked on his toast at the sight of

Lisa. She was wearing a pale pink gown that suited her coloring beautifully. In fact, at first glance he'd almost been tricked into thinking she wasn't wearing a gown at all, it matched her skin so well. It was also extremely low cut, revealing a good deal of cleavage he just wasn't used to seeing on her. The gown was also plainer than he was used to her wearing, without the usual ruffles, and she had also left her hair down in a mass of tousled, loose curls that fell around her shoulders and trailed down her back. It was the hair that had him nearly choking; it reminded him of how she'd looked yesterday when he'd found her at Mrs. Morgan's, and his body responded much as it had then, snapping to attention.

"Good morning, Richard. I hope you slept well," Lisa said pleasantly as she moved to the sideboard to collect a plate and begin piling food on it.

"Very well, thank you," Richard said easily. "And you?"

"Yes, thank you," Lisa said cheerfully, her concentration on the food she was selecting from the offerings. "But then I was nicely worn out after the ball. Slept like a dream."

"Yes. I'm surprised you're up so early after the late night we had," Richard commented.

"Well, I didn't plan to be," Lisa said with

a laugh, turning to head to the table. "But Bet came in and woke me early. She had found out Robert was here and was under the mistaken impression that I would want to breakfast with him. I didn't," she added with amusement, "But once I was awake, I couldn't get back to sleep, so . . ." She shrugged and settled in the seat on Richard's left, directly across from Robert.

"Ah," Richard murmured and Robert was aware he was glancing at him to see how he was taking this news, but Robert simply continued to stare at Lisa. She hadn't even glanced his way to acknowledge him since entering, and continued to ignore him now. It left him free to ogle her in her new incarnation, or at least one he'd never seen before. Until yesterday, he'd never seen her with her hair down. She'd always worn it in pigtails, then a ponytail and then in those fussy, upswept dos the women all graduated to for the balls. He liked her better this way. She looked soft and luscious, like she'd just rolled out of bed.

"So what are your plans for the day?" Richard asked after several moments of silence had passed.

"Well, I hadn't had any really," Lisa admitted, glancing to her brother-in-law with a wry smile. "However, I noticed there

118

were a bunch of calling cards in the salver in the entry on my way downstairs and stopped to see what that was all about. It appears I have several requests for calls today."

Robert frowned at this news. He'd noticed the cards in the silver salver by the door on his way by, but hadn't stopped to look at them.

"Yes, I noticed them myself," Richard murmured with amusement. "It appears you were quite a hit last night. There are at least six cards from men hoping for permission to call today."

"Hmm." Lisa nodded, and then swallowed the bit of egg she'd taken a bite of. "It was fun, and fortunately all the cards are from men I wouldn't mind seeing again. I suppose I shall send replies agreeing to see them."

"Is there something wrong, Robert?" Richard asked, startling him out of the scowl he was giving Lisa.

"She shouldn't be agreeing to visits until we find out who the suitor was," he growled, more irritated than he should have been at this news.

"Well, they will hardly drag her from the house," Richard said reasonably. "I'm sure it will be fine. Although, I don't suggest you have all six come today," he added, glancing back to Lisa. "It might cause a brawl in the parlor."

She laughed gaily at the suggestion. "Oh, surely not, Richard. They are all gentlemen."

"All but the one who paid Mrs. Morgan to drug and strip you naked for his pleasure," Robert snapped, finally garnering her attention.

Lisa turned a scalding look his way. In contrast, her voice was dead cold when she spoke. "I was not naked, Robert. You were not looking very carefully if you thought I was. I was wearing a very lovely gown. In fact, it's so lovely I think I shall keep it to wear on my wedding night for my husband."

"For your husband?" he asked with disbelief.

"Yes, my husband," she said with a shrug, turning her attention back to her plate. "I plan to marry this year. I just haven't decided which lucky man shall get me."

Robert stared at the top of her head blankly, his whole world shaken for some reason. He supposed it was because he was used to having her silent adoration and had never considered the possibility of losing it. Really, it was rather good for a man's ego to have a pretty girl's cherishing eyes following him about, and every word from her mouth sweet and complimentary. However, it seemed Richard and Daniel were right. She had given up on him and was actively seeking a husband. Someone who would replace him in her affections.

"It's foolhardy to have those men here when one of them could have dishonorable intentions. I forbid it," Robert said grimly and knew that was the wrong thing to say at once. The way she stiffened and the icy expression on her face when she lifted it to peer at him made him wish he'd thought more carefully before speaking.

"You forbid it?" she asked silkily. "I'm sorry, Robert, but despite your thinking of me as a little sister, you are *not* my big brother and don't have the right to forbid me *anything*. Besides," she added dryly, "no one would be stupid enough to call and then try to snatch me away so openly."

"I may not have the right to forbid you seeing any of these men, but Richard does," Robert said quietly and glanced to him, fully expecting the man to back him up on this.

Instead, Richard hesitated, then said apologetically, "I'm sorry, but she is right, Robert. If the suitor is among her callers today, he is hardly likely to try to take her away from here under the noses of the whole household. He's more likely to try another sneak attack as he did using Mrs. Morgan. It should be safe enough for her to have gentleman callers here. Besides, you'll be here to keep an eye on things."

Robert frowned, but couldn't argue with the logic of that. He wanted to, though. The idea of a passel of men trailing through the house to see Lisa bothered him a great deal. And not just because he was worried one of them might have arranged for her to be kidnapped with the intent to ravish her. If he hadn't gotten there in time . . . The image of some faceless man pawing at Lisa in the see-through gown rose up in his mind. It then turned into Robert himself, caressing and kissing her, suckling at her breasts through the gauzy cloth, licking his way down over her belly as he urged her back onto the bed —

"Then I should go send replies before I bathe and let Bet fix my hair," Lisa announced, pushing her plate away and standing.

An empty plate, Robert saw and wondered how long he'd been sitting there imagining ravishing her. Little Lisa Madison. The girl he'd looked on as a sister for nearly two decades. Christ, he was losing his mind, he realized watching Lisa leave the room, his eyes dropping over her body as she went.

"Are you all right?"

Robert gave a start at Richard's question and glanced to him blankly.

"You're looking a bit flushed," Richard said gently. "I hope you aren't angry that I sided with her rather than you. I simply don't see any reason not to let the men visit. I really don't think if her suitor is among them, that he'll try anything here, Robert. It would be incredibly foolish."

"No. Of course, you're right. I'm not angry about that," Robert said quickly, and then added, "And I'm fine. Just a little worried is all."

"Of course," Richard murmured, but Robert could have sworn there was amusement twinkling in the man's eyes and suspected he had some idea of exactly where Robert's thoughts had gone.

"All of yer gowns?" Bet asked with amazement.

"Yes," Lisa said firmly, stripping off the pale pink dress she'd worn to breakfast and stepping into the tub. "Every single one."

"But . . . the ruffles are lovely. They look —"

"Young and sweet," Lisa said grimly. "And

I am done with that. I am here to find a husband, Bet. I have to look like a woman, not a child."

Bet was silent for a moment, and then held up two dresses and pointed out, "But all the unmarried ladies wear gowns like these."

"Then I shall stand out among them," Lisa said with a shrug as she sank into the water. She released a little sigh as the warm, soft water enveloped her, and then picked up the soap as she added, "And I think we should try a simpler hairstyle as well. Something more like what Christiana wears."

Bet was silent for a moment and then shook her head, "All right then. I shall start on the dresses while you bathe. Tell me when you're ready for me to help wash your hair."

Lisa nodded and began to work the soap into a lather, a small smile playing about her lips. She hadn't missed Robert's reaction to her on entering the breakfast room that morning. The man's eyes had practically been on fire as they'd scraped over her. Until that moment she truly had given up on him, but after that reaction . . . well, it just seemed to her that perhaps he wasn't as immune as he pretended. So, she was redoubling her efforts, only she was changing tactics. By the time she was done with making herself over, there would be no way the man would be able to see her as anything like a child again.

Lisa wasn't naïve enough to think that would be enough to move him to claim her though. She was going to take a page out of that story about Lady Silvia and Lord James and use other men to drive Robert wild with jealousy. If that didn't work . . . well, she would give up on him then. But she would try this first. Which probably meant she was an idiot. She should really give up on the man, if for pride's sake only. After all he'd been pretty insulting with that comment about being loose and he wasn't exactly being nice to her at the moment. However, it was the first time he'd ever been anything close to rude to her and she had known him her whole life. She was willing to put it down to his present confusion. At least she hoped it was.

"Right, so I'll get some men on this right away. Have them question everyone they can find at the docks here in London and then move further out to the coastal towns. We'll figure out where she sailed from and where the ship was headed to and then go after her."

"Good, good," Robert muttered, nodding at Mr. Smithe, the Bow Street runner he'd arranged to meet with today. He was supposed to be the best in the business and his price reflected that, but Robert felt it was worth it if it meant sorting this mess out and letting him get back to his own townhouse and his nice peaceful life. A life where Lisa Madison wasn't prancing around in low-cut gowns while flirting with every man who walked through the damned door of Radnor.

His eyes shifted to the office door as a burst of laughter came muffled from the hall. Another suitor arriving, he supposed with irritation. Five had already gotten here before Mr. Smithe arrived for his appointment. But they just kept coming . . . and none of them appeared to want to leave despite the arrival of the next.

"Keep me posted," Robert growled, forcing his attention back to Smithe. "And try to track Mrs. Morgan down as quickly as you can."

"Of course." Mr. Smithe nodded his graying brown head and then tilted his head and asked, "Do you need a couple of men stationed here to help keep an eye on the gel until we sort this out?"

Robert sighed at the suggestion. It was what he would have liked, but with Christiana with child . . . "No," he said finally. "That's taken care of. Just find Morgan and sort out who the suitor is."

"Right." Smithe nodded and stood. "It's a bad business this. Keep an eye on the gel."

"I plan to," Robert assured him, moving around Richard's desk to walk the man to the door. "She will not be left on her own until this business is sorted."

"Good. I'll set things in motion then," Smithe said as they walked out into the hall.

Robert merely nodded, his gaze seeking the parlor door where Lisa and her callers were all having tea. It had gone quiet after that earlier burst of laughter, and he wondered with a frown what they were doing in there, but he turned his attention back to Smithe, murmuring a few more instructions as he led him to the door and saw him out.

He closed the door behind the man a moment later with a little sigh and took a minute to rub his face wearily. He didn't really want to go back into the parlor. Watching the other men compliment and court Lisa while she beamed smiles and fawned over them all was just . . . well, it was annoying as hell. Nauseating even. However, he was here to keep an eye on her and keep her safe, so he had no choice.

Straightening his shoulders, Robert forced a pleasant expression to his face and headed for the parlor. The expression froze, however, when he pushed the door open and found the room empty. For one moment, he simply stood there, and then he turned from the door with a bellow for Handers.

The butler appeared at once, pushing out of the kitchen door and heading up the hall toward him at the highest speed a good butler ever dared use, a dignified walk. Growling impatiently, Robert strode to meet him, asking, "Where are they?"

"If you are referring to Miss Lisa and her guests, I believe they have gone to the park so that Lord Findlay and Lord Pembroke could prove who had the faster phaeton," the man answered calmly.

Robert stared at him silently for a moment with disbelief, and then whirled on his heel and headed for the front door. His mind wasn't silent however. It was having a good old rant. Here he was giving up his bed for a guest room in the Radnor townhouse to look after her, and what did she do? She rushed off to the park with a gaggle of lords, any one of whom could be the mysterious suitor who had planned to kidnap and have his way with her.

Had she gone mad? Because the Lisa Madison he knew and had grown up being chased about by would never be this stupid and reckless. Did she want to be kidnapped and ravished? Was she so devastated by his seeing her as only a little sister that she would risk herself this way? He would wring her beautiful little neck when he found her.

"Bravo!" Lisa yelled, jumping up and clapping her hands as the phaeton she rode in left the open path and was first to the agreed-upon finishing line. They had won the race. Well, Charles had, she acknowledged with a laugh. She had just been lucky enough to ride along for the race, Lisa supposed, and turned to grin down at the man at the reins.

Findlay chuckled at her enthusiasm, but switched the reins to one hand and raised his other to catch her arm and steady her. "While I am happy you are happy, Miss Madison, you should really sit down. I would not want you to catapult out of the carriage when we slow down."

"Call me Lisa," she said on a laugh, dropping back to sit beside him. She then hugged him excitedly. "You showed Pembroke, Lord Findlay. Beat him by at least three carriage lengths. Well done, my lord!"

"Call me Charles," he murmured by her ear, his arm slipping around her waist to prolong what she'd intended to be a quick congratulatory hug.

Lisa hesitated, very aware that they were now on a much more secluded path leading through the woods. She eased back and smiled up at him crookedly. "Charles, then. But we should turn back. The others will wonder where we have got to."

She glanced over his shoulder then, wondering where Pembroke's carriage was. He had been three lengths behind them when Charles had raced the phaeton into the trees, the end point for this race. But his phaeton was nowhere to be seen now. Actually, there was no one on the path. They were quite alone, she realized as he began to slow the phaeton.

"I will turn around at the first opportunity," Charles assured her, removing his arm as she eased from his embrace to sit beside him more properly. "There is a small turnaround ahead on the right that we can use."

Lisa nodded, trying not to look nervous. Surely Findlay wasn't the suitor. He was far too handsome and refined to need to kidnap young women. Besides, even if he was, he wouldn't be foolish enough to simply ride off with her now. Everyone would know he had taken her. Bet, Lord Pembroke, Lord Tibald and two other gentlemen all knew where she was, or at least who she was with.

"Here we are," Charles murmured, distracting her from her thoughts and she glanced around to see that he was turning them into a small roundabout in a clearing.

"Oh, it's lovely," Lisa cried, her gaze sliding over the small field of purple flowers bordering the roundabout.

"Yes, it is," he agreed, slowing to a halt halfway around.

"What kind of flowers do you think they are?" she asked leaning to the side to get a better look.

"I have no idea. I'm afraid I have little to no knowledge of flowers," he said apologetically shifting behind her to look as well. He was close enough his breath brushed her cheek as he added, "But they are lovely. They match your gown. Would you like some?"

Lisa glanced down to the lavender gown she'd changed into after her bath and smiled as she said with surprise, "They are the same color, aren't they?"

"Yes, they are," he said simply, and then asked, "Shall I pick some for you as a remembrance of our win?"

She grinned at the suggestion and nodded. "Yes, please. That would be lovely. I shall put them in a vase in my room and think of you every time I look at them."

"Then you must have them," Charles said firmly, and set aside the reins to disembark. When Lisa stood up to follow, he waved her back. "You wait there. It's a bit muddy and you'll ruin your shoes. I won't be a minute."

Lisa sank back in the phaeton with a little sigh of pleasure. Really, this was very nice. It was a rare sunny day and she had enjoyed the race. She'd also enjoyed having men vying for her attention all afternoon, and watching Robert's irritation with it all until his appointment with the runner had intervened. At least she suspected that's who the man had been. She'd caught a glimpse of Handers leading a tall man with salt-and-pepper hair to the office and then Robert had disappeared in there with him. It wasn't long after that the men had begun to argue good-naturedly about who had the fastest phaeton and horse, and . . . well, some little devil in her had made her suggest a race to settle the matter. Everyone had been eager to agree and off they'd gone.

Of course, Lisa knew Robert would be furious, but then that was half the fun. She'd decided that his anger with her last night had been mostly jealousy. The man might claim that he had only big brotherly feelings for her, but he had never in his life said anything unkind to her before last night. Even as a child. So, she had some hope that his anger at the ball had been because of jealousy. If it was and there was a chance for them still, fine. If not . . . well . . . there were half a dozen handsome, seemingly nice men paying her a great deal of attention right now. She felt good. She felt like she had choices for a change. And it was nice.

"Here you are."

Lisa turned to see Findlay approaching with a bouquet of the beautiful purple flowers in hand. Smiling, she leaned over the side to accept them and then paused to glance at him with surprise when he didn't release them at once. His expression was solemn, his eyes on her mouth, and she wasn't terribly surprised when he moved closer and raised his face toward hers. He was going to kiss her.

The thought went through her head, chased by the sound of a rhythmic pounding she recognized as hoofbeats. Charles's lips had just brushed against hers when the sound exploded into the clearing. Both of them immediately drew apart and turned to see who had arrived.

It was a very harried and irate-looking Robert on horseback and Lisa didn't know whether to laugh or cry. She was really becoming quite curious to enjoy her first kiss, but Robert did seem to keep interrupting Charles's attempts to give it to her. On the other hand, she might just want that first kiss to be with Robert anyway. She just wasn't sure yet.

"Lisa, you — I cannot believe — this is —" Apparently at a loss for words, Robert drew himself up short, and just glared at her.

Lisa bit her lip to keep from laughing at his sour look. Glancing to Charles, she said apologetically, "Perhaps it's time we returned to the others."

"Home," Robert growled. "The townhouse."

"Oh, but —"

"It's growing late and you'll want to prepare for the Hammonds' ball," he said firmly.

"Ah, yes, the Hammonds' ball," Charles murmured, drawing her gaze to him again. "Don't forget you promised to save me a waltz, and a quadrille."

Lisa relaxed and smiled. "Yes, of course."

He smiled in return, pressed the flowers into her hand and then moved silently around the carriage to get back in. Lisa glanced over her shoulder as the phaeton moved forward again. Robert was directly behind them, his back straight, expression grim, and eyes burning.

"Langley appears to be quite concerned with your well-being."

Lisa glanced to Charles at that comment and grimaced slightly. "He's just protective. We grew up together and he thinks of me as a little sister."

"Little sister?" Findlay asked, glancing her way and allowing his eyes to slide over her in her newly de-ruffled lavender gown. "I find that hard to believe."

"Thank you," she said on a laugh.

Charles smiled slightly, but added, "Still, he seems . . . his interest appears almost overdone for just a family friend," he ended delicately.

Lisa glanced away. She would have to point out to Robert that he would give people ideas with his behavior were he not careful. Aloud she said, "Oh well, my brother-in-law, Lord Radnor, asked Robert to help keep an eye on me while I am in town. I fear they worry that having grown up in the country I may not be aware of all the dangers and pitfalls of the city."

"Hmm," Charles murmured, and then

glanced to her, his eyes dropping to her décolletage and back. "Then I shall be happy to help keep an eye on you too."

"My lord, I suspect you are one of the possible pitfalls," Lisa said with a laugh, and he offered a sad moue.

"Oh, now you wound me, Miss Madison. I have been a complete gentleman."

"So far," she agreed with amusement.

"So far," he allowed. "And I promise I shall remain so in your presence . . . for the most part at least," he added wryly and then explained, "Eventually, I will manage that kiss I have been trying to claim."

Lisa merely smiled faintly, wondering if it would be too forward to admit she was looking forward to it. Her first kiss. She had always planned and hoped that Robert would be her first kiss. However, it looked as if that wasn't going to happen. That being the case, she supposed she would just have to suffer and accept a kiss from the very handsome Lord Findlay instead. It didn't seem like much of a trial at that point. While her interest was primarily in Robert, he wasn't behaving very nicely, while Lord Findlay was being an absolute dear. Complimenting her, dancing with her, picking her flowers . . . And at least he *wanted* to kiss her. Which made a nice change from Robert's constant claims that he thought of her as nothing more than a sister.

CHAPTER SEVEN

"You were not supposed to leave the house."

"No one said anything about not leaving the house," Lisa said calmly, starting up the stairs with Bet on her heels. They had stopped to collect the maid on the way back to Christiana and Richard's home, as well as to wish the other men good day, and then Lord Findlay had returned her and Bet to the townhouse with Robert at their back every minute of the journey like some disapproving parent.

"You are being deliberately obtuse, Lisa," Robert said grimly, following them up the stairs. "I am here to watch over you. How can I do that if you are not even in the house?"

"Well, if you had been there watching me then I wouldn't have gone without you, would I?" she asked mildly. "Besides, I was perfectly safe."

"I was meeting with a Bow Street runner

to arrange for the capture of Mrs. Morgan," he hissed, moving up beside her to avoid the possibility of one of the servants hearing. "It was necessary. And I was just up the bloody hall. As for being safe, you don't know that. Findlay could have been planning to run off with you at any moment."

"I don't think running off with me was the plan," Lisa said calmly as she reached the landing and started up the hall.

"No. He was too busy kissing you," he muttered.

"*Trying* to kiss me," Lisa corrected mildly. "However, you do keep interrupting his attempts. I wish you would stop that, Robert."

"You wish . . . You want him to kiss you?" he asked with outrage.

Lisa stopped at her bedroom door and turned to face him as Bet opened it and entered. "Of course I want him to kiss me. Why wouldn't I? He's handsome, eligible and I've never been kissed. I should like to see what it's like. After all, I wouldn't want to marry him do I not enjoy his kisses."

"Marry him!" he squawked with amazement.

"Well, that is what I am in town for, Robert. To find a husband, and Lord Findlay is the handsomest of the options so far. So, I should like him to kiss me so I can see if I like it, or if I should turn my attentions to one of the other men instead, one whose kisses I might like better."

"Are you telling me you intend to just let him kiss you? Then if you don't like it, allow someone else to kiss you, and then someone else?" he asked with slow disbelief.

Lisa nodded. "That seems the most sensible plan to me. If I find them physically attractive, then I talk with them to see if I like their personality, and if so, well then I should see if I like their kisses."

"What?" he asked with horror.

She rolled her eyes with exasperation at his expression. "There is more to marriage than sitting across the table every morning talking," she pointed out. "It does seem to me I should see if the man I plan to marry can stir some passion in me. I should like a marriage as wonderful and heated as Christiana and Suzette were lucky enough to find."

"Dear God," Robert muttered and then shook his head. "Lisa, you cannot simply run about allowing every man in London to kiss you until you find the one who —"

"Why not?" she interrupted. "It is just a kiss, but according to Sophie, a kiss can tell you a lot about what kind of lover a man is.

Surely I'm not expected to go into marriage just hoping I will enjoy my marriage bed?"

Robert's mouth moved briefly with nothing coming out and then he asked with irritation, "Who the devil is Sophie?"

"She is a . . . er . . . Bird-of-Paradise," she whispered, glancing up the hall to be sure there were no servants about to hear.

"A Bird-of-Paradise?" Robert bellowed. "For God's sake, Lisa. You are friends with a brothel owner *and* a Bird-of-Paradise?"

She scowled at him for shouting, but said, "Of course not, Robert. I read Sophie's memoirs. And I didn't know Mrs. Morgan was a brothel owner."

"The memoirs of a Bird-of-Paradise," he muttered, running his hand wearily through his hair. "Dear God, you read the most horrid . . . Does your father know about these books of yours?"

Lisa rolled her eyes and turned toward her door, only to be swung back by Robert's hand on her arm.

"Lisa Madison, I forbid you to allow anyone to kiss you," he said firmly. "It is —"

"My choice," she interrupted firmly, and then said more gently, "Really Robert, while I love you like a big brother, you aren't one, and have no right to forbid me anything."

Tugging her arm free, she shook her head and turned to enter her room, adding, "I fully intend to kiss whomever I wish. I don't know why you care anyway. It is not like you're jealous."

The door closed behind Lisa, leaving Robert standing there staring at it blankly with her words echoing in his head. She loved him like a big brother? When had that happened? She used to adore him. Good Lord, had a couple of days of having men like Findlay, Pembroke and Tibald fawning over her made that much difference? Impossible.

Or was it? he wondered. Other than servants, he had been the only male around while the Madison sisters were growing up. Perhaps it shouldn't be surprising that she would have a crush on him. But now she was surrounded by men. They were flocking to her like bees to honey. It seemed that was enough to cool the longstanding ardor she'd had for him and turn her adoration to filial affection.

He should be relieved, Robert supposed. But, oddly enough, he wasn't. He felt . . . betrayed. Abandoned. And even . . . Dear God, he *was* jealous. The very idea of her kissing any man, let alone several, had him wanting to gnash his teeth. The problem was, he didn't know if he was jealous because he was just used to her being in love with him, or because he actually wanted her for himself.

Robert really had thought of Lisa as something of a little sister for years, finding her adoration of him amusing and annoying by turn. But finding her in that brothel, dressed in that damned see-through gown . . . the one she planned to wear on her wedding night to another man.

It wasn't just that though. Lisa was changing and quickly. The attentions of all these men were building her confidence. She laughed more gaily, a full, infectious laugh rather than the shy twitter he was used to hearing. She walked taller, her chin up, and her eyes positively twinkled with life and enjoyment. She was blossoming like a rose in bloom. And it made a pretty, quiet girl into an irresistibly beautiful and charming woman. The kind of woman a man could fall in love with and that many men would want and pursue.

"Damn," Robert muttered and turned wearily from the door. He had no idea what to do with these realizations. He had no desire to be having these feelings for Lisa. And he definitely had no desire to marry and suffer the humiliation and heartache of an adulterous wife. The hell of it was that prior to this trip he would have been hard-pressed to believe that Lisa even could be unfaithful. But now, with her wanting to kiss every man in London . . . well, it did seem more likely. And adulterous wives were something of a curse in his family. So much so that, despite her behavior, it probably wouldn't even be her fault in the end.

It just seemed better all the way around for Robert to ignore his changing feelings and keep the girl at arm's length. He would sort out this business of the suitor, but then he would get the hell away from her and let her live her life. It was her best chance of happiness and his best chance of avoiding getting hurt.

"Okay. So what is going on between you and Robert?"

Lisa glanced to Suzette with surprise. "Whatever do you mean? Nothing is going on."

"Right," Suzette said dryly. "He has been standing in that exact same spot across the ballroom, his eyes locked on you all night."

"And you have studiously avoided looking at him all night as well," Christiana added with amusement.

"I have no reason to look at him. As for his watching me . . . I cannot control what he does," Lisa said with a shrug, but wished she could. Robert's eyes had been following her since they'd arrived, and she hadn't glanced in his direction because she didn't have to. She could feel his eyes burning holes into her. She wished he'd stop that.

Lisa supposed she wouldn't mind if his look was admiring or something, but it wasn't. Robert had taken an emotional step back. She could feel it. He was watching her with a purely professional disinterest, as if he were a hired bodyguard. She didn't know what had done it, but something had made him erect a wall between them.

There was nothing she could do about that of course, so Lisa just accepted it and smiled and danced with the men on her card, vetting out those who she liked and those she didn't. She was not going to sit around waiting on any man, not even Robert.

"Miss Madison."

Lisa glanced to the man before her and smiled cheerfully. "Lord Pembroke. Is it your dance now?"

"I believe so," he murmured with a smile she suspected would have made the hearts of most girls flutter. Lisa's heart didn't twitch, but he was a nice man and she did appreciate how attractive he was and allowed her smile to widen as she placed her hand on his arm to let him lead her onto the dance floor.

"I hope you do not think less of me for losing the race this afternoon," Pembroke murmured as he took her in his arms.

Lisa glanced up with surprise and shook her head at once. "Of course not, my lord. It was just a bit of fun. In fact, I thought you had let Findlay win so that I could enjoy it more," she added lightly, not surprised to see him puff up a bit.

"Well, you did seem to be enjoying it," he said with a smile, suggesting that might be the case when she was quite sure it wasn't. She didn't mind though. He was now standing tall and smiling again where he hadn't been moments ago.

"Oh, I did enjoy it," she assured him with a laugh. "It was quite exhilarating."

"Then I am happy to have lost and given you such joy," he assured her.

Lisa chuckled. "I appreciate it, my lord. It's very kind of you."

"What else do you like to do, Miss Madison?" he asked, spinning her around the floor. "Perhaps we can endeavor to do it tomorrow afternoon. 'We' being myself and all your other admirers," he added with a teasing grin.

Lisa chuckled with appreciation at his teasing and then considered the question, "I enjoy riding, or did in the country, and long walks. And there is a river by our country home where I enjoy paddling a boat." She paused and shrugged. "I do not know, my lord."

"What of plays and such?" he asked.

"Oh my, yes. I have only seen one or two, but quite enjoyed them," she said easily.

"And do you like flowers?"

"Always, my lord. They are quite lovely and cheering."

"And your favorite sweet?"

"My favorite sweet?" Lisa grinned and teased. "Will you cook it for me?"

He laughed at the suggestion. "Not I. But my cook is known to make the best pastries in London and I would be pleased to have her make whatever you like. I could then bring it to you tomorrow if you would allow it."

Lisa considered it briefly, but finally said, "Of course I will allow it. I'd be happy to see you again tomorrow. As for what to have your cook make, surprise me, my lord. Have your cook make whatever she makes best. Something you like."

"I know just the thing," he assured her. "You shall love it."

"I shall look forward to it, my lord," she said with a laugh.

"As shall I," Pembroke assured her and then glanced around with a frown as the music came to an end. Grimacing, he murmured, "I guess this is the end of our dance."

"Oh," she said with surprise and glanced around. It had seemed to go by quickly as they talked. Smiling faintly, she turned her gaze back to him and said, "Well, thank you for the dance, my lord."

"Thank you, Miss Madison. It is always a pleasure," he assured her.

"Yes it is."

Lisa glanced to the side at that comment to see Lord Findlay had approached.

"My waltz, I believe," he said with a grin, and then nodded to the other man. "Pembroke."

"Findlay," Lord Pembroke murmured, giving Lisa up to him. Before he left, however, he smiled at Lisa and said, "Till tomorrow."

"Yes." She smiled and then turned her attention to Charles as the waltz began.

"Tomorrow?" Findlay asked mildly as he swept her into the dance. "I take it Pembroke plans to call on you again?"

"It would seem so," Lisa said with a grin.

"He is bringing me sweets from his cook who he claims is the best in London."

"I have heard that," Findlay allowed. "I suppose this means I shall have to come as well, bearing something to top his offering."

Lisa chuckled at the suggestion. "Surely it would have to be something special to top the best sweets in London, my lord."

"Yes, I suppose it shall," he acknowledged and then smiled wryly. "I shall have to consider carefully on what to bring."

"Hmm," she said with amusement, finding it heady that two of the most eligible, not to mention the handsomest, bachelors in town were vying for her attention thusly.

"In the meantime," Charles murmured, steering her about the floor. "I believe there is the question of that kiss I have been trying to claim."

"Ah yes, the kiss," she said, lips twitching. "Well, surely you will not try to claim it here on the dance floor, my lord? That would cause quite the scandal."

"Oh, I would never do that and risk damaging your reputation," he assured her.

"I am glad to hear it."

"And of course, if I wait for the quadrille and try to escort you outside for fresh air, your watchdog, Lord Langley, would be on us and no doubt drag you away again before

I could do more than take you in my arms."

"No doubt," Lisa agreed dryly.

"Fortunately, I thought of that and made my plans accordingly."

"Did you?" she asked with interest. "And what plans are those?"

"Well, at this very moment a couple of my friends are talking with him, and blocking his view of us. Unintentionally, of course."

"Oh, of course," she said on a laugh and turned to glance toward where Robert had been standing all night. Sure enough, a group of three men were surrounding him.

"And, I have danced us to the terrace doors," Findlay added.

Lisa turned her attention to her other side to see that they were indeed only feet from a set of terrace doors.

"All I am waiting for is your permission to whisk you out for a breath of fresh air and a kiss," he said quietly. "Do I have your permission?"

Lisa turned to face him, taking in the solemn question on his face as she debated her response. It was one thing to decide to allow a man a kiss should he make the attempt. It was another thing entirely to be asked and actually have to give permission. For some reason saying yes felt, well, a bit bold. It turned it from allowing something to be taken, to actually giving. Which was just silly, she supposed. Was she not eager for this first kiss business? Had she not been disappointed that Robert had interrupted them now twice? She really did want to know what it was like, and if she would like it.

Forcing her head up, Lisa opened her mouth but couldn't actually find it in herself to say yes. Instead, she closed her mouth, swallowed and simply gave one small, quick nod.

Fortunately, it was enough. In the next moment, Charles was turning, whirling them out through the open doors and onto the terrace so fast that she felt sure no one had noticed. Once out in the cool evening air, he broke their embrace and walked her to the railing at the shadowed edge. Lisa went silently, her head bowed now as nervousness roared up within her. He was going to kiss her. Dear God. Her first kiss and it wasn't going to be Robert.

That didn't matter, she reminded herself grimly. What did matter was . . . what if she was a bad kisser? She hadn't a clue what she was supposed to do in a kiss. Did she just stand there with her eyes closed and lips puckered? Was she expected to kiss back? If so, how? Her sisters and their husbands had kissed in front of her, but mostly they were merely quick pecks. However, she knew from her reading that there was much more than a simple brushing of lips in a proper kiss. There was nibbling and thrusting tongues and sucking and all sorts of things that sounded rather silly but were apparently quite delightful. On the other hand, perhaps he wouldn't give her a proper kiss. Perhaps he would just brush her lips with his this time and —

"I can almost hear your mind whirring."

Lisa glanced up with surprise at Findlay's amused words to find that while she was fretting, he'd urged her back up against the railing and stepped in front of her.

"You look nervous," he commented solemnly, slipping one arm around her to draw her closer, while using his free hand to tilt her chin up and then let his fingers trail down her throat. "Have you never been kissed before, Lisa?"

Eyes wide at the goose bumps his touch raised in her, she shook her head.

"Ah." For some reason the news made him smile, and then his expression turned solemn and he said, "Never fear. It is like dancing. The man leads, the woman follows. I will teach you. All right?"

She gave a jerky nod, and then held her

breath as his mouth lowered toward hers. Some part of her mind was waiting for Robert to bark out her name and interrupt again. In fact, she was quite surprised when Charles's lips brushed over hers without that happening. She was even more surprised when the pressure of his lips increased and then softened as his mouth opened and he nipped at her lips teasingly.

Lisa moved instinctively closer then, feeling some of that warmth she'd read about slide through her body, along with a desire to feel more. Her own mouth opened a bit, her lips nipping back as he was doing and her arms slipped around his shoulders. The action raised her breasts, which were suddenly pressed against his chest as he tightened his embrace and the action sent a frisson of interest through her that had her pressing closer still.

When his hand slid up the back of her neck to cup her head and tilt it slightly to his preference, that sent another little shock of pleasure through her. She quite liked his handling her so. Certainly, she had no idea what to do with her head. It was all very pleasant and making her tingly, so when he suddenly broke the kiss and eased back, she opened her eyes to peer at him with disappointment.

"Is that all?"

A surprised chuckle of amusement burst from Findlay. Once it passed, he shook his head and said solemnly, "No, my dear, that is certainly not all. However, that is as much as a gentleman would permit himself with a lady such as yourself."

"Oh," Lisa breathed, and smiled crookedly as he eased her out of his arms. She supposed it was good that she wanted more. That was certainly a promising sign. But at the moment she just felt a bit frustrated, as if she'd been given a taste of something that might be quite delicious, but hadn't got enough to tell for sure.

"We should go back in," Findlay murmured, easing her to his side. "My friends cannot keep Langley busy forever."

"Yes, I suppose we should," Lisa agreed quietly as he walked her back across the terrace. They were nearly to the doors when movement out of the corner of her eye made her glance to the side. Her step faltered and her eyes widened slightly when she saw the man watching them. Robert. Stock still and silent in the shadows, his expression unreadable. It seemed Charles's friends hadn't been able to keep him busy for long at all. She wondered how long he'd been there . . . and why he hadn't intervened this time as

he had the others . . . and what he was
thinking as he watched them slip back into
the ballroom.

CHAPTER EIGHT

"It seems your Mrs. Morgan took her carriage north and sailed from Dover," Smithe announced, lifting his tea to his lips for a sip before continuing. "The ship was heading for Calais. I have passage booked for myself and two of my men leaving tomorrow morning. We will search for her, follow if she traveled across land from there, or question her if we find she is still in Calais."

"Good," Robert murmured, thinking this could all be done and dusted quickly if Mrs. Morgan was staying in Calais. The sooner they found out who the suitor was, the sooner he could handle the man and get the hell back to his own life and stop being tortured by watching Lisa with her gaggle of gentlemen callers.

After having to witness her dancing with nearly every other single man in London last night, not to mention being forced to stand by and watch Findlay paw and kiss her out on the terrace, Robert didn't think he could stand much more of this job he'd given himself. He'd rather hoped that today Daniel or Richard would be here to keep an eye on her so that he could go visit his mistress and work off some of the excess energy and frustration that was presently building in him.

However, none of them had expected this turn of events and today, like yesterday, Richard and Daniel already had prior engagements, meaning Robert was once again on duty. Even Christiana and Suzette were away again at one of the charity teas they had taken to aiding in. Not that he would have left Lisa with just the women to watch her, but their presence in the parlor would have meant he could at least avoid it himself and simply watch from the office with that door open to be sure Lisa didn't try to slip out with her admirers for another phaeton race or some such thing.

"Of course, I doubt Morgan stayed in Calais. Paris is much more likely a place for her to set up trade again," Smithe commented. "I suspect traveling to Calais was just a red herring to try to lead us off the trail."

Robert sank back in his seat with a sigh. Paris was a large city and Mrs. Morgan wouldn't exactly be flaunting her presence. She wouldn't want to be found. It could take days to track her, days he would rather not have to wait and watch over Lisa.

"But I shall return as quickly as I can, either with the information of who paid her to kidnap Miss Madison, or the lady herself," Smithe assured him.

"Yes, of course. Thank you," Robert said grimly. The man could only do as much as he could do. Wishing it was otherwise wouldn't make it so.

"Don't thank me, my lord, until I bring back what you want," Smithe suggested calmly. "Then you can thank me with coins."

Robert smiled faintly. "Of course. Speaking of that, you will need a draft to cover your expenses."

"Yes, I will," Smithe said simply and suggested a sum that seemed reasonable to Robert. He quickly wrote up the draft and slid it across the desk to the man, then stood to see him out.

This time when he returned to the parlor and opened the door, Lisa and her admirers were all still present. Forcing his shoulders up and a bland smile to his lips, Robert slipped inside and positioned himself unobtrusively beside the largest flower arrangement in the room. It was one of several. While Pembroke had brought her pastries, Tibald and the other men had all brought collections of flowers. The room was positively awash in fresh, colorful blooms.

But the loveliest flower in the room was Lisa. Rosy-cheeked and beaming under all this attention, she held court, smiling and laughing, teasing and chattering. He didn't think he'd ever seen her look quite so happy or adorable. She positively shone under the admiration of all these men, drawing every eye and even more appreciation from her callers.

"I was hoping to arrange for a ride down the river for this afternoon since you mentioned enjoying that. But, I fear I couldn't arrange it all on such short notice." Pembroke's words caught Robert's ear, drawing his attention to the conversation taking place. "However, if you would be pleased, I have managed to rent a boat for the day after tomorrow to take a large party up the coast for a picnic."

"Oh, how lovely," Lisa said, clapping her hands happily. "Who all shall be there?"

"The invitations are being prepared and delivered as we speak," Pembroke said. "I have invited everyone here, of course." His expression was tight as he nodded toward the other men in the room and it was obvious, at least to Robert, that he hadn't been pleased to do so. "As well as your sisters and their husbands, Lord Langley," He nodded at Robert who had thought his entrance had gone unnoticed. "And I have invited several other single young ladies who are making their debut this year to add to the numbers."

And to hopefully keep the other men occupied, Robert supposed with amusement. Though he doubted that would work. In his opinion, no woman stood a chance next to Lisa. All these other women would do was make her value even more obvious. But bully to Pembroke for trying it, he thought.

"That sounds lovely," Lisa said happily and the men all murmured their agreement, though a little less enthusiastically, he noted, and guessed they were wishing they'd thought of it.

Much to his relief the visitation ended shortly after that when Findlay suggested they should leave Lisa to rest before she had to prepare for that night's ball. There was a general, if disappointed, murmur of agreement from the other men and they all began to slowly gather their things and make their departure.

Robert stood silently by while Lisa saw

each man off with a smile and assurances that she'd enjoyed their company. While Findlay was the first to suggest it might be time they left, he was the last to actually leave, dallying until an annoyed Pembroke finally shuffled out the door.

Lisa wasn't the only one to turn a curious gaze on Charles Findlay once the others had left. Robert eyed him suspiciously, sure the man had hoped he would leave them alone for a moment, but Robert had stood by and watched him grope Lisa last night and that was enough. He wasn't doing it again, he decided grimly, and simply raised an eyebrow at Findlay when he glanced his way expectantly.

Apparently coming to the realization that he wouldn't be left alone with Lisa, Findlay smiled wryly and then reached into his inside coat pocket as he approached her. His expression was somewhat chagrined as he pulled out three slender books.

"I didn't wish to give these to you in front of the others," he admitted, offering them to her.

"Oh, Charles," Lisa breathed, taking the books as if they were the finest jewels.

Robert immediately scowled at her use of the man's first name, but neither of them noticed.

"I wasn't sure what you enjoy reading, and I haven't read any of these myself, but a friend assured me you should like them," Findlay said uncertainly, and then frowned and added, "I hope you haven't read them yet."

"No," she said at once, quickly checking each title to be sure. Lisa then glanced up and beamed, before simply throwing her arms around him and hugging him tightly. "What a wonderful man! These are the perfect gift."

"Oh, well," Findlay chuckled faintly and let his arms slip around her back. He started to tighten his arms around her as well, but then his eyes suddenly shot to Robert and he eased his hold and then stepped back, releasing her. "I should be going. You probably do wish to rest before having to prepare for tonight's ball."

"Thank you," Lisa said sincerely, clasping the books to her chest as she walked him from the room and to the front door. "I shall start reading one right away and tell you what I think tonight."

"I'd like that," Findlay assured her. "And perhaps we could go for a picnic sometime later in the week and you could read to me. Or I could read to you. Or we could take turns reading to each other."

162

"That sounds lovely," she agreed with a grin.

The hell it did, Robert thought irritably. He and Lisa used to do that when they were younger — taking sandwiches and a blanket, enjoying lunch by the river between their homes and then reading aloud to each other. It had all seemed innocent enjoyment then. It didn't with Findlay inserted in his place.

"Check your calendar then and tell me tonight when you will be free and I shall have my cook arrange a basket for us," Findlay suggested, opening the front door.

"I will," Lisa said, her expression becoming more solemn. For some reason that was more disturbing to Robert than her obvious pleasure had been. It sounded to him like a vow, as if she were agreeing to more than a simple picnic. He got the feeling Findlay had just taken the lead in her husband hunt . . . and the thought disturbed Robert more than he cared to admit. While she had so many men to choose from, he didn't really have to consider someone winning her heart, but now . . .

He scowled at Findlay as the other man brushed a hand down Lisa's cheek in parting and then turned and started up the walk. Lisa watched him go briefly, then

163

closed the door with a happy little sigh and immediately charged upstairs, clasping her books to her chest like treasure.

Robert stood in the empty hall for a moment, a frown curving his lips. Lisa hadn't even glanced his way before rushing upstairs. It was as if she'd forgotten he was even there. Which was what he wanted, he reminded himself firmly. She was supposed to move on. He had no desire to marry anyone. If he were interested in marrying, she would certainly be at the top of the list, but he just wasn't. The Langley men didn't do well in marriage, he reminded himself firmly. It was better she had her hat set on someone else. Robert just wished he was actually glad she had.

"Oh dear, maybe we should cancel and not attend the Kittriches' ball either."

Lisa lifted her head from the basin she had been bent over for the last several hours and shook her head miserably. "No. It's okay. You go ahead. Suzette and Daniel are expecting you. Besides there is nothing you can do for me here. I shall just —" Hang over the basin tossing up my guts, she finished silently in her head as another round of heaving claimed her. Dear God, her sides ached horribly from the retching and there was nothing left to bring up but bile and still her stomach insisted on heaving.

"Oh dear," Christiana murmured again, rubbing her back sympathetically. "And all you had to eat today was the pastries Lord Pembroke brought?"

Lisa nodded miserably and sagged as the latest round of heaving stopped.

"Did you not even break your fast?" Christiana asked with a frown.

Lisa shook her head. "I was late rising today and only got below just before Pembroke arrived with his offering." She grimaced and admitted, "I'm afraid that made me gobble them up like a greedy child. I probably just had too many."

"Eating too many shouldn't make you this violently ill," Christiana muttered, rubbing her back again as Lisa once more began to retch.

"Oh Christiana, go," she said wearily as the latest round eased. "Once my stomach settles enough to allow it, I am just going to lie down and rest."

"But I hate to leave you alone like this," Christiana protested unhappily.

"She won't be alone," Robert announced from the door.

Lisa glanced to the side unhappily to see

him crossing the room to join them where she knelt on the floor beside the bed, her head hanging over the water basin Bet had brought her. Part of Lisa flinched at his seeing her like this. Another part just felt too weak and poorly to care.

"I shall stay with her until she sleeps and then keep an ear out in case she is sick again," Robert assured Christiana, nudging her out of his way so that he could replace her in kneeling at Lisa's side. "You go ahead. Richard is downstairs and the carriage is out front waiting. Go have fun. I shall take care of Lisa."

"Are you sure?" Christiana asked uncertainly.

"Positive," Robert said firmly, beginning to rub Lisa's back as Christiana had been doing. It wasn't nearly as soothing when he did it however, Lisa noted as he said, "Go ahead. I will send a message if she gets worse or doesn't improve."

"Very well then," Christiana said with a sigh. "But do send word if she worsens, and try to get some liquids down her throat if you can. Well, once she seems capable of keeping them down," Christiana added dryly as Lisa began to heave again at the very suggestion.

Despite her distraction, Lisa heard a heavy

sigh from her sister and then her footsteps left the room and faded as she walked away up the hall.

"Go away," Lisa mumbled the moment she was sure Christiana was gone.

"No," Robert said simply, and held her forehead as she heaved again. Once her stomach eased in its violent rebellion, he asked, "So Pembroke's pastries are the only thing you've eaten?"

"Heard that, did you?" she asked irritably.

"Yes," he said, brushing her hair back from her cheeks and turning her face so he could look at her. Lisa just sighed. She knew she must look horrid, but was too exhausted and feeling too weak to care. However, whatever he saw made Robert frown and it was something to do with her eyes. She was too exhausted to even ask what it was.

"Was Pembroke going to the ball tonight?" Robert asked quietly.

Lisa frowned, but then shook her head. "No. All the other men were asking me to save them a dance, but when I glanced to him to see if he wanted me to as well, he said he wished he would be there, but had a previous engagement."

"A previous engagement, huh?" Robert asked grimly.

"Hmm," she said wearily and found herself leaning against his shoulder, her eyes closing. All she wanted to do was sleep, but she was afraid that shifting back into bed would bring on another bout of heaving and she was desperate to avoid that. Her stomach and ribs were already screaming in pain from the activity so far.

"Poor little Lisa," Robert murmured, running his hands over her hair gently. "You feel like hell, don't you?"

She nodded, not bothering to open her eyes and felt him press a kiss to the top of her head, but couldn't even find the energy to be pleased at the affectionate gesture. Who cared anyway? It was an innocent caress, brotherly even, she supposed wearily as consciousness began to slip away. She stirred and murmured sleepily when he gathered her in his arms, but when she felt the soft bed beneath her, Lisa let herself drift off again. Sleep was definitely preferable to heaving anymore and she was desperate to avoid more heaving.

Robert straightened from laying Lisa in bed. He pulled the covers over her and peered down at her silently. Even sick she was still lovely. The bruising around her eyes and the pallor of her skin didn't detract much from it. And while she was wearing a loose white sleeping gown that looked ages old and comfortable rather than actually attractive, it didn't hide the curves he'd seen so clearly when she'd been wearing that see-through creation Mrs. Morgan had put her in.

"Has her stomach finally settled?"

Robert glanced around at that whisper to find Bet crossing the room to his side to examine her mistress. He nodded in answer, and whispered back, "Hopefully it's done and won't start up again."

"Aye," Bet agreed on a sigh. "She's been miserable with it for hours. Started almost as soon as she got up here to the room."

"Right after the men left," Robert murmured.

"Yes, thank goodness," Bet whispered. "She would have been doubly upset if it had started while they were here."

"Hmm," Robert murmured and turned to head for the door. "I will be in Richard's office. Call me if she starts up again or anything else happens."

"Aye, my lord," Bet responded quietly, settling in the chair beside the bed to watch over her mistress.

Robert left the door open so he would hear if Bet called. He started downstairs as he'd intended, but then changed his mind and moved to his room instead. He had planned to go downstairs and read to pass the time, but he'd been reading before bed last night and the book was on his bedside table. Once in the room, he decided it would be better if he read there and left his door open as well. He would be closer and could better hear if he was needed.

Lisa stirred sleepily and turned on her back, her head rolling to the side and her gaze falling on the person slumped and asleep in a chair beside the bed. Bet. While there were no lit candles or oil lamps in the bedroom, the door was wide open and enough light was splashing in from the hall that she could see well enough to make out the woman's identity. A small smile curved Lisa's lips at the sight. Bet was the best maid a girl could ask for. Honestly. They had pretty much grown up together and were friends as much as anything else.

A scratching sort of sound drew her attention toward the window, and Lisa peered sleepily that way to see a branch brushing against the pane. She started to glance away then, but the movement of the branch caught her attention. It was bobbing up and down against the window . . . which just seemed odd. It took her a moment to realize why. Surely a breeze would be moving it from side to side, not up and down?

After the briefest hesitation, she sat up cautiously in bed. When her stomach didn't immediately begin to rebel, Lisa released a relieved breath and slid her feet to the floor, then stood up shakily. Her bout of vomiting might be over, but the aftereffects remained. Her stomach muscles were complaining something fierce at their abuse and she felt shaky and in need of liquid if not a full-course meal.

Ignoring that for now, Lisa made her way carefully to the window to see what was causing the strange action. She was halfway there when the branch stopped moving. Curious and a little sleepy still, she paused at the window and looked out but the light from the hall was reflecting in the glass and she couldn't see anything. After a hesitation, she opened the windows, unlatching them and pushing one out to look about.

A calm, breezeless night met her once the window was open and Lisa peered curiously at the tree outside her window, but it was now still. An owl or some other night creature must have been on the branch, she supposed, her eyes shifting upward to take in the night sky. It was starless tonight and dark as sin, she noted, breathing in the cool night air.

It was only then she noted that the smell in the room was a little unpleasant. Deciding a little fresh air would be good, she left the window open and turned to move back to the bed, debating donning her robe and going below in search of food. While her stomach was no longer rebelling, it was gnawing with hunger. Not surprising, Lisa supposed, since it was completely empty.

Grimacing at the memory of what had seemed like hours of retching — the cause of her empty stomach — Lisa paused at the bed and was reaching for the robe laid across the bottom of it when a soft shuffling sound from behind caught her ear. She stiffened and started to turn, and then managed a muffled gasp as she was grabbed from behind, something snaking around her waist and pulling her back hard against a strong hard body, even as a hand slapped across her mouth to stifle the small sound that escaped her.

Before Lisa had even fully registered what was happening, she was kicking wildly as she was lifted off the ground and dragged backward across the room toward the window. It was good fortune that saved her in the end. Her captor moved too close to the table and chair where Lisa liked to sit to read and her wildly flailing feet caught the chair and sent it tumbling.

The stubbing that her foot took made Lisa grunt into the hand over her mouth, but the sound was drowned out by the crash of the chair hitting the floor and then she saw Bet startle awake. Much to her relief, in the next moment, the maid was shrieking at the top of her lungs and on her feet, coming around the bed to try to help.

Whether it was the oncoming Bet, or the fact that her screech surely hadn't gone unheard and help would most likely be on the way that put off her attacker, Lisa didn't know. But in the next moment she was released and crashing to her knees on the bedroom's hardwood floor. Bet halted in her forward charge to kneel beside her, her gaze sliding from Lisa to the man making his getaway as she asked, "Are ye all right, Miss?"

"Aye," Lisa gasped, glancing over her shoulder in time to see her attacker just pulling himself onto the window.

"What the hell?"

Robert's voice drew her head around as he crashed into the room. She opened her mouth to explain, but apparently he'd spotted the man climbing out her window and was already charging forward. Lisa shifted to the side on her knees to get out of the way, but the fellow was already gone by the time Robert reached the window. That didn't stop him, however; quick as a whip he was following her attacker's path and climbing out of her window as well.

"Oh dear," Lisa muttered and struggled quickly to her feet with Bet's help. She staggered to the window then, wincing as her knees, shins and stomach muscles all complained of their distress and recent mistreatment. Ignoring that, she bent to rest on the ledge and leaned out to see what was happening. She was just in time to see her attacker drop from the tree and race from the yard. Robert was still a good distance from the ground when he allowed himself to drop from the branches to the grass below. He landed with a grunt and then gave chase, but Lisa could see the fellow had a good start on him. He was also moving like the devil himself was on his heels, while Robert had apparently injured himself and was limping somewhat.

"Lord Langley'll never catch him," Bet said with disappointment.

"Nay," Lisa agreed on a sigh and pulled the window closed once Robert left the yard and disappeared from sight.

"Shouldn't ye leave it open for Lord

Langley to return?" Bet asked with a frown.

"I'm sure he'll use the front door rather than climb back up the tree," Lisa pointed out.

"Oh, aye," Bet muttered and quickly drew the drapes shut over the window, then turned to follow as Lisa limped back to the bed to lay claim to her robe as she'd intended before she was grabbed from behind. The maid's voice was worried as she asked, "How are you feeling now?"

"My stomach aches, my knees and shins hurt, and I am hungry," Lisa answered shakily, and then forced some strength into her voice and added, "I would kill for a cup of tea."

"Do ye think it'll stay down?" Bet asked with concern. "Ye don't want to be heaving again."

"I think it will stay down now," Lisa said wearily as she drew the robe on and tied the sash. "At least I hope it will because I could do with a cup to steady my nerves."

"Aye," Bet said with sympathy. "Well you just sit yourself down and relax then. I shall fetch you up something." She urged her toward the toppled chair, and then rushed forward to straighten it for her to sit in.

Lisa sat. Mostly because she was even shakier than she had been when she'd first woken up. She also didn't protest when Bet settled a blanket across her knees and tucked it around her, but she released a rather relieved sigh when the maid stopped fussing and departed to find her a drink and a snack.

Once she was alone, Lisa leaned back a little wearily, her eyes closing as she reviewed what had happened. She had no idea where her attacker had come from. She was pretty sure the tree had been empty when she'd peered out, but then it was extremely dark and with all the leaves and shadow coating the branches, Lisa supposed he may have been hidden from view. And she'd left the damned window open for him to come in after her, she thought with self-disgust.

"Lisa?"

Blinking her eyes open, she watched Robert enter with a lit candle and set it on the table by her bed before moving to stand before her.

"Are you all right?" he asked with concern.

"Aye," Lisa assured him, sitting up a little straighter in her chair. "Are you all right, Robert? You were limping as you gave chase."

He grimaced with irritation, and admitted, "I landed badly and twisted my ankle is all. Which slowed me enough to let him get away."

"Sit down," she suggested, waving to the bed. But rather than simply back up and settle on the edge of the bed as she'd intended, he limped around it to retrieve the chair Bet had been sleeping in. He brought it back to set in front of hers. Sitting in it with a relieved little sigh, he ran one hand through his hair and then said, "Tell me what happened."

Lisa quickly explained about waking up, the bobbing branch and her investigation and then the attack. Once finished she sat back to await his next question. It wasn't long in coming.

"Did you see his face?"

"He was wearing some sort of hood with holes cut out for the eyes, but I didn't even get a good look at his eyes. I'm sorry," she murmured, but he shook his head.

"It's not your fault. He obviously had no desire to be recognized," he murmured, his gaze moving past her to the window, his expression thoughtful.

"You think it was my suitor," she said quietly. "Someone I would recognize if I'd seen his face."

"Or someone who works for him that you might have recognized as well," Robert said with a shrug.

Lisa nodded, not arguing the point.

"I want you to stay away from Pembroke in the future," Robert said after a moment and she glanced up with surprise.

"Pembroke? Why him?" she asked with surprise. He was second on her list of possible husbands, right behind Findlay. The man was handsome, thoughtful and trying very hard to try to please her by arranging the picnic and such.

"Because if it weren't for his pastries making you sick, you would have been at the ball tonight."

"It is hardly his fault if his cook's pastries made me ill," Lisa pointed out with amusement.

"It is if he added something to make you deliberately ill, Lisa," he said quietly and she blanched in dismay.

"You think he put something in the pastries to make me ill?"

"All the other men were expecting you to be at the ball tonight," Robert pointed out. "In fact, most of them are probably only realizing now that you aren't going to attend tonight. But whoever attacked or sent someone to attack you knew you would not be attending the ball before that."

"Oh, surely it is late enough that —"

"It has been exactly one hour since I left you sleeping in here, Lisa," he said quietly. "I doubt Christiana and Richard have been at the ball for more than a matter of minutes. If they have even made it through the lineup of disembarking carriages to the door yet."

"Oh," Lisa murmured, recognizing the truth of his words. Getting into the more popular balls could be rather tedious. The narrow streets were always crowded and the carriage traffic slow on the way there, and then the lineup of disembarking carriages was always long. That was then followed by the long lineup at the actual ballroom entrance as guests waited to be announced. It could take a while to get in. Leaving was never quite as bad, but it was something of a trial as well if you waited until everyone else was leaving to head home.

"Just stay away from him for now," Robert repeated and this time she nodded, though a bit reluctantly. Really, Pembroke seemed very kind. Besides, she had rather been looking forward to the ride up the river and the picnic that was to follow the day after tomorrow. Well, she was now that she wasn't hanging over a basin. Although, now that she thought of it, if his cook was preparing the picnic, perhaps it was better

179

to avoid it anyway. She didn't wish to be hanging over the basin again the night after tomorrow.

"Here we are," Bet said cheerfully, entering the room now with a tray in hand. "I brought ye tea and some food too, Lord Langley. I thought ye might want it after yer efforts."

"Thank you, Bet." Robert stood at once and moved the table beside Lisa's chair, shifting it between them for Bet to set the tray on. "That was kind of you."

"My pleasure, my lord," Bet said, blushing slightly at the compliment as she set the tray between them. She straightened, hesitated, and then headed for the door saying, "Cook asked for my help with mending her apron so I'll just go see what I can do while you eat. Send for me if you need me."

"Thank you, Bet," Lisa murmured as the maid left. She then turned her attention to the contents of the tray. Cold chicken, cucumber sandwiches and bumbleberry tarts filled two plates on the tray. There was also a steaming pot of tea and two cups. Lisa smiled with anticipation and pulled the nearer plate a bit closer to begin on the chicken, but paused with a drumstick to her lips, eyes widening when Robert did the honors and began to pour the tea.

"I'm sorry," she said, setting the chicken leg back. "I'll do that."

It was always the woman's place to pour the tea, but Robert just chuckled and shook his head. "No. Go ahead. You are obviously hungry. I will pour the tea."

"Thank you," Lisa murmured, picking up her drumstick again and this time taking a bite. A little sigh of pleasure slid from her lips as the flavor of roast chicken filled her mouth. It was heavenly, even cold. But then she was hungry enough that she suspected even porridge would have tasted delicious at that point, and she disliked porridge.

"Slow down," Robert cautioned as she swallowed and immediately took a second bite. "Your stomach may still be a little tender. You don't want to make yourself sick again."

"No, I don't," Lisa agreed dryly, forcing herself to set the drumstick down and instead pick up the tea he'd just poured for her. They were silent for a bit after that, both of them eating and enjoying the tea. It was only after they'd both pushed their plates away that Lisa glanced to him and said quietly, "Thank you, Robert."

"For what?" he asked with surprise. "I didn't bring the food. Bet did."

She smiled faintly at his confusion and

explained, "Not for that. For . . . well, everything else," she said wryly. "For coming for me at Mrs. Morgan's. For looking out for me since then and for chasing after that man tonight. I know I have given you a hard time, but I do appreciate it. I guess my pride was just hurting a bit after that business in the carriage. But you were right," she rushed on when he would have interrupted. "While I had a crush on you while growing up, we have been too close for too long ever to turn our relationship into anything more than one resembling siblings. Now, I can't even imagine you kissing me or caressing my cheek the way Charlie did the other night. The very idea is laughable."

Standing up, Lisa moved around the table to bend and kiss his cheek, then straightened and moved to the bed, undoing and removing her robe as she went.

"Good night, Robert," she finished around a yawn. "I hope you sleep well. I certainly shall, knowing you are here, just a shout away, to watch over me."

She then slid into bed, pulled the covers up to her chin, and closed her eyes.

Robert stared at the bed for several minutes, her words replaying themselves in his head. She couldn't even imagine him kissing or caressing her as Findlay had? Well, he bloody well could. And he'd have done a damned sight better job than the tepid efforts he'd witnessed from Findlay at the ball the night before, he thought.

But it was a fleeting thought. His mind was full of the image of the way her robe and gown had gaped as she'd bent to kiss his cheek. He'd seen damned near all the way down to her belly button as she'd done it, though he was sure she had no clue of the view he'd had. And then when she'd tugged off her robe to crawl into bed, the neckline had dropped off on one side, revealing a good expanse of one creamy shoulder. Now she was lying there, not more than a few feet away, naked but for a thin nightgown, completely unconcerned that a red-blooded male was still sitting there. And he *was* red-blooded. That blood was pulsing through his body hot and strong right then.

But did Lisa care? Hell no. It seemed she'd decided he was right and she was better off with one of those addlepated idiots who had been fawning over her the last few days.

Damn. She was going to be the death of him if he didn't get this business resolved soon and get away from her, he thought grimly and stood to quickly gather the tray and carry it from the room.

"Good night, Robert," Lisa murmured as he reached the door and it was the sexiest damned sound he'd ever heard: soft and sleepy, almost a whisper. He could imagine her saying his name just that way, but in sleepy greeting as he slid into bed next to her, his naked body sliding against hers.

She was definitely going to be the death of him, Robert decided. He didn't respond to her words, but simply headed silently up the hall, his expression unhappy.

CHAPTER NINE

"I hope you are feeling better, Miss Madison."

Lisa turned from Suzette to peer at the man who had spoken, her eyes widening slightly when she saw that it was Lord Pembroke . . . whom she was supposed to stay away from. She should have realized he would attend the ball.

"Oh, yes, I — How did you know I was ill?" she asked suddenly, suspicion crowding her mind.

Pembroke's eyebrows rose slightly at the sharp question, but he explained gently, "Because when I sent a calling card today, your sister responded that you were feeling poorly and not accepting visitors in favor of resting up and recovering for tonight's ball. And then Tibald just told me that you were apparently unwell last night and didn't make an appearance then either."

"Oh, yes," Lisa murmured on a sigh, feeling guilty for her brief suspicions. Really, after some thought she found it hard to believe Pembroke could be behind her sudden illness. He seemed a very nice and likeable man. And handsome as he was, it was hard to believe he had to kidnap young women. Most would probably throw themselves at his feet, which reminded her of something Mrs. Morgan had said about the suitor and made her suspicions rise again.

"Are you feeling better?" Pembroke asked gently, reminding her of his earlier question.

"Oh, yes, thank you," she responded, her smile a bit forced now. "Much better."

"Good," he said with a nod. "Then I hope you saved a dance for me."

"Oh . . . I don't think . . ." She made a show of searching the bag at her waist for her dance card, her mind working as she tried to word the lie that she didn't have a single dance left.

However, she was stymied in her efforts to do as Robert wanted and avoid the man when Suzette said, "I have your card, dear. Remember Daniel asked you to save a dance for him and I was filling it in for you."

"Oh, yes, of course," Lisa muttered, turning to her.

"And you do have a dance or two left,"

Suzette said cheerfully. "See? A quadrille and a waltz. In fact, the waltz still available is the first song of the night and should be starting any moment."

Lisa froze as Suzette stuck the card under her nose so she could see.

"Delightful. I would love to dance the waltz with you," Lord Pembroke said, seeming quite pleased with how things had turned out.

"Oh, yes, of course then," Lisa said faintly, accepting the card to pencil in his name. What else could she do at that point?

Nothing that she could think of, unfortunately, and Lisa instinctively looked around for Robert. He was going to be annoyed, of course, but there was nothing she could do about that now, she thought, almost relieved when she saw that he was leading Daniel and Richard from the ballroom. No doubt in search of someplace to tell them about the events of the night before, she supposed. She knew he hadn't got the chance before now. Christiana and Richard had been very late returning from the ball last night, and Robert had said he'd dozed off and missed their arrival. Richard had also apparently been up and gone before Robert rose that morning, returning just in time to rush above stairs and change for the ball.

She was quite sure they were about to get the news of last night's events now.

"It's starting. Shall we?"

Lisa forced a smile and accepted Lord Pembroke's arm, assuring herself as she went that all would be well. He would hardly try to drag her kicking and screaming from the dance floor. And, hopefully, the dance would be over before Robert returned to the room.

"Are you sure you are feeling well, Miss Madison?"

Lisa glanced up and managed a smile. "Yes. I . . . well, actually no, not really," she said, thinking she'd found a way to avoid this dance after all. "Perhaps I should skip this dance, my lord."

"Yes, of course," he said, all solicitous at once. "I suppose I shouldn't be surprised if you've been ill for the last day and night. Perhaps you shouldn't have even come tonight."

"No, I probably shouldn't have," Lisa agreed as he began to lead her from the floor, but even as she said it, she realized that was a mistake. Her dance card was full. How would it look if she were to dance with everyone else after claiming she didn't feel well enough to dance with him? Lisa was so vexed at the pickle she'd somehow got herself into that it wasn't until a cool breeze brushed her cheek that she realized he'd led her outside on to the terrace. Damn, this was worse than dancing with him. Robert would be beyond furious with her.

"I thought some fresh air would help," Pembroke said with concern, apparently noting her dismay. "You have a full dance card and some gentlemen aren't as understanding as myself about these things and might insist you dance. Perhaps some fresh air will help you through the rest of the night."

"Oh, I — Yes, of course. Hopefully it will help," she ended lamely, glancing nervously about and relieved to see that they were not alone on the terrace. She was less relieved when he began to lead her to the stairs down into the garden, however.

"Oh, my lord, I don't think we should venture far. My sisters will worry," she said anxiously, dragging her feet.

"We won't go far," he assured her soothingly, urging her along. "There is a bench just there and I thought you might do better to sit quietly for a bit and breathe deeply. It might make you feel better."

"Oh." Lisa bit her lip and glanced from the house to the bench he was gesturing to. It was close enough she could see it, but it

189

was in shadow. It was possible he planned to knock her out and cart her off, or simply drag her off as the man last night had tried to do. Although it would mean getting her over the wall surrounding the large gardens. But the man last night hadn't seemed worried about dragging her out a window and down a tree.

Come to think of it, how the heck had he thought he would accomplish that? She wondered about that suddenly and found herself halfway to the bench before she managed to shift her thoughts to the problem at hand. But it mattered little. She couldn't come up with a single thing to make him turn back toward the house. Lisa supposed she would just have to hope he didn't have any nefarious plans and that she was returned safely to the house . . . and before Robert returned from talking with Richard and Daniel.

It was a lot to pin her hopes on, Lisa acknowledged unhappily as Pembroke led her the last few feet to the bench.

"Here we are," Pembroke murmured. "Please sit and we shall just enjoy the night air for a bit. It is nicer this way anyway. We can better talk. Although, of course, it means losing out on the chance to hold you in my arms," he admitted wryly as he settled beside her and then added, "But then perhaps I can do both."

"Er," Lisa said uncertainly and then cut herself off on a gasp of surprise as he suddenly turned to slide his arms around her and draw her against his chest.

"Relax," he said soothingly. "I am just going to hold you while we sit here. After all, it is really not that different to my holding you on the dance floor, is it?"

Lisa stared at the shoulder she was pressed against, her eyes wide. It certainly was different. On the dance floor he would never dare hold her this closely. Nor would he let his hands roam over her back so freely as he pressed her tight to his chest.

"My lord," she said, trying to ease away by leveraging her arms against his chest. "This really isn't proper."

"I know, but I can't help myself," Pembroke sighed, squeezing her closer still despite her efforts. "I find myself quite overcome in your presence, Lisa. May I call you Lisa?" Before she could reply, he continued, "I have never encountered quite such a lovely creature as you in my life. The things I dream about doing to you." He released a gusty sigh, and then added, "Of course, I would be most pleased if you would consent to be my wife too."

"Er . . ." Lisa said, still struggling to put some space between them. Honestly, she was beginning to have trouble breathing with his pressing her so tightly to him and she began to worry that perhaps that was the point. Smothering her into a faint, perhaps, and then dragging her off to ravish and marry. Mrs. Morgan did say that the suitor wished to do both.

Good Lord, she never should have come out here with him. The thought was enough to send panic through her, followed closely by a sudden rush of strength that caught Pembroke by surprise and allowed her to break the embrace. She almost sent him crashing to the ground in her fervor to be free, but he managed to save himself. By the time he regained his balance and straightened, however, Lisa was on her feet and hurrying back the way they'd come.

"Miss Madison!"

"Miss Madison."

One call came from Pembroke behind her, but the other came from in front and Lisa chose to turn her attention to the one in front, beaming a relieved smile on Lord Tibald as she recognized the man walking down the steps toward her.

"My lord," she greeted the newcomer a little breathlessly as she paused before him.

She took a quick nervous glance over her shoulder to see Pembroke hurrying toward them, and skirted around the other man, toward the stairs.

"Go ahead," Tibald said gently, giving her a gentle push. "I shall handle him. He had a bit too much to drink before the ball and is notoriously difficult when in his cups."

"Thank you, my lord," Lisa said with relief and hurried up the stairs and across the terrace. She had nearly reached the doors when a dark shape swooped out of the shadows, caught her arm in a steel grip and urged her along the terrace to the doors of a dark room. Lisa was so taken by surprise, she didn't even scream or struggle until it was too late and she was being bundled into the lightless room.

"What the devil did you think you were doing? I told you not to go near Pembroke and yet I return to have Suzette tell me that you were dancing the waltz with him. Only you weren't anywhere on the dance floor; you'd allowed him to take you outside."

"Robert," Lisa said with relief, recognizing his voice as he closed the terrace doors, enclosing them in darkness.

"Dammit Lisa, I am doing my best to keep you safe," he muttered as he struck a match and used it to light a candle on a nearby table before continuing. "But it would help if you would use some common sense and not throw yourself into danger at every turn."

"Throw myself into danger at every turn?" she gasped with amazement as he turned to glare at her.

"Yes," he snapped with frustration. "Running off to tea in brothels, opening your window to kidnappers and disappearing to the gardens with a man who could be the one behind all your trouble. What the hell are you thinking?"

"I didn't know Mrs. Morgan ran a brothel!" Lisa protested with outrage. "And I certainly didn't open the window for that man, I just wanted some fresh air and — dammit! I didn't want to leave the ballroom tonight. And I didn't want him mauling me as he was. In fact I was struggling to get free."

"Well, you certainly didn't look like you were struggling in Pembroke's arms down there in the gardens," he snarled. "You looked as cozy as a two-bit —"

His words broke off in surprise as her hand connected with his cheek in a sharp slap that echoed in the sudden silence.

Lisa was rather shocked that she'd done it. She hadn't intended to, didn't even realize she was going to until her hand connected with his face. Now she watched Robert raise a hand to the cheek she'd hit, and arch an eyebrow as he rubbed it.

"Interesting. You'll slap me, where you didn't slap him, yet claim you were unwilling. I guess that says just how unwilling you really were."

Lisa's hand flew up again, but this time he caught it.

"Once will do," he growled, holding her by the wrist firmly. "Try it again and I shall have to punish you."

In response, Lisa let her other hand fly. She was so mad she wanted to flail at him; hit, slap, scratch and even pull hair. But she suspected it wasn't just anger at Robert for what he'd nearly said. She was furious that he was too obtuse to love her, angry that she'd felt so helpless in Lord Pembroke's hold until she'd broken free. Mad as hell that a woman she'd thought was a friend had tried to kidnap and drug her, primp and present her for the pleasure of some unknown man, and downright enraged that that unknown man thought he could and should be able to ravish and marry her if he so chose, against her will or not. She was mad about everything, and Robert was a handy target, so she let her other hand fly too.

But he caught her second hand as well. They glared at each other briefly, both breathing heavily with an excess of emotion, and then Robert suddenly used his hold on her wrists to tug her forward against his chest and then swung her arms down and behind her back, forcing her closer against his chest as he covered her mouth with his.

As punishments went . . . well . . . she rather liked it, Lisa decided as his mouth moved firmly over hers and urged her lips open. He definitely kissed differently from Lord Findlay. There was no softness here, no nipping, or nibbling, no teasing or that feeling of wanting something more, something that was undefinable to her. She was now getting the something more — Robert's tongue thrashing her own and then receding before returning to slide around hers again. That was what had been missing with Findlay, Lisa realized as she responded to the kiss, her body pressing instinctively closer and her tongue entering the dance.

"Christ," Robert muttered, tearing his mouth from hers to pepper kisses across her cheek and then down her neck to nibble, suck and nip there.

Lisa moaned in response, struggling instinctively to free her hands to touch him.

"You're driving me insane," he growled, shifting her wrists to one of his hands so that his other could slip around and move up her waist.

Lisa gasped, rising up on tiptoe as his hand closed over one breast through her gown, trying to escape the caress even as she instinctively arched to press into it. She moaned when his mouth then trailed down across her collarbone, toward her neckline and then whispered his name urgently as she felt him tugging at the neckline of her gown, trying to free her breast as his tongue crested the slope above it.

Much to her relief, he freed her wrists then, allowing her to slip her arms around his shoulders as he brought his other hand around to work at the difficult neckline of her gown until he got one breast free. Robert immediately latched onto it, squeezing the soft globe as he sucked the entire nipple and aureola into his mouth.

"Robert," Lisa gasped, shocked by the bursts of pleasure that sent shooting through her. This then was the warm tingly stuff Fanny and Sophia had spoken about in their books. They really hadn't described it very well at all, she decided, clawing at Robert's shoulders with excitement until she couldn't stand it anymore and had to grab him by a handful of hair to drag his mouth back to hers again.

Robert obliged, his kiss this time demanding rather than punishing. But his hands continued to caress and squeeze, one at her exposed breast and the other now on her behind and urging her hips against his as his tongue worked its magic.

Lisa was vaguely aware of his moving her backward, but didn't understand why until she felt something press into her bottom, and then his hands gave up their squeezing and caressing to catch her by the waist and lift her to sit on that something. A desk, she thought, or a table. Lisa was too busy to look around and see. And then his one hand was back at her breast, but the other was tugging her skirt up one leg until he could slip his hand beneath and run it up from her knee along her outer thigh.

Lisa moaned and squirmed under the caress, her bottom shifting on the hard surface she sat on, and her own kiss becoming wildly demanding now. Her fingers tugged eagerly at his hair even as her palms pressed him closer. When his hand then slid back down her thigh only to ride back up, gliding along the inside of her thigh this time, she began to squirm in earnest, little gasps of excitement puffing from her mouth to his. When his fingers brushed against the curls between her legs, Lisa positively jumped, bucking up and back at the same time and legs squeezing together trapping his hand there.

Distracted as she was by what Robert was doing, Lisa wasn't at first aware that her actions and their weight had set the small table she was sitting on tumbling backward. Robert was a little quicker on the uptake and did try to save them both, but he was off balance and merely managed to stumble and fall with her. His weight crashed down on her chest even as her back hit the hard floor. Lisa groaned in pain from both that and the pain suddenly radiating from the backs of her knees which were caught on the edge of the table.

"Damn," Robert muttered, scrambling to get off of her. "Are you all right?"

Lisa winced, but opened her eyes and managed a crooked smile. "I think so. A little bruised maybe, but otherwise all right."

"I'm sorry," he apologized, shifting to help her up.

Lisa stood carefully, grimacing at the pain in her back and legs.

Once he had her on her feet and was sure

nothing was broken, Robert immediately turned to quickly right the table and replace the few things that had been on it besides her and him. Realizing that she was standing there with one breast still out, Lisa quickly tucked it back in her dress. She then checked her hair with her hands, and blindly tried to repair any damage that may have been done, but it was difficult when she couldn't see what damage the incident may have caused.

Frowning, she glanced around the room and spied a mirror hanging on one wall. Moving to it, Lisa was relieved to find that not too much damage had been done. She quickly straightened her hair and then brushed down her skirts before turning nervously back to Robert to find he had finished with his task and was now eyeing her silently. The look was one she recognized. She had known him a long time after all. That look was the one he wore when contemplating a troubling puzzle or problem he couldn't quite sort out.

It was rather lowering to be considered a troubling problem after what they'd just done and Lisa instinctively raised her shoulders in self-defense against whatever he was about to say.

But all he said was, "We should probably

return to the ball. Suzette said you have a full dance card. Your absence will not go without notice."

Lisa stared at him silently for a moment, as disappointed as if he had insulted or slapped her, and then she simply turned away toward the door.

"Of course, you're right," she murmured, and then as she reached the door, she added, "After all, I am not going to find a husband in here, am I."

She dragged the door open and strode quickly up the hall toward the music and chatter coming from the ballroom.

"There you are. I have been looking everywhere for you. Our dance is about to begin."

Lisa paused abruptly and forced a smile when Lord Findlay suddenly appeared in front of her as she entered the ballroom.

"I —" She paused and glanced over her shoulder when his gaze suddenly moved past her and narrowed. He'd spotted Robert, of course. Following her. Only Lord Langley hadn't thought to stop and check his appearance and his hair was disheveled as were his clothes. He looked like . . . well, like he'd been ravishing a young woman, she supposed, and wondered with dismay if her lips were as swollen and bruised as his.

"The music is beginning, my lord," she said desperately.

Lord Findlay shifted his gaze back to her face and then gave a small nod and smile. "Then we should dance."

Lisa let her breath out on a small puff of relief, hoping that meant she didn't look like she'd just been kissed silly, and allowed him to lead her onto the dance floor. But her hopes were dashed when Lord Findlay took her into his arms murmuring, "Do I need to call Langley out to defend your honor?"

Sighing, she sagged briefly in his arms and then forced herself upright again and blurted, "We were arguing."

Not surprisingly, that brought a dubious rising of one eyebrow.

"And then I slapped him," she continued reluctantly, before babbling, "and then I slapped him again, and he kissed me for punishment and then the table fell over and he picked it up and we came back out." She grimaced as she finished, aware that she was probably blushing furiously.

Lord Findlay was silent for several seconds and then cleared his throat and asked, "And does he often punish you with kisses?"

"No, of course not, never," Lisa assured him, and then babbled nervously, "Well, except tonight, but you see he wanted me to stay away from Lord Pembroke, but I had to dance with him because of Suzette. Only Pembroke could tell I was uncomfortable and thought it was because I'd been sick and insisted on taking me out for air. Then he grabbed me, and I got away and Lord Tibald took care of Pembroke for me while I tried to come inside. But then Robert saw everything and dragged me off to rant at me about being with Pembroke, which is when I slapped him and . . . well, all the other followed and we returned to the ball," she ended weakly.

"I see," Findlay murmured.

Lisa was doing her damnedest to avoid looking at him, afraid of what she would see in his eyes. But when his shoulder began to shake under her hand, she glanced at him nervously, amazed to see him struggling to stifle what appeared to be mirth.

"Are you laughing, my lord?" Lisa asked with amazement.

"I am sorry," he assured her sincerely, but the sincerity cracked under amusement as he added, "Truly you are the most delightful female. Sometimes I simply cannot make heads or tails of what you're saying."

"Oh," she muttered and supposed her

explanation had been a little less than coherent.

"Why are you supposed to stay away from Pembroke?" Langley asked.

"Because —" Lisa paused abruptly, and avoided telling the truth by repeating what Tibald had said. "Because he is notoriously difficult when in his cups."

"Ah, yes, he is," Findlay agreed solemnly. "I take it he is in his cups tonight?"

"Lord Tibald seemed to think so," Lisa muttered.

"Right." He nodded. "And how is it that you had to dance with Pembroke because of Suzette?"

"Oh," she sighed unhappily. "He came up asking about a dance and Suzette announced that the first waltz was still free, so of course I had to dance it with him."

"Of course," Findlay agreed wryly. "And did you enjoy Langley's punishing kiss?"

Lisa was so startled by the unexpected question that she actually stumbled in the dance. Lord Findlay immediately tightened his hold on her, drawing her closer against his chest to prevent her falling and she took refuge there briefly to avoid answering the question.

"Are you all right?" he asked, easing her back a moment later. It was the smart thing to do. It really wasn't proper to be hanging on a man like that.

Lisa nodded, still avoiding his eyes. "I — yes, thank you."

He allowed a moment of silence to pass, and then pointed out gently, "You have not answered the question . . . but then perhaps that is answer enough," he added quietly, sounding disappointed.

"I — it's not — I liked your kiss," she said finally if a little weakly.

"Did you?" Charles asked, cheering somewhat, and then tilted his head and said, "Better or less than his?"

He would have to ask that, Lisa thought with vexation and then said, "They were two entirely different kisses. Yours was gentle and . . . er . . . sweet. His was . . ." She briefly sought her mind for an acceptable description. Certainly, hot, passionate and overwhelming wouldn't do. Finally, she said, "Hard."

Lord Findlay blinked at the word. "Hard? What was?"

"His kiss," she said with a frown. "That is what we are talking about, my lord. If you will insist on discussing this, please at least try to follow the conversation."

"Yes, of course, my apologies," Charles murmured quickly, his lips twitching again.

"So you see, they were two entirely different kisses. Impossible to compare."

"I would imagine," he said agreeably.

"However, perhaps if you were to kiss me hard, well, then I could compare the two," she suggested as the idea came to her. Robert's kisses had been heart stopping. He'd wrung passion from her as easily as the maids at home wrung water from a soaking rag. Really, it had been the most exciting, most enjoyable experience of her life. She was not willing to live with a lesser passion in her marriage bed. But she wasn't likely to get Robert to marry her with him being such a dense and stubborn idiot of a male. But surely he wasn't the only one who could wring such passion from her?

Perhaps if Lord Findlay used a bit more fervor in his kisses and didn't treat her as if she were so fragile she might crumble under his passion . . . well, perhaps he too could stir those depths of passion from her.

It seemed perfectly reasonable to her. Findlay had already kissed her once. It was just that his had lacked the passion and fervor of Robert's, but then it was possible that he had just been considerate of her being a lady.

She raised her head to peer at Lord Findlay to see what he thought of the suggestion and found him staring down at her with quite the most startled expression.

"Are you . . . ?" He paused to clear his throat and then said carefully, "Are you suggesting you would like me to give you a punishing-type kiss?"

"Well I would rather that than ask Robert to give me a gentle kiss," she admitted wryly, and Lord Findlay released a burst of startled laughter that made the arms holding her shake and vibrate. Lisa smiled wryly, glad she'd amused him this time, and then, in the next moment, Charles began to whirl them to the side and right out of the ballroom.

Lisa glanced around with surprise as he walked her across the terrace. She hadn't realized they'd been so close to the doors while speaking and hadn't expected the moment to come quite this soon. Actually, she hadn't really been thinking at all when she'd made the suggestion: she'd mostly been desperate to have Lord Findlay wipe the memory of Robert's kisses from her memory, and hopefully stir the same passion he had. If Charles could . . . well, perhaps all would be well after all.

Lord Findlay stopped walking and she glanced around to see that he'd led her to the darkest corner of the terrace where no one was likely to notice or see. When he then turned her to face him, she shifted nervously, her eyes shooting everywhere but to his face.

"Punishing, huh?" he murmured thoughtfully, seeming reluctant.

Lisa was about to call it off, and let him off the hook when he suddenly caught her arms, dragged her up against his chest and planted his mouth on hers. This was definitely punishing, Lisa decided as his mouth crushed hers bruisingly against her teeth. Had Robert really been trying to punish her? Not bloody likely if this was punishing, because this was nothing like what Robert had done, she thought with dismay as Charles bit at her lip and forced her mouth open with his tongue. When it then swept inside, it wasn't with the questing grace of Robert's, but with a conquering fervor, filling her until she thought she would choke on it or suffocate.

Robert may have called it punishment, but his kiss hadn't been punishment at all compared to this. Good Lord, and she'd asked for it, she thought with dismay as Lord Findlay continued to mash his mouth over hers. What on earth had she been thinking?

The kiss, if that's what it was, seemed to

be interminable, and Lisa was more than relieved when it finally ended and he lifted his head.

"Well?" he asked, breathing a bit heavily.

Lisa stared at him blankly for a moment and then cleared her throat and offered, "It was much more masterful than . . . er . . . you know."

Really, it was the best she could do under the circumstances. She could hardly criticize it when it was exactly what she'd asked for.

"Lisa!"

Sighing as she recognized the owner of that sharp voice, she turned and grimaced at Robert as he paused a few feet away. He was angry, of course, his hands clenched and back stiff as a board, but then he always seemed to be angry with her lately, she thought unhappily.

"I am right here, my lord," she said grimly. "There is no need to bark at me like a dog."

"Inside," he growled, which really wasn't much better than barking, in her opinion.

CHAPTER TEN

"Did you try the tea cakes?" Suzette asked, leaning forward in her seat to select another one. "You should have one."

"No, thank you," Lisa murmured despite her growling stomach. She was not eating a single thing Pembroke had presented for this picnic. She may be hungry right now, but a short bout of hunger was better than hours of vomiting followed by still hours more of dry heaves. She had learned her lesson. Still, it was very hard sitting here watching the others eat so eagerly while she was hungry. But she supposed it was just punishment in Robert's eyes.

The thought drew her gaze to the man in question. He had chosen to sit at another table, leaving her, Christiana, Suzette, Richard and Daniel at their table.

It was Pembroke's picnic, which Lisa had thought they weren't going to attend. However, Christiana had seen the invitation before Robert could get to it and had wanted to go. And they hadn't been able to refuse without telling her the truth of things, which Robert was reluctant to do for some reason. All he would say was that they shouldn't upset Christiana. She didn't know why he cared so bloody much about upsetting her sister. He certainly had no problem upsetting her.

The man had been an ogre ever since the night before, growling and snapping at her every couple of minutes. One would almost think he was jealous at catching her and Charles in what he must have thought was a most passionate embrace. However, he would never admit it if he was. Robert took stubbornness to a new level.

Thoughts of Charles had her glancing around even though she knew he was not there. Pembroke had said Findlay had sent word of a prior engagement, but she suspected he simply hadn't invited the man. She couldn't help noticing that Lord Tibald wasn't there either — also a prior engagement. She had come to the conclusion that Pembroke had simply decided to eliminate the competition during this excursion by neglecting to invite them. She didn't know why he'd bothered, since he himself hadn't approached her even once since the beginning of the journey. Lisa didn't know if he was embarrassed about last night's tussle in the garden, angry that she had rebuffed him, or just too busy seeing to everyone else to find the time to speak to her, but he had spent most of the journey fussing over his mother and seeing to her comfort. The man was definitely a mother's boy.

This excursion was certainly an impressive one though. They had all gathered at the docks, piled on a boat and sailed up the coast to this rather lovely clearing. Pembroke had then herded everyone ashore and while the guests had all wandered about surveying the pretty flowers, trees and a nearby spring, a small army of servants had filed out of the bowels of the ship with tables, chairs, tablecloths, dishes and platters of food. It wasn't really a picnic at all, but open-air dining, she decided. And the spread was really a quite impressive one too. However, she wasn't willing to risk it and end up hanging over the basin all night. Besides, her stomach was still tender and she wasn't really hungry.

"Oh, the torte is lovely too," Christiana moaned. "Really, Pembroke's cook outdid herself this time."

Lisa forced a smile and then stood.

"I think I shall just walk along the shore

while you all finish," she said and moved away before anyone could protest.

Some of Lisa's tension eased as soon as she had moved away from the tables, but she didn't truly relax until she'd walked far enough that she couldn't hear the chatter of the diners anymore. In that silence though, she became aware of the sound of footfalls behind her and glanced over her shoulder with a frown that dissolved into a sigh when she spotted Robert following her about ten feet back. Her watchdog was there. She should have known she wouldn't be allowed to take even a moment for herself. The only peace she got anymore was in her room at Christiana and Richard's. It was the only time Robert let her out of his sight. But that began to feel claustrophobic pretty quickly. It wasn't that it was a small room or anything, it was simply that even the largest room shrank in size when you felt trapped in it.

Muttering under her breath, she ignored Robert and simply continued to walk. She hadn't intended to go much farther, but his presence goaded her into continuing along the shoreline and around the bend, out of sight of the others.

"We should probably head back," Robert said quietly behind her and Lisa gave a start at how near his voice was. His words had been spoken practically in her ear. She ignored them, however, and continued without a word.

"Lisa."

"What, Robert?" she asked wearily, turning finally to scowl at him. She then quickly took a couple of steps back when she realized just how close he was. They had been close enough to kiss when she first turned.

"Where are you going?" he asked, rather than repeat that they should head back.

"Just . . . wherever," she murmured, gesturing vaguely with one hand. "I just want a few minutes of peace and quiet."

Robert nodded and moved up beside her. "You've been attending a lot of balls and teas. I suppose you're not use to all the busy-ness and people after so long in the country."

"Yes, that's it," Lisa said sarcastically. "It's all the people around me. Not the great, grumpy ogre who follows me everywhere."

He paused and peered at her with amazement. "I am trying to keep you safe."

"I don't know why. You act like you hate me," she snapped. "Why would you bother keeping me safe when you hate me? And why is it you who is keeping me safe anyway? You could just hire someone to do it. Then you could go on about your happy bachelor's life and forget about me."

"We can't hire someone. Christiana would want to know who he was and why he was needed and Richard doesn't want to worry her in her delicate condition."

Now it was Lisa who stopped walking. Turning on him blankly, she asked, "Her delicate condition?"

"She is with child again, but doesn't want anyone to know until she is further along . . . in case she loses it again."

Lisa stared at him with amazement, several thoughts running through her head. First and foremost was a sense of betrayal that Robert had known about it before she did. And she was Christiana's sister. It seemed like everyone was treating her like a child, the last to be trusted with news.

Shaking her head bitterly, she turned and continued to walk.

"And I don't hate you, Lisa," he said, sounding reluctant to make the admission. "I'm just finding this all a bit taxing on my patience."

Lisa snorted at the understatement in the words.

"What was going on with you and Lord Findlay last night?" he asked suddenly, as if the question were torn from him.

Lisa bit her lip and remained silent for a moment, but then shrugged. "You saw what was going on."

"He was kissing you, but he appeared to be rather rough about it," Robert said grimly.

"He — I —" Lisa paused and frowned, then shook her head, finding it impossible to even attempt to explain the debacle she'd instigated. It certainly hadn't tuned out as she'd expected.

"If he was forcing himself on you —"

"No, he wasn't," she said quickly, and then realizing there was no help for it, admitted, "He saw us after you — last night when we returned to the ball. He figured out something had happened. I admitted you had punished me with a kiss for that nonsense with Pembroke and he asked if I'd enjoyed it and if it was better than his kiss. I said they were completely different, and then I suggested he give me a punishing kiss to compare yours to." Lisa rolled her eyes even as she admitted that, realizing now just how stupid that had been.

"And he did," Robert said quietly.

Lisa nodded. "However, it wasn't like your punishment at all. His was rough and . . . well, rather nasty really. Punishing I guess, just as I'd requested." She was silent for a moment and then added, "Which made me realize that your kiss hadn't been a punishment at all."

"We should really turn back," Robert muttered, stopping and turning away.

"I never saw you as a coward," Lisa commented idly, glancing back to seeing the way he stiffened as he paused again. "But that's what you are, isn't it Robert? Afraid to marry, afraid to admit you want me, afraid to admit that that kiss wasn't punishment at all, but just an excuse to unleash the passion you feel for me. And you do have passion for me."

"We have to return to the others," Robert growled, not turning back.

"So go back to the others. I'm safe enough out here on my own. It's not like Pembroke can escape his mother or his other guests and come kidnap me. Besides, what would he do with me then? Bundle me into the hold of the ship with the servants for the return journey?"

Robert hesitated, but then nodded once grimly and headed away, leaving her on her own.

Lisa really hadn't expected that. She'd expected an argument. Hoped for it even, and had hoped it would lead to another bout of his unleashed passion. Because after

Robert's kiss last night she was right back to where she'd been at the start, wanting him and no one else. Lord Findlay and the others were all very nice and sweet and complimentary, but Robert stirred her passion and she suspected none of them would ever be able to make her tremble, quiver and moan as Robert had. She didn't even want them to. It had always been Robert for her. And she suspected he wanted her as well. She just didn't know how to break down the walls he'd erected around himself so that he'd give in to what he wanted and claim her. She didn't even know why he was hesitating to do so.

Sighing, Lisa turned back the way she'd been headed and then froze in surprise when she found herself facing a rather large man all in black with a hood. It was the same damned hood the man who had broken into her room and tried to take her away had been wearing.

"Ro— !" she began instinctively, but never finished shouting his name before one meaty fist slammed into the side of her head, knocking her senseless.

Robert almost didn't turn back at Lisa's shout. It was a broken sound, but he simply thought the wind had captured the rest of his name and taken it away. However, then he heaved a sigh and stopped again. Annoyed with her or not, irritated by her claims as he was, he couldn't simply ignore her. He would have to face her eventually and counter her arguments somehow, because while she was right, he wasn't ready to admit that he did want her. Because she was also right that he was afraid.

He started to turn back, caught movement out of the corner of his eye as he did and instinctively ducked and swerved, narrowly missing the ham-like fist that had been aimed at his head. Blinking in surprise at the large man now confronting him, he glanced past him to see Lisa lying unconscious on the sand back where he'd left her, and then ducked and rolled to the side as the man in black swung for him again.

Robert was popping back to his feet, mentally preparing himself for the next blow when he saw the fellow pull a long, large blade from the back of his trousers and toss it from hand to hand as he crouched slightly before him.

Bloody brilliant, Robert thought grimly. Fisticuffs were one thing, but a one-sided knife fight was not good. Not good at all. It was even more worrisome because if he failed at overcoming the huge bastard now moving in on him, Lisa would be lost. Which meant he'd better not lose if he wanted to keep her safe.

Very aware of that fact, Robert began glancing around for something he could use as a weapon. The only thing handy was sand at the moment, and he didn't hesitate but bent to grab up a handful even as he leapt to the side to avoid the knife now plunging toward him. He wasn't quick enough; the tip of it sliced into him, scraping across his ribs as he went, but he ignored the stinging pain and straightened, tossing the sand at his adversary's eyes.

The trick worked. The man stumbled back, reaching for his face and Robert charged, bending at the waist to ram his shoulder into the man's chest. The tackle took the fellow down and Robert landed on him hard and then began slamming his fists into his hood-covered face and stomach until he simply couldn't hit him anymore.

Much to his relief, when he stopped and knelt over the man, his attacker didn't move or suddenly rise up to start hitting back. It appeared he was unconscious. At least he could see that his eyes were closed through the eyeholes in his mask.

Robert sank back on his haunches with relief and then glanced down at his chest, grimacing when he saw the long slice in his shirt and the blood staining it. His gaze then shifted to where Lisa lay in the sand. It was probably good she was unconscious. She would have fainted if she'd seen the blood anyway, he thought wryly. Lisa had never been very good with blood.

His gaze swiveled back to the attacker and he started to lean forward, intending to remove the man's mask, but paused as the cut in his stomach protested. Sighing, he sank back without removing it. He would send Richard and Daniel for the fellow and they could unmask the man and tell him who he was. Right now, the more important thing was to get Lisa safely back to the others. His wound was bleeding quite a bit, and Robert was growing weaker by the moment. Should the hooded man wake up and have another go at him, he wasn't at all sure how he'd fare.

Taking a breath, he forced himself to his feet and then stumbled through the sand to Lisa.

Lisa moaned and turned over, wondering why her head felt like someone was dancing on it. She then opened her eyes slowly. She was in bed in her guest bedroom at Christiana and Richard's home.

"Oh, thank goodness. You're awake," Christiana murmured, suddenly appearing in her line of vision as she pent to peer at her.

"Chrissy?" Lisa said uncertainly. "What happened?"

"Don't you remember?"

That question from her other side brought Lisa's attention to the fact that Suzette too was there. She glanced at her uncertainly and then peered back to Christiana, her gaze sliding over the dresses they wore. The same dresses they'd been wearing at Pembroke's picnic.

"Oh," she breathed, recalling heading out for a walk, her words with Robert and then the big man with the hard fists. "Did Robert save me?"

"I'll say, and damned near died in the doing," Suzette said grimly.

"What?" Lisa asked with horror.

"It's all right. He's fine," Christiana assured her, glaring at Suzette for scaring her. "But he took a nasty wound to the chest saving you. And he bled quite a bit while carrying you back to the picnic. But the doctor thinks he'll be fine."

"He carried me wounded?" she asked with dismay.

"Yes. He didn't want to leave you there

unconscious and unprotected," Christiana explained gently. "And as it turns out, that was smart. He knocked out the fellow who attacked you, but when Richard and Daniel went back to find him he had regained consciousness and gone. If Robert had left you behind . . ."

She let her words trail off, but Lisa supposed they didn't really need to be said. If Robert had risked leaving her behind while he went for help, she might very well have been gone too. Sighing, she massaged her forehead unhappily trying to ease some of the aching there.

"Is your head hurting?" Christiana asked with concern.

"Aye," Lisa said with a grimace, and Christiana turned to pick up a glass beside the bed.

"The doctor left a tincture for you. He said it would help, but would make you a bit woozy. So don't get up and try to move around after you take it."

Lisa sat up with Suzette's help to drink the tincture. Once she'd downed the last of it, she sank back with a little sigh and then asked, "Is Robert here?"

"Across the hall," Christiana answered, setting the empty glass down.

"Oh," Lisa said quietly, and then glanced

at Christiana sharply. "How are you?"

Christiana's eyebrows rose slightly. "I am fine. I was not the one knocked out or stabbed."

"Yes, but all this excitement cannot be good for the baby. You should rest," Lisa said firmly.

"The baby?" Christiana said blankly.

"Robert told me that you are with child," Lisa said solemnly. "I wish you had told me yourself. I —"

"With child!" Suzette squawked, glaring at Christiana. "And you did not tell me?"

"I did not tell you because I am not with child," Christiana said dryly to Suzette and then glanced back to Lisa. "Robert said I was?"

"Yes. He said that was why he had to watch over me and we could not hire a body guard. You would ask questions and might get upset and lose the baby again," Lisa explained.

"Well, that might be a concern if I were with child. But I'm not," she said impatiently and then asked with bewilderment, "Where the devil would he get an idea like that?"

"Ah." That sound from the door made all three women glance that way to find Richard standing there with Daniel at his back.

At least Daniel started at his back, but Richard now collared his friend and urged him forward into the room, saying dryly, "Ask Mr. I've-got-a-plan here."

"Daniel?" Suzette asked with surprise. "Did you tell Robert that Christiana was with child?"

"Yes, actually, my love, I did," he admitted without shame as he moved around the bed to stand behind her. He bent to press a kiss to her forehead as she tilted her head back to look at him, and then shrugged and said, "It was the thing to do."

"Why on earth would you do that?" Christiana asked with amazement, covering Richard's hand with her own when he paused behind her and set it on her shoulder.

"Because it meant a guard couldn't be hired to watch out for Lisa and that Robert would have to do it himself," Daniel said simply. "Which he really wanted to do anyway. I just gave him the excuse he needed to move in here and do it."

"What?" Lisa asked with bewilderment.

Daniel glanced to her and smiled gently. "Lisa, my dear, Robert loves you. And not like a little sister," he added dryly. "But he's allowing his fears to prevent him doing anything about it. He needed a nudge, so I supplied it. When this business with Mrs.

Morgan came up, he suggested an around-the-clock guard on you, but I said Christiana was with child again and that the worry of this business might cause her to lose the child. We would have to look out for you ourselves."

"But you haven't looked after me at all," she pointed out dryly. "It is Robert who has been with me night and day since —"

"Wait. What business with Mrs. Morgan?" Christiana interrupted with a frown and then glanced to Lisa. "Have you seen that woman since coming to London?"

When Lisa grimaced, it was Richard who quickly explained about her tea and all that had followed.

"Damn," Suzette muttered. "We should have known she was up to no good. No proper lady would be giving young girls books like that one about Fanny."

"Never mind that," Christiana said impatiently and turned to glare at her husband. "Why did you not tell us about this Mrs. Morgan business?"

"Because then you and Suzette wouldn't have let Lisa out of your sight," Daniel explained for him.

"Too right we wouldn't have," Suzette said dryly.

"Which wouldn't have given Robert the

226

chance to realize his feelings," Daniel pointed out calmly, and then returned his glance to Lisa and added, "And, no, Richard and I haven't been watching out for you. We trusted that to Robert. In fact, we've been keeping Suzette and Christiana away as much as possible to leave him here alone with you." He paused and raised an eyebrow. "How has that been going?"

Lisa scowled at her brother-in-law. "Not all that well, thank you very much. He's stubborn and stupid and . . . male," she finished with disgust.

"Has he kissed you or anything?" Suzette asked.

Lisa snapped her mouth closed, but could feel the heat of the blush that bloomed on her face.

"He has, hasn't he?" Suzette crowed.

"Once," she acknowledged shortly. "But he's also been a horrible ogre, nasty and short-tempered and most unpleasant."

"He's jealous that all your suitors are fawning all over you," Daniel said with a shrug. "That's a good sign."

Lisa peered at him uncertainly. She'd come to the sad conclusion that Robert simply didn't love her and that explained his lack of interest in marriage. That if the right girl had come along, one he did actually love, he would change his mind. But Daniel was suggesting that Robert did love her. Biting her lip, she asked. "Why do you think he loves me?"

When Daniel merely burst out laughing at the question, it was Richard who said gently, "Lisa, every other word out of his mouth is your name when we are with him. Lisa likes these almond pastries too. Lisa is coming to town next month, next week, tomorrow. Lisa would have enjoyed this play. Lisa would have liked that." He smiled gently. "We have known he cared for you for quite some time, and had hoped he would get over his worries about the supposed Langley curse on his own."

"What curse?" Suzette interrupted with surprise.

"Surely you know about his father's marriage? The rumors floating around about Lady Langley's affair with Gower?"

"Oh, well yes," Suzette admitted with a frown, and then added, "But that is just gossip."

"I'm afraid it's not," Daniel said solemnly. "Gower has been bragging for years about his long-standing affair with Lady Langley."

"Oh dear," Christiana murmured.

"Hmm." Richard nodded and squeezed her shoulder. "But she is only the latest in a long line of unfaithful wives to the Lords of Langley. Robert's father raised him on the belief that it was a curse on the Langley men and told him he may as well get used to the idea that one day he would find his own wife grunting in a stall with his stable master."

"Oh my," Christiana said with distaste. "What a horrid thing to tell him."

"Why did he never tell us any of this?" Suzette asked with a frown.

"It isn't exactly proper conversation for ladies," Daniel said dryly, and when she looked about to protest, added, "I know the three of you have been as close as siblings to him. And that is probably what saved him. But —"

"What do you mean by saved him?" Lisa interrupted.

Daniel raised his eyebrows. "Well, what kind of man do you think would come out of having his ear filled with such rot by a bitter father?"

Lisa considered it, her eyes widening as she realized it would have been a bitter, woman-hating man.

"Exactly," Daniel said as if she'd spoken the words aloud. "I suspect his friendship with the three of you, and knowing you were all fine females and faithful friends is all that kept him from becoming as bitter and angry as his father and grandfather before him."

He let that sink in and then added, "However, even knowing the three of you hasn't completely eradicated the effects of being fed such drivel all his life. He fears that if he gives in to his feelings and marries Lisa, he too could incur the curse and find himself cuckolded."

"He thinks I would be unfaithful?" Lisa squawked with outrage.

"Do not take it personally," Richard said soothingly. "I suspect it is so ingrained, he thinks it is impossible for it not to happen. That the curse would make you do it."

"What rot," Lisa snapped. "Nothing and no one makes me do anything I do not wish. And I simply would not be unfaithful to my husband, no matter who he was or what he did. I would not break vows made before God."

"She wouldn't either," Christiana said staunchly. "Our Lisa is as faithful and loyal as a dog."

"Thank you," Lisa said, and then frowned because really, faithful and loyal as a dog simply didn't sound very attractive at all.

"Yes, well it is not I who think you would be unfaithful," Daniel said reasonably. "And

Robert probably doesn't even really believe that himself, it is simply what he has been raised to believe it will most certainly happen. An irrational fear, but it's keeping him from what he wants most anyway."

Lisa frowned over this and plucked at the blanket covering her, but finally asked plaintively, "Well, how am I supposed to help him over this fear?"

"I am not sure you really can," Daniel admitted regretfully. "I suspect your best bet is to compromise him and force him to marry you."

Lisa's mouth dropped in amazement and then she asked, "Are you suggesting I seduce him, ensure we are caught and that he has to marry me?"

"No, of course he isn't," Richard said coldly, glaring at his friend.

"But of course," Suzette said at the same moment. "That would work. Robert is too much a gentleman not to marry you if you were caught in a compromising situation. And once you are married, he will see that you are faithful and good and give up his fears."

"Oh, Suzette, I don't know," Christiana said uncertainly. "Forcing him into marriage . . . Well, Robert might be very angry. It could start them off badly."

"But it would start them off," Suzette argued. "Which is surely better than her marrying someone else and longing for Robert all her life while he mopes about kicking himself for losing her. At least they would be miserable together rather than apart."

"Something without misery would be better still," Richard said dryly.

"All right," Suzette said with a shrug. "So what do you suggest?"

There was silence as Christiana and Richard exchanged glances and then Christiana sighed. "I don't know. I guess we should all think about it."

"You'd best think quickly then," Daniel said quietly. "Robert is here now and in bed, which would surely make her seducing him easy. But once the Bow Street runners return with the name of the suitor . . . Well, there will be no reason for him to even stay here. And I suspect he will retreat as quickly and far away as he can once that happens and when he does, her chance will be lost."

Lisa frowned at his words, knowing they were true. Time was ticking away. If she wanted to win Robert, she had to do it soon, or she might lose her chance altogether.

CHAPTER ELEVEN

"Are you sure you want to do this?" Christiana asked with concern.

"Of course she's sure," Suzette answered for her. "Lisa has loved Robert forever. It will be all right."

"Suzette, don't push her into this," Christiana said quietly. "This is not a game. He could be very angry if he works out it was a setup. He might never forgive her."

Lisa bit her lip as Christiana's words ran through her head. It was a scary thought, but not as scary as the thought of never having him, she acknowledged. And if she did not do this, she very much feared she would lose him. Or never get to claim him, Lisa supposed, since he wasn't hers to lose yet.

Straightening her shoulders, she nodded firmly. "I want to do this."

"Good girl," Suzette said cheerfully, rubbing her shoulder. "You can do this. You've read all those books and know what to do.

Just pretend you are Fanny or Sophia and do all those delicious things you've read about. He will not be able to resist you."

"Right," she murmured, her mind scrambling to pull up all the bits of information she had read over the years. Unfortunately, the only thing she could remember just then was that the first time was supposed to be terribly painful and bloody. The thought was not an encouraging one. Hardly something to look forward to and she felt herself begin to wilt. Then she recalled those moments at the ball when Robert had kissed and caressed her after pushing her into the dark room. Those memories managed to push back the fear and trepidation.

"Good." Suzette patted her back. "So we will head out to the ball, and you go sit with him in his room while he eats, and then seduce him. We will return early and check on him and catch you in there, hopefully naked in bed," she added. "You can do this."

"I can do this," Lisa agreed, shoulders straightening, and then she asked with worry. "What time are you returning?"

"We hadn't decided on a set time," Christiana said with a frown when Suzette hesitated.

"It's better that way, then you will not have to fake being surprised," Suzette assured her when Lisa looked worried.

"But what if I haven't seduced him by the time you come back?" she asked plaintively.

"Well, you should seduce him right away," Suzette said firmly. "Or at least as quickly as possible. The doctor has given him a tincture so he should be manageable enough and suffering no pain."

"But —"

"Blow out the candle when you've done it," Christiana suggested. "If we return and the candle in his room is still glowing, we will wait to make our entrance."

"Oh, okay," she murmured with relief. It would be just her luck for them to return before she'd worked up the courage to seduce Robert and ruin everything.

"All right," Suzette smiled encouragingly. "Chin up. This will work. This time next year you and Robert will be happily married and laughing about all of this."

"If he forgives her," Christiana said gloomily. She was still not keen on this idea, but was giving her support because she loved Lisa and wanted her happy. And because she couldn't think of another way to handle the matter. Lisa appreciated that.

"Chrissy, stop being such a pessimist about this," Suzette reprimanded grimly. "We have been considering the problem for the last two days since the attack and there is really no other way to handle him. And it has to be handled soon. Those runners could return at any moment with the name of the suitor."

"Yes, I know," Christiana said on a sigh. "That's the only reason I have stopped arguing against it." Forcing a smile, she patted Lisa's shoulder. "Everything will be fine, I'm sure."

Lisa nodded solemnly, though she wasn't sure of that herself.

"Are you ladies ready to go?"

The three sisters glanced to the door together to see Daniel smiling brightly. "Richard is arranging for the carriage to be brought around right now. We need to get going if we wish to avoid the worst of the crush of arrivals."

"Yes, we're ready," Suzette said and gave Lisa's arm an encouraging squeeze before crossing the room to slip her arms around her husband.

"Good," he said and bent his head to kiss her forehead affectionately. Glancing back to Lisa, he said solemnly. "Good luck, little sister."

Lisa nodded and managed a smile, then turned her attention to Christiana as she moved in front of her.

"All will be well," Christiana whispered, giving her a bracing hug. "You don't have to do this if you don't want to. But it will be all right. At least I hope it will. It will be fine. Maybe."

On that confusing note, she released her and followed the other two out of the room.

Lisa stared after them briefly, then turned to pace to the window and peer out at the night sky, trying not to think about what she was supposed to do. Seducing Robert. Good Lord, she didn't have a clue what she was going to do. How was she supposed to seduce him? It wasn't exactly something she'd been trained in. Did they even have training in that? Was there a school for Birds-of-Paradise and other light skirts? Classes on kissing? Caressing? Or on how to not scream like an idiot when he tore through your maidenhead and sent the blood gushing?

"Dear God," she muttered, pushing that thought firmly away.

She would just go in there and . . . well, she would eat with him, talk, laugh, and . . . hopefully, something would inspire her. It would be easier though if he were doing the seducing. She would respond most eagerly if he did. However, that wasn't likely to happen.

"Here we are."

Lisa turned from the window as Bet entered, a tray in hand. "Cook put together quite a feast for the two of you. She says Lord Langley needs to build up his strength. I managed to refrain from saying more than she knew," Bet said with a naughty grin.

Lisa managed a rather sickly smile, and moved to take the tray from her. Everybody was so bloody cheerful and happy about this plan. It seemed to her most households would not be so happy at the thought of the deliberate ruination of a young unmarried lady of the family. She truly had an unusual family.

"Good luck," Bet murmured as she re- leased the tray. "I shall be thinking of ye."

"Oh, dear God, please do not," Lisa whispered shakily. "This is going to be hard enough without knowing you are thinking about what I am doing."

"Oh, aye," Bet muttered. "I'll . . . er . . . think o' something else then."

"Thank you," Lisa said dryly and headed out of her room to the one Robert was oc- cupying. She paused, her gaze sliding from the tray she held to the doorknob, and then sighed and glanced around. She smiled with relief when she saw that Bet had recognized the problem and was now rushing forward

238

to open the door for her.

"Good luck," she whispered as Lisa nodded and slid inside. "God be with ye."

Lisa turned with a start at those words, just in time to see the door close.

God be with her? She was planning to seduce a man, compromise herself and force him into marriage. God was not likely to approve of that plan, or stay at her side to help her through it. Good Lord, they'd all gone mad.

"Lisa?"

Sighing, she offered a smile for Robert's benefit as she moved toward his bed.

"Good evening. I've brought you dinner and thought I would stay to eat it with you," she announced cheerfully, carrying the tray to the bedside table

"That is kind of you," Robert murmured and started to pull himself up in bed.

"Just a moment and I'll help you," Lisa said with a frown when he winced and paused.

Setting the tray quickly on the table, she turned to bend to him. Lisa caught the way his eyes shifted to her chest as her robe gaped open, but pretended she didn't and acted very businesslike as she helped him sit up.

"Er . . . Lisa?" Robert muttered as she

fussed over tucking his blankets more securely around his waist.

"Would you like a robe or something? Are you chilly?" she asked as she straightened.

Robert glanced down at his chest, bare but for the bandaging around his ribs and grimaced. "A shirt will do."

"Of course." She moved to the chest at the foot of the bed and bent forward to open and begin searching it, knowing as she did that she was once again revealing a good deal of what she was wearing under her gaping robe.

"What the hell are you wearing?" he asked in a near growl as she pulled out a shirt and briefly examined it.

"Oh, a robe and night wear," Lisa answered absently as she straightened and moved back around the bed to help him don the shirt.

"What kind of night wear?" he asked, distractedly allowing her to tug the shirt on for him. Lisa didn't close it properly or bother with buttons.

"A nightgown, Robert," she answered on a laugh as she turned to the tray. "What else would I be wearing?"

"Yes, but . . . it is not that gown Mrs. Morgan put you in, is it?" he asked fretfully.

Lisa glanced at him with feigned surprise.

"As a matter of fact it is. How did you know?"

"Because when you bent over I saw damned near down to your belly button and there wasn't much in the way to prevent it but a gauzy film," he said dryly. "What the devil are you doing wearing that damned thing?"

"It is extremely comfortable," she said with a shrug, removing her own plate and glass of wine, leaving his on the tray before she turned toward him with it as if to set the tray on his lap. She paused before setting it down though and raised her eyebrows, then turned to set the tray back. Lisa then settled herself on the side of the bed and reached for the buttons of his shirt, murmuring, "You did not do up your shirt. I suppose your wound makes such things difficult."

"I can do up my own shirt," he muttered, but didn't try to stop her as she reached for the buttons, allowing her fingers to brush as much of his skin, by accident, as she could. Not that he seemed to notice. His eyes were on the opening of her robe. Which appeared to be parting a little more with every movement she made. "I can't believe you are actually wearing that damned gown."

"As I said, Robert, it is comfortable," Lisa

responded with unconcern, finishing with one button and letting her fingers trail down his chest to the next. "It feels as if you're practically wearing nothing at all, and brushes light as feathers against your skin when you move. It's quite nice. Here, feel."

Releasing the button she'd been about to slip into its hole, Lisa took his hand in one of hers while tugging the top of her robe to the side with the other. Then she pressed his hand to the material between her breasts. "It's quite lovely, really."

While she pressed the backs of his fingers against the material between her breasts, it was he who turned his fingers over to run them down the V she'd revealed, following the swell of one breast.

"Beautiful," he murmured, his eyes burning.

Lisa held her breath, waiting as little tingles began in the trail of his fingers and swept smoothly outward in both directions, bringing her nipples erect. She could see them pebbling beneath the thin material of her robe and even thinner nightgown. She wasn't the only one. Robert had noticed, she saw. His gaze appeared to be fixed on the flesh rising beneath the cloth as his finger moved.

"You shouldn't be here," he growled, but

his fingers continued to run over her skin through the delicate cloth.

"Of course I should. You need to eat," she whispered back, pressing gently forward into his caress until her breath brushed his lips as she spoke.

Robert shifted his eyes to her face, a frown beginning to pluck at his lips and she knew he was about to start thinking and ruin everything.

"Kiss me, Robert," she pleaded. "I so enjoyed your kisses at the ball. They made me burn and tingle everywhere. Just a kiss. Please?"

Lisa saw the struggle on his face as he hesitated, and decided to add to her persuasion. Releasing his hand, she quickly undid the sash of her robe and pulled it apart, baring herself to him from the waist up. Well, she did still have that gown from Mrs. Morgan's on, but it covered nothing. She might as well have been naked.

Robert groaned, his hand moving now under its own power to allow his fingers to drift to the side and crest one breast and then brush across the now erect nipple.

Lisa moaned in response and pressed closer, her mouth instinctively seeking his. Robert didn't push her away, but slipped his other hand into her hair and tilted her head to the angle he wished as his mouth claimed hers. She knew then she'd won. She'd actually done it. She'd seduced Robert.

Damn, she thought with amazement. That had been a hell of a lot easier than she'd expected, and then she stopped thinking altogether as his hands began to roam over her, pushing the robe off her shoulders to leave it pooling around her waist as his fingers then sought both breasts, squeezing and kneading the eager flesh through the gauzy cloth as his mouth devoured hers.

When Robert suddenly urged her back, Lisa feared for a moment that he was going to send her away and that perhaps she hadn't won after all, but he only pressed her back enough to break their kiss. He then caught her by the waist and dragged her farther up the bed until he could claim one nipple through the gauzy material of her see-through gown.

Lisa gasped as his mouth closed over her tender, excited flesh, her body humming with a growing need. She slid her hands into his hair, cradling his head to her breast and murmuring little, senseless sounds of encouragement as he laved the cloth-covered nipple and then suckled at it by turn.

When one hand dropped away to find the

bottom of the gown and begin to slide it up her leg, Lisa groaned and shifted under the touch, her thighs rubbing together as a tingling began between them. She remembered this and felt anticipation build in her as his fingers brushed up her outer leg. But this time he didn't run it back down once he reached her hip and then slip it back up the inside of her leg. Instead, he simply followed her hip bone around in front of her and then let his fingers drop and slip between her legs.

Lisa gasped, her legs opening slightly to allow his fingers entrance, and then snapping closed again the moment they brushed against her core. Robert wasn't put off. Rather than retreat, his fingers pressed forward more firmly, sliding between the folds to find the silky flesh beneath.

"Robert," she groaned his name as his fingers stirred all sorts of delicious sensation in her.

His response was to begin tugging at the neckline of the gown, dragging it off her shoulder and down her arm. Lisa was sure he would rip it with his actions, but the cloth seemed to stretch to accommodate and within seconds he'd revealed one breast. Leaving off his attentions to the first breast, Robert turned his mouth to the now uncovered one and began to lave and suckle it.

Lisa gasped and arched into the action as his hand now tugged fretfully at the other side of the gown, pulling it off her shoulder to bare that breast for his attention. He covered it with his hand and squeezed, kneading the tender flesh and then plucking at the nipple with his fingers as he was doing with his mouth to the other.

"Oh," Lisa moaned, clasping his shoulders now, her legs spreading slightly at his urging to allow his hand more freedom there.

"Christ you're so wet and hot," he growled, releasing her breast.

Lisa barely registered the words. He was suddenly erupting beneath her, his body shifting and blankets flying and then he had removed his hand from between her legs and caught her by the waist and was dragging her from her sitting position, rolling her onto her back on the bed. Suddenly she was beneath him and he was bent over her, his body shifting down along her body so that she lost her hold on him. His tongue, lips and hands seemed to be everywhere, grazing her throat, chest and breasts. Then he was forcing the gauzy gown down with fingers that scraped across her skin, pushing the material before them to allow his mouth to lick and nip its way down her belly.

"Robert, your wound," Lisa muttered, shifting and squirming under the attention and trying to reach his shoulders again. She needed something to hold on to, something to ground her. Unable to reach him, she finally grabbed for the pillow on either side of her head, clutching at it almost desperately and gasping and moaning as first his fingers pushed the cloth over her hips and then his mouth followed. Finding her hip bone, he nipped and licked his way across it.

Lisa lifted her hips instinctively when he continued to push the material along, allowing him to slip it down off her bottom and past her thighs. Robert paused to remove it completely then, sitting back on his haunches to the side of her to slip the material down her legs and off her feet. Then he tossed the gauzy material to the floor and turned back to peer at her.

Suddenly self-conscious, Lisa tried to cover herself; one arm moving to cross over her breasts, while her other hand dropped between her legs. For some reason the shy action made Robert smile. And then he clasped one ankle and lifted her leg, raising it up and over his head so that he knelt between her legs.

"Robert?" she said uncertainly, sure he

was now going to do what one of the books she'd read had described as planting his victory flag in her turf. When he suddenly shifted and sort of dove forward, she braced herself, but he didn't land on top of her, planting his flag. In fact, he didn't land on top of her at all. He fell short, his shoulders coming down between her knees and his head dropping between her thighs.

Lisa thought it was an accident. That he'd simply undershot, so was shocked when he suddenly pressed her thighs farther apart and planted his mouth over the core of her.

For one moment she was confused and didn't know what was happening. Then she cried out and bucked as he spread her folds and his tongue lashed over her most secret place. This was just not — none of the books had mentioned — dear God! Her mind screamed with confusion, but mostly with the pleasure he was wringing from her. He was doing things to her that — hell, she wasn't even sure what he was doing. All she was really aware of was a terrible, overwhelming pleasure shooting from the center of her and swelling with terrifying speed. Her body was suddenly shaking and rocking, her blood roaring in her ears, as she arched and thrust into a caress she'd never come across in all of her reading.

Lisa groaned as he continued to lave and suckle, and drew her knees up. She then dug her heels into the bed and pushed, raising herself slightly into whatever he was doing. She was vaguely aware that she was making little noises, pleading sounds and prayers, but if asked wouldn't have known what she was saying. Her mind was completely focused on her pleasure.

She was so far gone that it hardly registered when he suddenly grabbed her ankles and shifted her feet to his shoulders, or when one hand wrapped around her upper thigh, anchoring and holding her down as he worked to drive her completely insane. At least that was how it felt. Lisa was losing herself in the sensations. Thought was impossible. She was merely a throbbing, vibrating thing of need, responding to the song he was playing. But God, it felt good. She never wanted it to stop. She could have died in that moment and gone with a smile, sure she'd experienced everything. And then the building tension suddenly snapped like a bow releasing an arrow, but this arrow exploded on release, shattering through her body and mind and making her scream as if she were dying. That scream surely would have drawn every single person in the house to the room had she not been gnashing on the pillow by that point and had the good sense to pull it completely over her face to muffle the sound.

When it ended, Lisa came back to awareness to find that she was lying limply in the bed, the pillow covering her head while Robert pressed kisses to first one of her quivering thighs and then the other. After a moment she was aware of his shifting and moving up her body, but she was too spent to even remove the pillow covering her face. It was he who lifted it away.

When a completely male smile of satisfaction claimed his lips, Lisa just smiled wryly back. The man had earned that arrogant smile, she acknowledged, and found the strength to raise her hands to his head and draw him down for a kiss. Lisa had meant it as one of gratitude and appreciation, but moaned and arched when it somehow became more and the fires she'd thought he'd banked suddenly roared up within her again.

Dear God, she'd thought surely there wasn't an ounce of passion left in her, but there was and he quickly stirred them back to life. Almost demanded a response with the passion of his kiss, and Lisa gave it to him, shifting restlessly beneath him as he lowered himself.

When she felt something hard press against her, she instinctively wrapped her legs around his hips even as her arms went around his shoulders. But that hardness merely rubbed against her again and again as he kissed her, helping to build the fires in her, and then he broke their kiss to drop his mouth to her breast again and suckled briefly as he reached between them and took himself in hand to rub against her with more precision. It made her moan and twist her head on the bed as the heat in her revved, and then she felt him pressing into her and he released his hold and removed his mouth from her breast to kiss her instead.

Lisa kissed him back, but her attention was on what his body was doing as it eased into her a bit, and then withdrew before easing in again a little further. It was a completely alien sensation and one she wasn't sure she liked. It just felt odd. And then his hand slid between them to find the center of her excitement and she groaned and tightened her legs around him as excitement jumped within her. Distracted by the pleasure he was eliciting, she began to instinctively move her hips, pressing into the caress. The hardness claimed more of her push by push and then his hand suddenly left her so that he could brace himself on the bed.

Lisa opened her eyes in confusion and disappointment and then gasped in shock as he suddenly thrust forward. This time there was no tentative easing in, but a full plunge that sank him fully into her.

For one moment they both froze. Lisa had no idea why he paused, but she was waiting for the shattering pain and blood to begin rushing out of her. However, that never came. Other than a slight pinching, and a strange stretching sensation as her body tried to accommodate this strange intrusion . . . well, really there was no pain at all. And as far as she could tell she wasn't suddenly gushing blood . . . she didn't think.

"Lisa?"

She blinked her eyes open, realizing only then that she'd been holding them tightly squinted closed. Robert was peering down at her, looking as if he were the one who had suffered all the pain. His face was scrunched up as if he were in agony, his eyes mere slits as he peered at her. None of the books had mentioned that men suffered pain the first time, she thought with surprise.

"Are you all right?" he growled.

When she nodded uncertainly, relief

washed over his face and then he lowered his head to kiss her and his body began to move again, withdrawing from her partway, before sliding smoothly back in. Lisa kissed back and shifted a little beneath him as he moved, and found if she positioned herself just so, he rubbed against the nub of her excitement, stirring that delicious excitement again. When he began to move more swiftly, his thrusts becoming more demanding, she untangled her legs from around him and pushed her heels into the bed to raise her hips to meet his thrusts. She was riding the waves, crashing toward shore again, her body trembling and quaking as it strained toward the explosion of pleasure she knew was coming.

When it came, Robert dropped his head to kiss her almost violently and caught her cry in his mouth. A heartbeat later, he tore his mouth away on a gasping cry of pleasure and threw his head back as his body pounded forward and arched, pinning her in place as they both rode the waves he'd unleashed. Moments later he sagged on top of her, then rolled onto his back, taking her with him and Lisa simply nestled against him, completely spent, her eyelids drooping closed.

Lisa wasn't sure how long she'd slept

when she suddenly woke up. She wasn't even sure what had woken her, but she found herself still curled up against Robert's side in his bed. Lifting her head carefully, she peered at his face, smiling when she saw that he was dead to the world, his eyes closed and mouth partly open to emit the faintest of snores.

Perhaps that was what had woken her, Lisa thought with amusement as she took in his relaxed face. He looked so peaceful in sleep, with none of life's worries troubling him, she thought, and wished he could always be so at peace. But of course, that wasn't likely. Especially after Suzette, Christiana, Richard and Daniel returned to "catch" them. He would be furious then. Or worried for her reputation. Or both. He probably wouldn't blame her unless he figured out that it had been a deliberate trap. But he would resent being forced to marry her when he had no desire to enter that blissful state.

That thought made her shift carefully away from him and she rolled onto her back, wanting to think without his smell and the feel of his body to distract her. But the move did not remove his smell. It was on her now like perfume. Eau de Lord Langley. He had marked her with his body and his scent. She was his. It was just a shame he didn't want to be married.

Grimacing at the unpleasant thought, Lisa glanced at the ceiling and then frowned when she saw the way the light was flickering on it. That made her shift her gaze to the candle on the bedside table. It was apparently a flawed candle, the wick not quite centered. The flame had burnt down one side, leaving a small mountain of wax around the other that was melting and pooling at the bottom. The light was about to be guttered by its own wax . . . and then the others would come, catch them in here and demand Robert make an honest woman of her.

Which he would do. Lisa didn't doubt that for a minute. But he would also hate her for it. Or at least resent her. He would blame her for this for the rest of their days.

Lisa didn't think she could stand that. And in truth, she didn't want to win him this way. She wanted him to want to marry her. She wanted him to trust her. She did not want him marrying her out of duty and then always watching her, waiting for her to betray him. Life would be unbearable like that. There had to be another way.

The thought had barely entered her head

when the candle gave its last flicker and
went out.

CHAPTER TWELVE

The sound of the door opening and a splash of light in the dark room startled Robert from sleep and had him blinking sleepily.

"Oh, it's dark in here, Chrissy. Let me grab a candle from the hall," he heard Suzette say, and the words for some reason made him suddenly recall Lisa. Panic roaring through him, he glanced to the other side of the bed, but was unable to place her in the darkness and then Suzette reappeared with a candle revealing everything; she and Christiana still in their ball finery and the empty bed beside him.

Robert stared blankly at the spot where Lisa should have been and then back to Suzette and Christiana, who had paused halfway to the bed.

"Hi," he said weakly, but his mind was racing as he tried to sort out where Lisa was and when she'd left. He shouldn't have fallen asleep after. He should have made himself stay awake and talked to her. He had ruined her. They had to marry now. There was no choice.

"We just got back from the ball and thought we'd check on you," Christiana said after a pause.

"Yes," Suzette said, suddenly moving forward again. "How was your night?"

"Are you feeling well?" Christiana asked, casting Suzette a warning glance though he wasn't sure what she was warning her of.

"I — yes," he said on a sigh and sagged back in the bed. He'd had one hell of a night and was definitely feeling . . . hell, he felt great . . . well other than a slight tenderness from his wound. He probably shouldn't have exerted himself this early after the injury, but Lisa in that damned gown of Morgan's had been irresistible.

"Well . . . good," Suzette said finally, though she sounded annoyed more than anything and suddenly turned back toward the door, taking the candle with her.

Christiana bit her lip and glanced after her sister, then she began to back away, following the glow of the candlelight. "We shall let you sleep then. We just wanted to check on you."

Robert nodded, but as the women reached the door, asked, "What time is it?"

For some reason, the question made them both pause and exchange a glance and then Christiana said, "Not yet midnight."

"That's rather early," he commented. They usually went much later, sometimes to dawn and even beyond, but supposed Christiana's being with child had some effect on their usual patterns.

"Yes, well, we are all a little tired and out of sorts after all the excitement lately. And then we were worried about you and Lisa so we decided to leave early," Christiana explained.

"Oh," he murmured, thinking it was good Lisa had woken and left. While marriage was inevitable now, he was glad she didn't have to suffer the humiliation of getting caught in his bed.

"Good night then, Robert," Christiana said softly and then the door closed, leaving him in darkness again.

Sighing, he settled back in the bed, staring into the darkness above him as he contemplated all that would need to be done. He would have to talk to Lisa first thing and tell her of his decision to marry her. She would no doubt be grateful and weep a bit, and then he would tell her they should head to Gretna Green right away. He hadn't been careful, hadn't even thought

259

of withdrawing or using any type of caution to prevent her getting pregnant. She could even now be carrying the Langley heir. A quick jaunt to Gretna Green would ensure there was no nasty little scandal. It would also mean he wouldn't have to wait to sink himself into her warm wet body again.

Damn, Lisa had been as responsive as a man could wish; writhing, moaning, whimpering, and crying out even as her body wept with pleasure at what he did to her. She might one day betray him with another, but their marriage bed would certainly be a pleasure until then. Well worth all the misery and betrayal later, Robert thought wryly. He just had to bear in mind that she would eventually betray him and writhe, moan, whimper and cry out for another, her body weeping its pleasure on another man. If he kept that in mind and simply enjoyed her while he could . . . well, perhaps it wouldn't be so bad when she betrayed him.

A soft *shush* of sound caught his ear, and Robert stiffened, trying to place where it was coming from and what it could be. It seemed to be coming from under the bed, he realized, and sat up to peer around.

Moonlight was pouring through the open curtain and his eyes had adjusted enough

260

that he could make out shapes and shadows. But his eyes widened incredulously when a small shape suddenly popped up beside the bed. They widened further when that shape shifted to stand and he recognized that it was a woman.

"Lisa?" he whispered incredulously.

"Shhh. They will hear you and come back," she hissed, shifting something about in her hands. Her robe, he realized when she drew it on and belted it.

"What were you doing under the bed?" he asked with amazement.

"What do you think I was doing, Robert?" she asked with low-voiced exasperation. "I heard Christiana and Suzette talking as they came up the hall, so slid under the bed to hide."

"Why?" he asked blankly.

"Why?" Lisa echoed with disbelief. "So I wouldn't be caught in your bed, of course. For heaven's sake, there would have been an uproar, and you would have been forced to marry me, and — Robert Langley, are you laughing?" she asked with disbelief.

"Come here," he said between chuckles and caught her hand to draw her onto the bed. She dropped onto it, mostly because she lost her balance, but he ignored that and her stiffness and wrapped his arms

261

around her, dragging her down to lie with him, "It was very sweet of you to try to protect me, Lisa. And I am glad you didn't have to suffer the humiliation of being caught in such a compromising situation, but it doesn't matter in the end anyway. We will have to marry now."

Lisa didn't squeal with joy or throw her arms around him with gratitude as he'd expected. In fact, much to his surprise, she seemed to go still and stiff in his arms.

"Lisa?" he said uncertainly and then frowned when she eased from his embrace and sat up.

"There is no need to marry me, Robert. No one knows we were together. We can just continue as if it never happened," she said coolly and stood.

"What?" he asked with disbelief and then lunged off the bed to stop her when her shadow moved around the bed and headed for the door. Catching her arm, he drew her to a halt and moved in front of her. "Just a minute, dammit. We have to talk about this."

"There is nothing to talk about. No one knows, and I am not making you marry me. Everything is as it was."

"The hell it is," Robert said grimly. "Lisa, you could be carrying my child even now. We have to marry."

"I am not marrying a man who doesn't want me and doesn't trust me and who will spend our entire lives together sure I will someday betray him," she said unhappily. "This was a mistake."

She tried to move around him then, but he caught her arm to stop her.

"Lisa," he began, but then paused, completely flummoxed as to what to say. While he could tell her that he definitely did want her, that wasn't what she meant. She meant he didn't want to marry her, and mostly that was true. He didn't want to marry anyone. And she was right, he would spend their entire lives together sure she would betray him and waiting for it to happen.

"Go to sleep, Robert," Lisa said and he frowned at the disappointment in her voice, suspecting she had been hoping he would deny what she'd said. That if he had, even if she hadn't fully believed it, she might have given in and married him. But even now he couldn't bring himself to lie to her.

"We will talk in the morning after we've both rested," she said quietly and this time when she moved around him, he let her. He just let her leave.

"What do you mean you were hiding under the bed?" Suzette snapped.

Lisa sighed at her sister's irritation and glanced at the other three people in the parlor: Christiana, Richard and Daniel. She had left Robert's room and slipped into her own to find Suzette and Christiana there questioning Bet, trying to figure out where she was.

All three women had been relieved to see her. It seemed they'd begun to worry that something had gone amiss, that the suitor had somehow got his hands on her and taken her away. They had been about to start the hue and cry to get the men searching for her when she'd entered. Instead, they'd rushed forward blurting questions, and after Lisa had shushed them for fear of Robert overhearing, they had dragged her down to the parlor where the men had joined them to find out what had gone wrong with their grand plan.

"Why the devil were you hiding?" Suzette asked now with disbelief. "That was the whole point of this business. You were supposed to get caught in his bed so he would have to marry you."

"Yes, well . . ." Lisa frowned and shook her head. "I decided that maybe that wouldn't work."

"Of course it would have worked. It — you did sleep with him?" Suzette asked with a frown. "Didn't you?"

Lisa's answer was a blush that she was sure covered her from head to toe.

"You did," Suzette said on a sigh and dropped back in her seat with a shake of the head. "I don't understand any of this. We had a plan in place. You were to sleep with him and we were to catch you. We stuck to our part of the plan. We left the ball hours ago and were just sitting in the carriages out front waiting for the candle to go out. Which took a hell of a long time and was a damned boring business, I might add," she pointed out irritably. "But it finally went out and we went up there all prepared to be shocked and horrified, only to find him in bed alone . . . and now you're saying you were there, hiding under the bed? What the devil are you thinking?"

Lisa hesitated, and then blurted, "I do not want a husband who is forced to marry me and will resent me for the rest of time because of it. And I do not want Robert if he will spend our entire married life doubting me and waiting for me to betray him with another. I could not bear it."

"Oh, Lisa," Christiana said sympathetically and left her own chair to move to the sofa where she sat to hug her. "We understand, dear."

"The hell we do," Suzette groused. "The idiots love each other. Anyone can see that. But they are never going to get together at this rate."

Daniel chuckled at her dissatisfied words and sank to sit on the arm of the chair she was in and slip his arm around her shoulders. "You are such a romantic, my love."

Lisa stared at them with disbelief as Daniel pressed a kiss to Suzette's forehead. What her sister had said hadn't sounded the least bit like the words of a romantic to her. What was the man thinking?

"What do you want to do?" Richard asked quietly, drawing her gaze to him as he followed Christiana to the sofa and settled on her other side.

"I do not know," she admitted wearily. "I wish he loved me."

"He does," Suzette said with exasperation.

"Love involves trust, Suzette," Lisa said solemnly. "And I don't think Robert *can* trust, or therefore love, anyone until he gets over his childhood."

"But —"

"Do you trust Daniel?" she asked quickly.

"Of course," Suzette answered with amazement.

Lisa nodded. "And does he trust you?"

"Yes," Suzette said without doubt and

Daniel hugged her, murmuring, "With my life."

Lisa ignored Daniel and met Suzette's gaze. "Well, how happy would you be if Daniel was always watching you out of the corner of his eye, expecting you to betray him in some way?"

Suzette scowled at the very idea and then sank back in her seat with a sighed, "Right."

"Lisa," Christiana said tentatively, drawing her gaze. "I understand that you might not wish to marry him the way things stand. But you could be with child now. And surely that child deserves —"

"If I am with child I will marry," she said simply. "But until I know one way or the other . . ." She shrugged and stood up. "I am ever so weary. I think I shall go to bed. Good night."

The room was silent as she left, but she heard the murmur of their concerned voices begin as soon as she closed the door. They would fret over her now, but there was nothing she could do about that. She would not marry Robert. Tonight had been beautiful, an experience she would never forget. But she was not going to spend her life with a man who didn't trust her and resented her.

Lisa just wished she'd realized all this before tonight. She never would have slept with him and known what she would be giving up by marrying another if it came to that.

"Shall I read to you?" Charles asked. "Or will you read to me?"

Lisa dragged her eyes from where they'd wandered to Robert and smiled faintly at the question. "Why do we not take turns? You can begin and I shall take over after a couple of pages."

"Very well," Charles said agreeably and settled back with the book he'd brought for her. Opening to the first page, he began to read aloud and Lisa found her gaze drifting back to Robert again. He sat under a tree at the opposite side of the clearing, glaring at them coldly.

He'd been glaring at her ever since the start of this outing. It seemed he wasn't taking her refusal to marry him well. She supposed it wasn't what he'd expected after her years of adoration. Lisa suspected that if she'd given him the opportunity, he would have dragged her off to a corner this morning to try to demand she marry him. However, she hadn't given him the chance. She'd remained in her room all morning, taking breakfast there to avoid him, and had only come below when one of the maids had come to tell her that Lord Findlay had arrived to take her on their picnic.

Charles had been waiting at the front door with a glaring Robert looming nearby when she'd descended the stairs. Lisa had ignored Robert, smiled at Lord Findlay and allowed him to usher her out to his carriage. She hadn't been at all surprised when Robert had followed them out and mounted his horse. The animal that had been waiting for him, saddled and ready for him to accompany them.

Lisa had done her best to ignore him since then, but it was difficult when she could feel his fury burning into the back of her head with every passing moment. He was angry that she'd refused his proposal, that she hadn't spoken to him today as promised, and no doubt that she was on this picnic with Findlay. But she didn't know what else to do. She could not marry him, would not marry him the way things stood, and talking to him about it would not change things. As for this picnic, she had agreed to it before the attack at Pembroke's outing and everything that had followed. It would have been rude to refuse at this late date.

"Perhaps you can carry on from here."

Lisa glanced back to Lord Findlay and accepted the book he was holding out, then glanced blankly over the two pages. She hadn't heard a word he'd said and wasn't sure where he'd left off or where she should begin.

"Here," Findlay murmured, pointing to the top of the right-hand page.

"Thank you," she murmured and began to read. Forced to concentrate on the words, she could not get distracted by Robert, and Lisa found herself relaxing and getting involved in the story. She was so wrapped up in the story line that it wasn't until Robert spoke that she realized the shadow cast over her wasn't merely a cloud blocking the sun, but him standing, looming over her.

"It's getting late."

She blinked and glanced up at those words and then frowned and glanced around, surprised to see that the sun was low in the sky. "Oh," she murmured. "Yes, of course."

Nodding, he turned and strode back to his tree where his horse was grazing, and Lisa smiled apologetically at Charles. "I suppose we should return, my lord. But thank you for a lovely time. The picnic was delicious and really, this is a wonderful story."

"Yes, it is," he agreed wryly, getting to his

feet and offering her a hand to help her up. "I was quite enjoying your narration of it. You have a delightful way of giving personality to the characters."

"Oh, thank you," she murmured, blushing faintly.

"Do not thank me. It is little more than the truth. I hope you will save our spot and continue on with the story when we next meet. I do not think I would enjoy it as much without you reading it."

"Oh, that's very kind," she said, flattered. Lisa then glanced around, eyes widening with surprise when she saw that their picnic was already packed away and only the blanket was left to be folded and put away.

"I tidied up a bit while you were reading," he said with amusement, bending to pick up the blanket and fold it. "You were so involved in the story you did not even notice."

"Oh," she murmured and then laughed, and repeated, "Well, it is a good story."

"I cannot agree more, and it pleases me that we both appear to have the same taste in books," he commented, then laid the blanket over his arm and moved closer to take her hands in his. "It would be nice to have a wife read to me at night by the fire."

Lisa's eyes widened slightly and then she

ducked her head, confusion rifling through her. "Well, that sounds pleasant."

"Doesn't it?" he agreed. "Would you be that wi—"

"It's going to start raining," Robert interrupted briskly, suddenly appearing beside them and catching Lisa's arm to drag her toward his horse. "You will ride back with me. It is quicker than a carriage trying to move through the traffic."

Lisa cast an apologetic glance over her shoulder toward Lord Findlay, but didn't protest. She was pretty sure the question Robert had interrupted was "Would you be that wife?" and she didn't have a clue what to say to it. Lisa was actually relieved that Robert had interrupted and dragged her off. She needed time to think. To figure out what she wanted. She'd thought she had given up on Robert and was looking for a husband, and then she'd decided to try to make him love her, and then she'd fallen in with the plan to force him to marry her, only to decide she didn't want him that way. Now she simply didn't know what she wanted.

That wasn't entirely true, of course, Lisa acknowledged to herself as Robert mounted and then helped her onto the horse behind him. She knew she wanted Robert. She just didn't want him if he had to be forced into marriage and didn't trust her. And that appeared to be the only way she would get him. So if she couldn't have him, what would make her happiest? Living alone for the rest of her life, surviving on memories of her one night with Robert? Or marrying another and perhaps at least managing a warm, friendly marriage of reading by the fire at night, easy conversation and children to distract her?

"Put your arms around my waist," Robert ordered and waited for her to do so before urging his mount to move.

They were silent as they rode out of the clearing, through the park and headed for the townhouse. Lisa simply sat behind him, her arms around his waist, her breath matching his as they rode. But the feel of him and his smell reminded her of the night before. The faint scent of his aftershave had stayed with her all night, filling her dreams with his kisses and caresses. She had been sorry to wake and wash it away in her bath. But she'd also been relieved. His scent had made it impossible not to think of the man, and thinking of him was a sort of torture.

It started to rain as they turned up the road where Richard and Christiana resided, so she was surprised when Robert didn't stop at the front door to let her dismount and hurry inside. Instead, he continued on around to the back of the property and right inside the small stables there before stopping. They both hesitated, waiting for the stable master to come rushing up. When that didn't happen, Robert frowned and muttered, "Harry must not be here."

"It's all right," Lisa murmured, removing her arms from around his waist. "I can get down myself."

"Just sit tight," Robert said, reaching back to keep her from trying to get off. He then shifted the reins to one hand and swung a leg over the horse's head and slid quickly off. He landed with a small grunt, but before she could ask if he was all right, raised his arms to help her down.

"What about your wound?" Lisa asked with a frown. Really, he had put undo stress on it last night. And he shouldn't have been riding around today. But lifting her off the horse seemed to be pushing it just a bit far.

"*Now* you worry about my wound? You did not seem worried when you had me bouncing around on the back of a horse, chasing after you and Findlay," he said dryly and then gestured impatiently with his hands for her to disembark.

Lisa scowled at him for the dry comment,

and allowed him to help her down, but once on the ground muttered, "I did not force you to come out today."

"Should I have left you to be dragged off and ravished then?" he muttered, turning to tend to his horse.

"That's ironic. You guarding me from being ravished," she snapped and then could have bitten off her own tongue. Damn, sometimes she wished she thought before she spoke. Noting how stiff and still Robert had gone, Lisa sighed unhappily and said, "I'm sorry. That was uncalled for. I was not unwilling."

Robert didn't respond. He simply finished removing his horse's saddle and tossed it aside before leading the animal into a stall.

Lisa followed, saying, "I really am sorry, Robert."

His only response was to pick up a brush and begin to run it silently over the horse's back, brushing him with a brisk efficiency that told her he was mad as hell.

Rolling her eyes, she tried to think of a way to ease the situation, but nothing was coming to mind. Finally, she sighed and turned away, intending to go into the house. She had stepped out of the stall and was starting toward the doors when he said coldly, "You are not marrying Findlay."

Lisa paused and turned back with surprise. "He has not asked me."

"He was asking when I interrupted," he said tightly, setting the brush aside and coming out of the stall. "And you are not marrying him."

"Robert, you have no say in who I marry," she said gently.

"The hell I don't. You could very well be carrying my child."

Lisa bit her lip at the words, and then shook her head. "I doubt it. I'm sure one time wouldn't —"

"It only takes one time, Lisa," he said impatiently.

Lisa shifted on her feet unhappily. "Then if he asks again, or manages to ask without being interrupted, I shall have to explain the situation and if he still wants to marry me —"

"He will," Robert interrupted harshly. "He wants you."

"You don't know that," she protested.

"Lisa, when you are not looking, his eyes are all over your body. He wants you. Trust me, I recognize the look. It's the same way I look at you."

When her eyes widened incredulously, he cursed and closed the small distance between them. He bore down on her like a wave, his arms sliding around her, his lips claiming hers and his body pressing into and forcing her back as he continued forward.

"Robert," she gasped when he broke their kiss to glance around, and then he changed direction, bearing her to the right and into an empty stall. "We can't —"

Her words ended on a gasp as he kicked the stall door closed and lowered her to the straw strewn floor. His mouth then covered hers again, smothering any protest, and pretty much pushing even the thought of protesting from her mind. His kisses were like wine, making her drunk with desire and Lisa gave up any attempt to be a good girl and stop him and clutched at his head, her mouth becoming demanding under his.

Robert groaned at the sudden change in her response, and then immediately began tugging at the top of her gown, managing to free her breasts with surprising speed. The moment they were free, he tore his mouth from hers to claim them.

Lisa moaned, her hands moving over his shoulders and tugging fretfully at his coat as he laved and nipped at one breast and then the other. She then gasped in surprise when one of his legs slid between hers and pressed against her core. The surprise passed quickly however, and she found herself shifting her hips to press into his thigh, enjoying the friction caused by both their bodies and their clothes. When she felt a hardness against her own thigh, she recognized it for what it was and rubbed her thigh from side to side, unsure but hoping he would enjoy it as much as she enjoyed what he was doing.

Lisa didn't know if Robert liked it, but he did suddenly give up on her breasts and rise up to claim her mouth again in a kiss that was almost violent in its need. She immediately began plucking at his clothes again, trying to remove them so that she could feel his skin against hers, but Robert suddenly caught her wrists and lifted them over her head, then held them there with one hand as his other reached down to drag up her skirts.

Lisa tore her mouth away on a gasp and tugged fretfully at her hands, her body writhing beneath his as he pushed her skirts up her legs.

"Robert, please," she groaned, and then cried out as his hand suddenly slid between her legs.

"Christ, you're already wet," Robert muttered into her neck, nipping her there.

"Sorry," she muttered with embarrassment, which simply made him laugh. Lisa didn't understand what amused him, but in the next moment didn't care as he slid one finger into her, forcing an "Oh God," from her lips and making her buck into the caress.

"Are you tender?" he growled with concern.

Lisa shook her head, incapable of speech as she shimmied under his touch.

"Thank God," he muttered, and released her hands to reach down between them without the necessity of having to stop caressing her.

Lisa immediately clasped his shoulders and held on as she bucked under his touch, but stilled briefly when his hand was suddenly withdrawn and something else pressed against her. She held her breath as he found the right angle, and then released a long groan as their bodies merged.

"Yes, please," she whispered, wrapping her legs around his hips. He claimed her lips again in a quick, hard kiss. Then he rose up, caught her ankles and lifted them to his shoulders so that he could hold her hips and pound into her.

Lisa stared up at him in amazement, shocked at this new position. She then closed her eyes and bit her lip on a moan as one of his hands reached for a breast. The other slid between them to caress her again even as he thrust himself in and out.

As fast and furious as it had started, it ended just as quickly. Within moments, Lisa was writhing in the straw and crying out as pleasure exploded over her. This time there was no delay and Robert joined her in that hazy explosion, his own cry joining hers. Lisa clutched desperately at his arms as they rode out their pleasure, and then clasped him tight to her when it ended and he lowered himself to lie on top of her. He stayed there only a moment though, his weight a pleasant caress, before he rolled onto his back in the straw, taking her with him.

Robert continued to hold her close and she felt him press several kisses to the top of her head before he relaxed. After a few minutes his breathing grew slow and steady and she knew he'd dozed off again, just as he had last night. Lisa had joined him in sleep then, but didn't now. They couldn't afford to be caught in the stables like this.

Easing from his embrace, she sat up and glanced around, wondering where the naïve, young, romantic Lisa had gone as she took in the setting they were in. She'd just had her skirts tossed up in a stable. Brilliant. The sad thing was, she couldn't find it in herself to regret it. It had felt too damned good.

Sighing, she pushed her skirts back down her legs, and then tucked her breasts away in her dress and eased to her feet. She had been telling the truth when he'd asked if she was tender. She hadn't been, but was a bit now and the realization brought a grimace to her face. But she supposed it was to be expected. Her body wasn't used to such activity.

Lisa quickly brushed down her skirts, removing the bits of straw stuck to her, then felt her hair and removed any stray strands there. She then glanced back to Robert uncertainly. She couldn't just leave him here like this, but on the other hand, she had no desire to talk to him at that moment. He would just say she couldn't marry Findlay, or insist she had to marry him now, or some such thing and she didn't wish to deal with it all now.

After a hesitation, she slid from the stall and moved to the open stable doors. Pausing there, Lisa glanced back, and then stepped out into the rain and slammed the door closed, making sure to make as much of a racket as she could. She then peered through a knothole, relaxing when Robert suddenly stood up, popping into view. The noise had done its job. He was awake.

Turning abruptly, Lisa raced for the house, heading for the French doors to Richard's office rather than risk running into anyone in the kitchens. What she hadn't counted on was finding Richard actually in, seated at his desk.

He glanced up with a start, eyes wide when she rushed inside and slammed the door, and Lisa paused briefly, her own eyes going wide. Then she rushed across the room with a muttered, "Sorry," and hurried out into the hall, headed upstairs to her own room.

CHAPTER THIRTEEN

"Are you sure you don't want to come tonight?" Christiana asked, eyeing Lisa with concern.

"Positive," Lisa assured her, avoiding her eyes.

Actually, part of her did want to go, the part that wanted to avoid any chance of being forced to speak to Robert. However, another part, the part that also wanted to avoid having to dance with and possibly be proposed to by Lord Findlay, definitely didn't want to go. She was basically stuck between a rock and a hard place at the moment. Avoiding two men.

Unfortunately, while Lisa could avoid Findlay by staying home, Robert was going to be a bit trickier. She could stay in her room of course, but there was no guarantee he wouldn't come harass her here. He had knocked at her door three times already since she'd charged up here after their

283

tumble in the stables. She'd refused to speak to him each time, and there had been little he could do but leave her alone with Richard and Christiana in the house. She suspected, however, that he wouldn't be quite as accommodating without them here.

"Very well," Christiana said finally, and turned to walk to the door, but paused there to ask, "Is there any message for Lord Findlay? He's sure to ask where you are."

"No," Lisa said on a sigh. "Just say I was not feeling well. Better yet, say getting caught in the rain has given me a cough or something."

Nodding, Christiana turned away and slid from the room.

The moment she was gone, Lisa turned and paced to her window to look out, her mind seeking some way to avoid Robert. He would come, she was sure. Probably the minute Christiana and Richard had left and the last thing she wanted was another argument with him. Her resistance to the man was pretty much completely absent at this point. The idea of marrying and enjoying the pleasure he stirred in her for the rest of her life was tempting. It was the time in between such sessions that worried her. The days of silent suspicion and accusation.

Lisa knew she couldn't bear that. Perhaps

she should just head home to Madison, she thought suddenly. She could not marry anyone now. Men wanted their wives to be pure on their wedding nights, not slightly used and possibly expecting. The thought made her grimace. There was now twice the chance that she may be carrying Robert's child. She didn't want to make it thrice. But if she stayed here, Lisa had absolutely no doubt that it would happen again.

Good Lord, her body was already hungry again for more. Now that her body had experienced the pleasure to be had, it was insatiable. Turning abruptly, she glanced to Bet.

"Unless you want to be trapped up here all night with me, I suggest that you leave now," she said and then turned to grab the chair by her window and began to drag it toward the door.

Bet's eyes widened and then she headed for the door. "I'll be downstairs if ye need me."

"I won't need you until morning," Lisa assured her and waited for her to slip out before jamming the chair firmly under the doorknob. Satisfied that she had done what she could, Lisa then turned and paced back to the window. She hadn't been there more than a moment when a knock sounded at the door.

"Go away, Robert," she said firmly.

"We need to talk, Lisa," he said just as firmly.

"I don't want to," was her response.

A moment of silence followed and then the doorknob twisted, but the chair held it closed. There was a heavy silence and then Robert growled, "Have you locked the door?"

"No. I jammed a chair under it," she announced. "I am not speaking to you, Robert. Just go away."

Lisa waited a moment, almost holding her breath, but when no response came, she moved cautiously to the door and listened. However, she couldn't hear anything and couldn't tell if he was still out there or not.

Frowning, Lisa turned away and peered around the room. She then paced restlessly toward the window only to stop halfway there and swing back impatiently toward her bed. She would not spend the next five hours pacing around like a caged animal. It would drive her crazy. She needed to sleep, or read, or something.

Thinking would be good too, Lisa acknowledged, but she had been trying to do that ever since returning. However, rather than think about what to do, her mind seemed fixed on Robert and all the delightful things he had done to her today and yesterday. That was the last thing she wanted to do now when Richard and Christiana were not here to prevent her from repeating her folly yet again.

Sighing, Lisa quickly removed her gown and set it across the foot of the bed, then moved to her chest to find a nightgown. The first thing she saw, of course, was the see-through gown of Mrs. Morgan's. Lisa sighed as she peered at it where it lay folded and resting on top of the clothes in the chest. She would have to tell Bet to burn the damned thing, she thought, but couldn't resist reaching out to caress it as her mind flooded with memories.

Shaking her head to try to remove the images filling it, Lisa grabbed a white nightgown and straightened, then whirled with a gasp as her window burst open with a crash.

"Robert?" she said with amazement as he swung himself into the room. "What the devil?"

"We shall have to put a better lock on that window," he said calmly, pushing the two sides closed, but not bothering to try to relatch it. It was dangling and definitely broken. Turning back, he added, "And it was incredibly foolish of you to jam the door

with the chair. If your hooded man returned, I wouldn't have been able to get in
to help you."

"I was more concerned about keeping you
out than anything else," she said dryly.

"Yes, well . . ." He grimaced. "That didn't
work very well."

She rolled her eyes at the ridiculously
obvious claim and then stilled as she saw a
small dark stain on his shirt. Biting her lip,
she asked shakily, "Is that blood?"

Robert glanced down at the spot, and then
to her and quickly covered the spot with
one hand. "No. I must have got some sap
on me or something when I climbed up
here."

Lisa frowned, not sure she believed him,
but wanting to. She really didn't handle
blood well. "You shouldn't be climbing
about in trees, my lord. You'll reopen your
wound."

"I'm fine," he assured her, moving toward
the door. "I'll just go change my shirt." He
removed the chair and then glared at her.
"Do not replace the chair. I will just climb
through your window again if you do."

Lisa grimaced, but gave a short, sharp nod
of assent.

Letting his breath out on a sigh, he nodded and turned to the door, but then

paused and asked, "Where is Bet?"

"Downstairs, why?"

"I have some mending I am hoping she will help me with," he muttered and slid out of the room.

Lisa stared at the closed door for a moment and then hurried to open it and rush out into the hall . . . and nearly ran over Robert, who had stopped to undo his shirt and pull the bandaging away to examine his wound.

Probably checking to see just how much damage he'd done, she thought and immediately averted her eyes. "Go to your room. I'll send Bet to sew you back up."

"No, that's all right. I didn't burst my stitches. I just pulled one a bit. I'm going to clean it up and rebandage it," he said, releasing the bandage. "Don't bother Bet."

"You can't rebandage yourself, Robert. Let me —"

"I'm fine," he interrupted, and turned to head into his room.

Lisa instinctively started to follow, but paused when she saw Bet appear at the top of the stairs. Concerned by her alarmed expression, Lisa moved to meet her. "Is something wrong?"

"Aye," Bet murmured. "I thought I'd best warn ye. I heard Handers mention to Cook that he saw Lord Langley go outside and I thought it odd since he's so determined to watch out for ye. But then it occurred to me he might try climbing the tree to come in yer window."

Lisa nodded wryly. "Yes, you were right. He did, and now he's pulled his stitches. Can you fetch some salve and . . ." she let the last of the request die away. Bet had already turned with a nod and hurried back up the hall to go after what she needed.

With nothing else to do, Lisa moved to the door of Robert's room and peered cautiously inside. She spotted him at once. He was seated on the opposite side of the bed with his back to her. He'd already removed the old bandage and was now mopping at his chest with a bunched up bit of the used cloth.

"Robert, wait for Bet, she —"

"I don't need Bet, I'm fine," he muttered, continuing what he was doing.

"The wound needs to be properly cleaned. Salve needs to be applied and then a fresh bandage has to be put on, Robert. You cannot do it alone," she said firmly.

"I can," he said stubbornly and Lisa shook her head, then glanced around as Bet appeared beside her with a basin of water, a cloth, salve and bandages.

Lisa stepped aside and gestured for the maid to enter, but remained by the door rather than risk seeing blood.

"Thank you, Bet," Robert said quietly when Bet moved to the bedside table to set down the items she'd brought. "That'll do."

Bet hesitated, but it was definitely a dismissal, so she turned and crossed back toward Lisa with a shrug. What else could she do?

Once the maid was gone, Lisa closed the door, but remained by it, watching silently as Robert cleaned the wound properly and applied the salve. It was when he then tried to rebandage himself that he ran into trouble. Which was exactly what she'd expected.

"Lisa?" he said finally after spending several minutes struggling to get the cloth around himself just once. "Do you think you could . . . ?" He glanced over his shoulder to her apologetically.

Tsking with exasperation, Lisa straightened from where she'd leaned against the door frame, and crossed the room to stand in front of him, very kindly not saying I told you so. Much to her relief the one round of bandaging he'd managed to get around his chest, while crooked, covered the wound and was a clean, fresh white with no sign of blood to be seen. Letting her breath out, she took the roll of bandaging from him and said, "Arms up."

"Lisa," he murmured, reaching for her instead. "You can't marry Findlay."

"Don't talk, Robert, it will just end in an argument," she warned.

"But —"

"Shall I have Bet do this?" she asked, raising one eyebrow. The threat made him fall silent and sit back. Relieved, Lisa quickly began to run the clean white cloth of the fresh bandage around his chest.

"You smell delicious," Robert murmured as she passed the bandage around his back, her arms around him and her face next to his.

"Thank you," she said stiffly, bringing the bandage around his front again.

"And you're beautiful."

"Robert," she said on a sigh as she began to run it around his back again.

"It's true," he said simply. "You smell good, you look good . . . you feel good," he added, his hands lowering to run from her shoulders and down her upper arms and back as she brought the bandage around his back to the front again.

"Robert." This time his name was a plea and she paused in her efforts, her eyes closing briefly. Just that light, almost innocent touch of her arms had her nipples hardening and her thighs clenching against a stirring there.

"You want me," he murmured, leaning forward to press a kiss to her neck that made her shudder. His hand rose to close over one breast then, and he squeezed gently. "You can't marry Findlay. He could never make you feel like this."

Lisa shook her head weakly and then brought the bandage around to his chest again and quickly tucked it under the cloth, trying, but finding it impossible to ignore the way he was caressing her. The moment she straightened, his other hand snaked around her hips to clasp her behind through her gown. He used the hold to urge her forward between his open legs as he massaged and kneaded her flesh.

"We could do this every night if you married me," he said quietly, his hand dipping between her legs from behind and caressing her through her gown.

Biting her lip, Lisa caught at his shoulders and closed her eyes as her body began to sing under what he was doing.

"Marry me, Lisa."

"Shut up," she muttered and caught his face in her hands to raise it so that she could kiss him. Lisa didn't struggle or demur when he suddenly turned, urging her onto the bed next to him.

A burst of laughter brought Robert awake. Frowning into the darkness, he listened briefly, slowly relaxing as he recognized the murmur of Christiana and Richard's voices drawing near. He heard Christiana suggest they check on him and felt a smile curve his lips as he glanced at the lump in the bed next to him, and then the door opened, light splashed in and he saw that the lump was merely the comforter bunched up. Lisa was gone.

"Oh, you're awake," Richard said from the door. "Everything all right?"

"Fine," Robert muttered, turning his head to scowl at him. "I was sleeping but your laughter woke me up."

Richard's eyebrows rose at the testy voice he used. "Sorry about that, then. Good night."

Robert sighed as the door closed. He shouldn't have snapped and felt bad about it, but dammit, Lisa had slipped away again when being caught here would have solved everything.

Damn, he thought. Next time he would make sure he made love to her in her room.

The thought made him blink in surprise. Hell. Was he really now contemplating compromising Lisa to force her into marriage? Well, she was already compromised, he just had to prove it. However, the point was that only a matter of days ago, he would have laughed at the suggestion that he wanted to marry anyone, and now he was willing to use dirty tricks to force Lisa into his bed and marriage.

What a difference a day or two could make, Robert thought wryly and then shook his head. He couldn't believe she was not willing to marry him. Most women would be screaming holy murder and demanding he put a ring on their finger after being bedded. But not Lisa.

Robert supposed it was that damned romantic nature of hers. Those bloody books had raised ideas in her. She wanted romance, proclamations of undying love, and happy ever afters. But that wasn't how the real world worked. People married and were miserable for the rest of their days. Well, most of them, he supposed, thinking of Christiana and Suzette's happy marriages to Richard and Daniel. Of course, both couples had only been together for a couple of years. There was still plenty of time for the misery to settle in. He was sure even his father and mother must have enjoyed a year or two of happiness at the start.

Sighing, he shifted on his side in bed, wincing as his chest gave a twinge of pain. He'd not been any more concerned with it tonight than he had been the first night or in the stables. The damned thing was never going to heal if he wasn't more careful. But he didn't really care about that when he had Lisa shivering and shaking in his arms, her nails biting into his skin and her pleas ringing in his ear. There was no way he would ever again think of her as a little sister. Robert couldn't believe that he ever had. The woman was as passionate as he, meeting him thrust for thrust and demanding more.

He would claim her for his own. Robert was determined. He just needed to figure out how.

Lisa turned over in her bed and peered toward the window as she heard her sister and brother-in-law's bedroom door close and silence return to the house. She'd woken up and slipped back to her room only moments before they'd returned. Just in time, she thought and almost sighed aloud with something like disappointment. If she'd been caught, she would have had to marry Robert. He would have seen to it.

And the thought was a tempting one. Enjoying such pleasure every night? Who would not be tempted?

"You cannot marry Findlay. He could never make you feel like this."

Robert's words from earlier rang through her head and she turned restlessly onto her back. The words just continued to repeat through her mind though. And she wondered . . . Could he? Could anyone? Surely Robert wasn't the only one in the world who could kiss and touch her in a way that roused her passions? The thought was a depressing one. While she didn't think she could live with his waiting for her to cheat on him, she was also beginning to think she couldn't live a celibate life in the country either. The man had brought her body to life and she didn't think it would easily or quickly forget the pleasures it had learned and enjoyed. She didn't even want to.

Surely, someone could make her feel at least some of this passion?

A quiet life with a man she liked, whose company she enjoyed and who could make her feel even half the passion she'd experienced so far sounded far preferable to the alternatives. And she liked Charles Findlay. She enjoyed dancing and chatting with him, had really enjoyed reading with him, the race and . . . well, she liked him. True, his first kiss had barely stirred her passions and had left her wanting. And yes, the second kiss had been painful, but that was her fault. She'd asked him to kiss her punishingly and that's exactly what he'd done. How was she supposed to know that Robert's kisses hadn't been punishing at all?

Perhaps if she asked Charles to kiss her passionately rather than punishingly it would make a difference, she thought. It was worth a try.

Of course, he might not be willing to marry her once she confessed that she had been with Robert. And she would have to confess, Lisa thought unhappily. She couldn't live with such a secret. Her conscience would kill her. But even if he turned from her then, at least if he kissed her and managed to stir her passion she would know that Robert was not the only man in the world who could do so.

Obviously, all this depended on her not being with child. But then Suzette and Christiana had been married for two years and she knew darned right well from their talk that they were enjoying their marriage bed often and well. Yet neither of them were with child. Okay, Christiana had been once, but she'd miscarried. So perhaps the females in her line didn't easily get pregnant and that would not be a worry.

The thought gave her hope. Ruined by itself was definitely better than ruined and with child.

Lisa turned onto her side again and stared at the window as she contemplated what she should do. She would ask Charles to kiss her passionately. If that worked out all right and he did ask her to marry him, she would tell him about Robert and see how he reacted, and then . . . She supposed the "and then" would depend on how he reacted.

It wasn't much, but it was the first bit of hope Lisa had felt in days. She might not be able to have the kind of marriage her sisters enjoyed, but then again she might. After all, neither Suzette nor Christiana had known their husbands for years before marrying them. Actually, they'd both only known them for a matter of days. There was still hope for her without Robert. She just had to keep her spirits up and resist the temptation he offered in the meantime.

It was the temptation that was her biggest worry. All the man had to do was touch her and her resistance crumbled like a house of cards. It was pathetic really, when she thought about it. She'd been raised better than that. But so long as he was guarding her, she very much feared —

Lisa sat up in bed abruptly. As long as he was guarding her . . . That was the problem. Richard and Daniel had arranged things so that he would have to guard her in the hopes that he would admit he loved her and give up this ridiculous idea about a curse on the Langley men. But Christiana wasn't with child, and the women knew about the suitor. There was no longer any excuse not to hire a proper bodyguard to trail her around rather than Robert. And doing that would remove temptation for her.

"Damn," Lisa muttered, dropping back in bed. She should have thought of this before. She would talk to Richard about it tomorrow. With any luck, Robert and his temptation would be out of the house by tomorrow afternoon.

"Oh, it's you."

Robert stopped his pacing of Richard's office and turned at that comment to find the man standing in the open office door.

"I heard someone in the hall upstairs and got up to investigate, but by the time I pulled on my trousers the hall was empty, so I thought to check the rest of the house," Richard explained, moving into the room and pushing the door closed behind him.

"I couldn't sleep," Robert muttered, turning away to pace to the fireplace again.

"How is the wound?" Richard asked, moving to the sideboard to pour himself a whiskey.

"Healing," he answered without interest. It wasn't his sliced chest that was bothering him. It was Lisa's refusal to marry him. He couldn't believe she'd rejected the proposal out of hand. For God's sake, she'd trailed him around like a puppy for most of their lives, following him with adoring eyes. And she'd slept with him, for pity's sake. She'd let him do things that no man but a husband should do. She could be carrying their child! And yet she refused to marry him? He would never understand women.

"So what has you up and pacing?" Richard asked, settling in one of the chairs before the fire and eyeing him curiously.

"Explain women to me," Robert demanded rather than answer.

Richard raised his eyebrows and lowered the glass he'd just raised to his lips. "Any woman in particular?"

"Lisa," he growled.

Richard nodded solemnly. "What would you like me to explain about her?"

"I asked her to marry me," he admitted

after a brief struggle, and then added, "Several times."

Richard didn't gasp in shock. He didn't even appear surprised, just asked, "And why did you do that?"

Robert turned away, unwilling to reveal the events that had led to the proposal.

"I thought you had no desire to marry?" Richard prodded. "That any woman you were foolish enough to shackle yourself to would surely be unfaithful and make your life a misery."

Robert grunted with a nod.

"So why ask Lisa to marry you?"

He scowled into the cold, blackened logs in the unlit fireplace and shook his head, unwilling to explain.

After a moment, Richard said, "Perhaps she refuses because she doesn't want to be painted an adulteress when she hasn't earned it."

Robert glanced around with surprise at those words. "What?"

Richard shrugged. "Trust is a part of love and necessary for a good marriage, Robert. I have to trust Christiana every day in many small and large ways and she me. If we didn't have that trust, our marriage could never survive the trials and tribulations of daily life." He took a sip of his whiskey and

302

then added, "And it is the same for Daniel and Suzette. Trust is important in a marriage. Lisa knows that. But you aren't offering it to her with your proposal."

"I trust her . . . mostly," he added uncomfortably.

"Mostly isn't enough," Richard said quietly. "And I suspect if you can't offer her your full trust, you will never win her."

Robert turned back to the fireplace with a frown.

Several moments of silence passed and then Richard asked, "Do you think I should trust Christiana as I do?"

"Of course," he said without having to think about it.

"And can Daniel trust Suzette?"

"Again yes," he said at once. "Neither of them have a deceptive bone in their body."

"Well I wouldn't go that far," Richard said with amusement, and then quickly added, "But my question is, why then do you not trust Lisa? She is their sister. Raised by the same parents with the same values. Why is she untrustworthy when her sisters are not?"

"I do trust Lisa," he said with a frown.

"Not if you think she would be unfaithful," Richard said firmly.

"That is different. It wouldn't be — it's not that I think she — it's —"

"The curse?" Richard suggested when Robert paused again.

"Yes," he said on a sigh and the other man shook his head.

"You do not even recognize how irrational that sounds, do you? Your father pounded that ingrained belief so firmly into your head, you cannot see that it was just the rantings of a bitter old man."

"They weren't rantings," Robert said quietly. "My mother was unfaithful."

"Has it occurred to you that he may have driven her to it with his beliefs and suspicions?" Richard suggested quietly. "I suspect your father was raised by his own father on the same milk of hate and mistrust for women as he tried to instill in you. I think had you not been such good friends with the Madison sisters, you would have grown up a woman hater like him."

Robert frowned. "He didn't hate women."

"Really?" Richard asked with a disbelieving laugh. "Give one example of a good or kind thing he ever said about women. Because I met your father a time or two over the years when I was younger and it seemed to me he was a bitter, nasty woman hater." Richard downed his drink then and stood up. "I am going back to bed to cuddle up to my wife. You should get some rest too. You

304

are still healing."

Robert merely nodded. His thoughts were now on his father as he sought for even one good thing the man had ever said about any woman. The only thing he could come up with was that Cook made damned fine pasties. Sadly, he'd followed that up with the comment that it was too bad she wasn't a man.

Frowning, he moved to the chair Richard had just vacated and settled into it, his mind going back over his childhood and his parent's interactions. What he recalled were a lot of fights and yelling, usually every time his mother came back from visiting one or another of their boarders or had tea with a friend. Which was almost daily. He recalled his father shouting accusations and his mother responding with frustration and despair. He hadn't understood at the time, but supposed now that his father had been accusing her of meeting a lover or being unfaithful. And since Robert had usually been with her on those visits and knew she hadn't been . . . well, all those battles had been for naught. They'd been nothing more than paranoia and false accusations against a woman who hadn't deserved them.

It must have been unbearable for her, Robert thought with a frown. How had he never seen this before? Somehow as a young man he had ended up taking his father's side in everything, sure he was right and she was nothing more than a faithless whore. And, yes, in the end she had turned to another man. But was it possible his father had driven her into the arms and succor of another man with years of what really amounted to abuse? To give her credit, the only affair Robert was even sure his mother ever had was the one with Gower and that had not started until his parents had begun to live apart.

This was casting an entirely new light on his parents . . . not to mention his beliefs in the supposed curse on the Langley men. It was possible it was nothing more than a case of believing it would happen bringing it about. Had Lisa consented to marry him, would he have driven her to leave him and take up with another for comfort?

"Jesus," he muttered.

CHAPTER FOURTEEN

"You are sure Robert is not up yet?" Lisa asked Bet for the third time as the maid finished with her hair.

"Aye. Handers said Lord Langley was up pacing in the office most of the night, and Lord Radnor said to let him sleep. He's sleeping."

Lisa nodded on a relieved sigh. "And Richard is gone already."

"Aye. He was up with the dawn and gone," Bet repeated, also for the third time.

Lisa nodded again, but this time with a grimace. She had hoped to talk to him about hiring a guard today so that Robert could leave. But there was nothing she could do about that now if Richard was gone. Still, she wasn't going to sit about here for Robert to lure her into bed again.

Perhaps she should go hire a bodyguard herself. The Bow Street runners did that kind of thing. Or at least she hoped they did. If not, surely they could tell her who would. She would have Handers hire a hack and take care of the matter herself, she decided.

"There you are," Bet murmured, stepping back as she finished with her hair. "Is there anything else?"

"Nay," Lisa murmured, standing to head for the door. "I have to go out for a bit. I shall —"

"Not by yerself," Bet said firmly. "That suitor fellow is still out there somewhere."

Lisa hesitated, recognizing the stubborn set to Bet's shoulders. "I was going to have Handers hire a hack. In fact, I am heading out to hire a bodyguard so that Lord Langley needn't bother with the task himself anymore."

Bet relaxed a bit and nodded with understanding. "Between me and the driver we should be able to keep ye safe. But we'll take one of the footmen just to be sure."

Lisa smiled wryly at the other woman as she moved to join her. "I take it you are not going to let me go alone?"

"With yer tendency to land yerself in trouble?" Bet asked with a snort. "Not bloody likely, miss."

Shaking her head, Lisa didn't bother to argue, but simply turned and led the way out of her room. They were descending the stairs when a knock sounded at the front door. Lisa slowed, but continued forward, watching curiously as Handers appeared in the entry to answer it. Her eyes widened, however, when she saw a grim-faced Findlay on the doorstep, a bouquet of flowers in one hand, and books and a small bag in the other.

"I came to —" Charles started and then paused when he saw Lisa coming down the steps. His face brightened at once, a wide smile replacing the slight frown that had been there before. "Lisa. I mean Miss Madison," he corrected himself quickly, his glance sliding to Bet and Handers.

"It's all right, Handers. I shall see Lord Findlay," Lisa said after a hesitation.

"Very good, miss. Shall I show him to the parlor?"

She smiled wryly at the question, but shook her head. "I think I can manage to lead him there myself. But perhaps some tea could be sent to us?"

"Very good, miss." The butler gave a half bow and turned to head up the hall.

"Shall I talk to Harry in the stables about hiring a hack for us?" Bet murmured behind her.

Lisa glanced over her shoulder and nodded. "Yes, please."

The maid nodded and slipped around her to follow the butler as Lisa stepped off the stairs and approached Charles.

"Please, come in," she said with a laugh, realizing the man was still standing on the front step.

Returning her smile, he stepped inside and pushed the door closed. "These are for you."

"Thank you," Lisa murmured, accepting the flowers he held out. "They're beautiful."

"Not as beautiful as you," he said solemnly, and then added, "I am glad to see you looking so well. I was worried when you didn't attend the Norstroms' ball last night. Your sister said you had a cough after getting caught in the rain. That's all my fault. I should have been paying better attention to the weather. I am sorry."

"Don't be. I am fine today," she murmured, trying to ignore the guilt his apology stirred in her. Sighing, she turned to lead him up the hall to the parlor, adding, "And it wasn't your fault, anyway."

"Still, I shall take more care in future," he assured her and then they both paused as a maid rushed out of the kitchens with a vase of water.

"Mr. Handers said ye'd be wanting this, Miss," the girl explained, holding up the vase.

"Yes, thank you, Joan," Lisa murmured, setting the flowers in the vase and then taking it from the girl to carry into the parlor. She set it on the table in front of the sofa as she settled on it and immediately began to fuss with the flowers, arranging them more attractively as Lord Findlay settled on the chair across from her.

"These are for you too," Charles murmured, leaning forward to offer her the books and the bag he carried once she was satisfied with the flowers.

"Thank you," Lisa said, accepting the offerings. Peering quickly over the titles, she smiled wryly, "You have discovered my weakness, my lord. I do love to read. Though I haven't had much chance to enjoy books since coming to London."

"It is always busy in town," Charles said, waving that away, and then added, "There is much more time to read in the country. I actually prefer life in the country for just that reason."

"So do I," she admitted. While this was her first trip to town, Lisa found the constant round of balls and teas a bit taxing. Of course, the rest of her time was not exactly relaxing, what with the kidnapping attempts, and with Robert's constant attentions.

"There is something else we have in common then," Charles said with a smile.

"Yes," she agreed with a smile, setting the books aside and turning her attention to the bag he'd handed her. Opening it, she peered inside, her eyes widening as she spotted the hard candies inside. The sight startled a "My favorite!" from her, and Charles grinned.

"Really? They are mine too."

"Something else we have in common," Lisa said with a laugh, and then glanced past him to the door as Bet appeared with a tea tray in hand. The maid set the tray on the table beside the flowers, and then bent to whisper by her ear, "Harry is arranging for the hack, and Handers has selected one of the largest footmen to accompany us."

"Thank you," Lisa murmured.

Nodding, the maid straightened and left the room, leaving them alone.

Once she was gone, Lisa hesitated and then busied herself pouring the tea.

"Thank you," Charles said as he accepted the cup she then offered him.

"Shall we have a candy too?" Lisa asked picking up the bag.

"Yes, that would be nice," Charles said, reaching in to take one when she held out the bag. Smiling faintly, he sat back and contemplated the little candy with a shake of the head. "I cannot believe we like so many of the same things. It's rather nice."

"Yes," Lisa agreed, popping one of the candies into her own mouth and considering him as she moved it around with her tongue. They did appear to have a lot in common. That had to be a good thing. Now if he could just manage to stir some passion in her . . .

"What are you thinking?" Charles asked suddenly, a curious smile curving his lips. "You have a very odd look on your face."

Lisa hesitated, and picked up her tea. She took a sip, and then rather than answer, asked, "My lord, what were you asking me when Robert interrupted us the other day?"

When he hesitated, she said, "I thought perhaps you were in the middle of asking me to be your wife."

Charles glanced down to his teacup, and then set it down with a sigh and nodded. "In truth, I was."

Lisa relaxed a bit and nodded. "I thought so."

They were both silent for a moment and then he raised his eyebrows. "And will you?"

Lisa bit her lip and dropped her eyes. She should have realized this would follow the question, but she didn't appear to be thinking terribly clearly at the moment. Which was a good deal of the problem. If she could just get some time without Robert hovering nearby, or seducing her, or even just sleeping across the hall from her, she was sure she could figure out what was best to do in this situation. But to get that time she needed to hire a guard and remove any reason for Robert to be at the house. Until she did that, she wouldn't be able to think and wouldn't trust any decisions she came to not to be simply knee-jerk reactions to Robert's effect on her.

"Lisa?" he prodded.

Sighing, she raised her eyes and asked, "Would you mind terribly if I asked for time to consider before answering?"

"Time to consider," Charles echoed quietly, sitting back.

"It is a very big decision," she said apologetically. "It decides the course of the rest of my life. And yours."

"Yes, it does," he agreed solemnly.

"And while I do enjoy your company and we do seem to like the same things, I —" She hesitated and then blurted, "Do you think you could kiss me again, my lord?"

Charles rocked back in his seat with surprise, his tea sloshing in his cup and slipping over the side to fill the matching saucer it sat on.

"I realize it is bold of me to ask," she rushed on, aware that she was blushing. "But it does occur to me that before deciding something so important, it might be good to learn if we could . . . I mean, if we suited each other in . . . er . . . less intellectual ways."

His eyes were wide now, his eyebrows halfway to his hairline and Lisa knew she was bright red with embarrassment.

Grimacing, she struggled on. "It is just that a lifetime is a very long time and while you have kissed me before, the first time I think you were being gentle with me and the second time was punishing at my own request, but I —" Lisa shook her head and then said, "I just thought if you kissed me passionately and . . ." She stared at him helplessly, and then stood abruptly, too embarrassed to continue. "I'm sorry. It was not well done of me to even suggest such a thing. I should probably —"

"No, no." Charles was on his feet at once and moving around the table to claim her hands. "You took me by surprise, but you are absolutely right."

"I am?" Lisa asked uncertainly.

"Yes, of course. Surely a proper kiss or two to ensure we . . . er . . . suit each other in other ways would be a sensible idea," he said with a crooked smile.

Lisa felt herself relax at his words and nodded. "Yes. It does."

"Very well." Charles hesitated briefly, and then released her hands to clasp her elbows and draw her into his arms. Lisa managed not to stiffen up. It was difficult though. This wasn't Robert and her body seemed very aware of that.

Charles smiled at her, and then lowered his head to press his lips to hers lightly, before beginning to nibble and nip.

Lisa waited for something to stir in her . . . and waited. Then his tongue brushed along her lips and she automatically opened to him, allowing his tongue to sweep in. Much to her relief, passion finally, slowly stirred to life within her. Sadly, it was only a weak echo of the passion Robert brought to life in her. On the other hand, Charles's hands were remaining chastely on her elbows, not traveling over her body as Robert's did when he kissed her, so perhaps that was the difference, she told herself.

A footfall at the door made them break apart then and Lisa glanced toward it, cursing herself for not closing the door when she saw Robert standing there.

"Langley," Charles said in greeting, releasing Lisa. He hesitated and then said, "You may be the first to congratulate us. I just asked Miss Madison to marry me."

Lisa bit her lip, but otherwise didn't react. He did ask her to be his wife. However, she had asked for time to think and the way he had phrased it made it sound as if she'd accepted. But then they had just been caught in something of a compromising position and she didn't doubt he was trying to protect her.

"Perhaps you should go for now," Lisa suggested when Robert didn't comment and simply continued to stand staring at them.

"Of course," Charles murmured, but asked, "Will you be at the Brewsters' ball tonight?"

Lisa nodded.

"Then I shall look for you there," he announced. He kissed her on the forehead and then moved across the room to leave.

Robert stepped out of the way at his approach, watched him exit and then pushed the door closed and turned on Lisa.

"I didn't agree to marry him," she said nervously when the silence drew out, and then could have kicked herself for it. Raising her chin, she added, "But I intend to if he still wants me after I tell him about . . . what we did."

"You cannot marry him," Robert said quietly.

Lisa scowled. "I can and I will, Robert."

"Marry me instead. Then you will not need to explain anything."

Sighing wearily, she shook her head. "I will not spend a lifetime trying to prove I will not be unfaithful."

"You could be carrying my child," he pointed out.

"Then I had best find a husband quickly," Lisa snapped impatiently and his head went back as if she'd slapped him.

"Another man is not raising my child," he growled.

"And I am not marrying a man who thinks I will be unfaithful before we have even said I do," she shot back.

"I don't —" Robert broke off and glanced to the door impatiently when a knock sounded. Growling under his breath with frustration, he turned to open it. "What?"

"There is a Mr. Smithe here to see you, my lord," Handers announced. "I showed him to the office."

"Dammit," Robert muttered, and then

hesitated a moment before turning to Lisa. "Wait here. I need to see him, but I won't be long. We need to talk about this."

He didn't wait for her agreement, but then turned and hurried out of the room.

Lisa heard him stride up the hall, but when she heard the office door open and close, she hurried out of the room, up the hall and straight out the front door. She couldn't talk to Robert. They would argue, he would kiss her, they would end up in a naked heap in the parlor, be discovered and the decision of who to spend the rest of her life with would be taken from her.

Her fleeing was a purely panicked reaction with no real destination in mind. But when she spotted the hack in front of the house, she immediately rushed to it, pausing just long enough to tell the driver where she wanted to go before climbing inside and collapsing on the seat. The coach was already moving before it occurred to her that she'd forgot to bring Bet and the footman with her.

"Sorry it took so long, my lord," Smithe said as soon as the greetings were over and Robert had ushered him to a chair.

"That's all right," Robert muttered, settling in the chair behind the desk and eyeing Smithe expectantly. "I presume you found Mrs. Morgan?"

"Yes, but it took some fancy footwork. She'd gone to ground. Was lying low and just vacationing. It made it harder to find her than it would have if she'd set up shop right away. We had to talk to countless people, and search all the way to Paris before we found someone who recognized her, and then that was just happenstance. They'd traveled over on the same boat. She'd told them she was heading to Paris, but they saw her get in a carriage heading north."

"North?" Robert asked with a frown. Paris was south of Calais.

Smithe nodded. "She traveled north along the coast to Amsterdam and then southwest to Dusseldorf, Weisbaden, Stuttgart, and then on to Milano and finally Firenze."

Robert scowled. It sounded as if she'd been on something of a rushed grand tour, a damned expensive venture. "How the devil did she afford that?"

"The suitor was apparently at the house when they discovered your Miss Madison had escaped," Smithe said dryly.

Robert's head went back at this news. He had apparently gotten Lisa out of there just in time. An hour hadn't passed between his getting her out of the room and returning to Morgan's brothel, but the woman had already packed and fled. It must have only been moments between his taking her from the room and the suitor's arrival to claim her.

"He has deep pockets," Smithe continued. "Told her where to leave from, where to go, and paid her well to keep her from setting up shop again until he sent her the all clear."

Robert nodded grimly.

"So the old hag wasn't out in the open to find, and she was traveling under several tales. In Dusseldorf she claimed to be a widow on her way to visit her daughter. In Weisbaden, she was gentry on the way to meet her husband. In Milano she was a lady seeking her son, who was on a grand tour, to give him the sad news that his sister had died." He shook his head. "And she changed her look with each stop like some master of disguise. It made it damned difficult to track her."

"I can imagine," Robert murmured and asked curiously, "How did you manage it?"

"To tell the truth, I don't think we would have managed it had there not been one thing that stayed the same no matter where she went," he said dryly.

"What was that?"

321

"She's a right old cow," Smithe said grimly. "Raised a fuss everyplace she stopped, demanding better service and complaining about this and that and what-not. Made everyone who met her hate her with a passion. In the end, all we had to ask after was a 'difficult Englishwoman.' She made enemies everywhere she stopped," he said dryly.

"Hmm." Robert sat back, and then asked, "But you did catch up to her?"

Smithe nodded. "Always get my man, or in this case, nasty old harridan," he said with amusement.

Robert smiled faintly at the words, but asked, "Did she tell you who this suitor was?"

"It took some persuading. For all that she's a bitch, she was scared of the fellow," he said solemnly. "But when we shackled her to bring her back, she started singing. Your man is one Lord Charles Findlay."

Lisa shifted nervously on the carriage seat, trying to prepare in her head for what she would say to the Bow Street runner. She had no desire to tell him everything. How embarrassing would it be to explain about unknowingly taking tea with a brothel owner, and getting herself drugged, locked up, bathed and dressed for a man? Too humiliating. She had no desire to tell the tale. On the other hand she had to give some sort of explanation for her need of a bodyguard or guards to replace Robert.

Perhaps she could just leave out the bit about the brothel and tell him about the attack in her room and on Pembroke's excursion, she thought. Of course, any Bow Street runner worth his salt would wonder why she had come to see him on her own and why a man of the house wasn't hiring him.

That consideration brought a scowl to her face and Lisa began to wring her hands fretfully. He would wonder why a supposed lady did not have even a maid with her for this journey too, she realized and thought perhaps she should tell the driver to turn back. Once back at Radnor, she could send him to the door to ask for Bet rather than risk getting caught and cornered by Robert. Or maybe she should call this off altogether and ask Richard to handle it. But that would mean probably waiting until the next day . . . another day and night with Robert there, kissing and caressing her, tempting her to do things she really shouldn't.

No, she wanted a guard now. She wanted Robert gone now. Lisa wasn't even sure Richard would be willing to hire a guard for her that would remove the necessity of Robert's staying at Radnor. Richard might not agree that he should leave. After all, he knew she'd slept with Robert.

Her eyes widened. Richard knew she'd slept with Robert. They all did. Why the devil was no one insisting that they had to marry? Every single one of them should be screaming for that, but especially Richard. She was an unmarried young woman, a member of nobility and his sister-in-law, and had been ruined in his care under his own roof. He should be squawking and roaring and demanding Robert make things right.

The fact that he wasn't was rather shocking now that she thought on it. It also made her suspect that there was something afoot here that she didn't understand. Was he in cahoots with Robert? And hoping the man would talk her into marriage so he didn't have to demand it?

Lisa's thoughts died as the carriage slowed to a halt. She sat forward in her seat and peered out the window, grimacing when she saw the dilapidated area they were in. She hadn't recognized the address for the runner when Tibald had mentioned it during one of the afternoon teas. He'd hired the fellow to track down a thief who had stolen some jewels from his country estate. Fascinated, Lisa had asked several questions about the runner, and, eager to entertain her, Tibald had told her everything there was to tell, including the man's address. He had also mentioned what a run-down area it was in, but she'd got the sense of just a poorer section of town, not this distressing, dingy street with buildings that looked ready to fall down and groups of men standing in shadows and on corners looking menacing and dangerous.

Lisa bit her lip, suddenly thinking that returning home might be for the best. But then her worries about what Richard might be up to made her rethink. It was not as if she would be on the street long. She just had to walk from the carriage to the building they had stopped in front of, Lisa encouraged herself and then wondered why the driver wasn't getting down to open the door.

Probably afraid to leave his seat and risk someone jumping into it and taking off with his hack, she thought on a sigh and opened the door herself. Really, Bet was right, she did have a tendency to get herself into some sticky situations, Lisa thought as she descended to the ground. Once there, she pushed the door closed, glanced nervously about and then hurried forward to the door ahead of her. She had nearly reached the building when the sound of the carriage hurrying off made her halt and whirl round in time to see the hack reach the corner and start around it.

Lisa gaped after it with amazement, hardly believing the man had just left her there. She hadn't even paid him yet, she thought and then wondered if the stable master had. If so, she would send him to get the money back. But —

Lisa drew her thoughts to a halt as she became aware that she was beginning to draw the attention of the groups of men on the street. Noting the looks she was getting, she whirled back to the door a bit desperately. Surely, the runner would find her a hack to take her back home after they'd finished their transaction, she assured herself. And he'd send a guard with her too. That was what she was here for.

Lisa reached the door and then hesitated, unsure whether she was expected to just walk in or knock. If it were a store she would have just walked in, but perhaps its being an office meant knocking. Biting her lip, she shifted from one foot to the other and then tapped at the door before glancing nervously over her shoulder. The moment she did, she wished she hadn't. Three men were now walking in her direction, eyes fixed on her like she was a mince pie and they were hungry.

She turned quickly back to the door, beginning a prayer under her breath. It was the hallowed old "Please hurry, please hurry" mantra. But when the door didn't open after repeating that three times, she knocked again, more firmly.

Lisa kept her gaze locked firmly on the panel of wood before her as she waited, almost terrified to look around, half afraid that if she did she would find the men on top of her. But the door wasn't opening and there wasn't a sound coming from inside.

Swallowing, she reached desperately for the doorknob, but paused at the sound of a carriage approaching. Her hired hack was returning, she thought hopefully. Or perhaps it was the runner returning home and that was why he wasn't answering. She risked a glance over her shoulder.

While they weren't on top of her, the three approaching men were much closer now and two other of the small groups of men were now moving in her direction as well. She felt like a small defenseless hare with a pack of wolves circling, and then her gaze slid to the carriage coming to a halt on the road.

Lisa recognized the crest on it just as the door opened and Lord Findlay stepped down. Spotting her, he paused abruptly, one hand still on the open door and his eyebrows flying up. "Lisa?"

With the first group of men perhaps six feet away now, Lisa gave up on the runner's door and rushed to Charles.

"Lisa, what ever are you doing here?" he asked, catching her arms and frowning as he peered past her to the men around them.

"I was going to hire a runner, but he's not in," she mumbled, her gaze slipping past him to his carriage, and then over her shoulder to see that the men had stopped and were now waiting and watching. Turning back to Charles, she asked, "Do you think you could take me home, my lord? My hack left without me and I —"

"Of course." Stepping aside, he helped her in, then moved to speak to his driver before climbing in to join her.

The carriage set off at once then, and they peered out the window at the men they were leaving behind. Each and every one of them was staring after the carriage with narrowed eyes and hungry looks and she suspected Charles had just saved her from a most unpleasant experience. Sitting back in her seat, she smiled at him with gratitude. "I am very glad you arrived when you did, I was growing a bit nervous."

"A bit?" he asked dryly. "Lisa, those men would have . . ." He paused and shook his head. "It is fortunate I happened to choose today to try to see Tibald's runner."

"You were there to see him as well?" she asked with surprise, and then wondered why she even asked. What else would he have been there for?

"Yes, I've had a little problem with theft myself recently. A new maid, I suspect, and since Tibald spoke so highly of this fellow I thought I'd see what he could do for me." He peered at her curiously. "What were you hiring him for?"

"Oh. Well, I just . . . something similar," she finished vaguely, not wishing to open that kettle of fish at the moment.

"Hmm." Charles eyed her solemnly and then said, "I cannot believe that Radnor allowed you to come down here by yourself."

"Yes, well, Richard did not know I was coming," she admitted unhappily.

Charles nodded, but added, "Still, I cannot believe Langley allowed you out of his sight long enough for you to come down here by yourself either. The man seems ever to be shadowing you."

"Yes, he does," Lisa agreed with vexation. "The man is —" She cut herself off abruptly and glanced toward the window, irritation wiggling its way through her. Finally she simply said, "Robert did not know I was coming either. In fact, he had no idea I was leaving or surely would have followed."

Findlay hesitated and then leaned forward in his seat to clasp her hands in his. When she raised her head to peer at him, he said, "Lisa, is Langley the reason you wanted time to think about my proposal?"

Lisa avoided his eyes uncomfortably and tried to tug her hands free, but he held them tightly and said gently, "It has become obvious to me that there is something more than family friendship between the two of you. Your feelings, at least, are deeper than that, though I don't know about Langley. He's a cold bastard and hard to read at times."

Lisa lowered her eyes and shook her head helplessly. Wondering if all of London could tell she had feelings for Robert.

"Do you love him?"

Lisa swallowed, fighting not to speak, but then it just came pouring out. "I have loved him my whole life. No one but him. And I think he cares for me too, but he is afraid I would be unfaithful like his mother and grandmother and refuses to marry. Or did," she added with a frown. "Now he wants to marry me, but only because —" She cut herself off abruptly, flushing as she realized what she'd almost revealed and rushed on, "But I will not be married to a man who thinks I would be unfaithful to him."

"Ah." Charles said quietly and squeezed her hands. "Then might I suggest you accept my proposal instead?"

A sharp bark of laughter slipped from her lips, and then she waved one hand wearily and said, "My lord, you do not want me."

"On the contrary. I want you very much," he said wryly.

"You wouldn't if you knew —" Lisa cut herself off again abruptly, but Charles finished it for her.

"That Langley has bedded you?"

CHAPTER FIFTEEN

Robert stared at Smithe blankly. "Findlay?"

"Hmm. Never heard much of the man myself. Know he's a respected Baron and such, or supposed to be. But it turns out he's one dissolute bastard for all that," Smithe said and consulted a small notebook. "Too fond of drink and gambling. Likes prostitutes, but they don't like him so much 'cause he apparently only finds his pleasure by inflicting pain on others. Has a violent temper and wants what he wants." He flipped the notebook closed and glanced to Robert. "Seems he's wanted Miss Madison for a while. Apparently had some plan to get her a couple years ago with the help of her brother-in-law." He paused and raised an eyebrow. "That would be Lord Radnor."

"His brother," Robert assured him grimly. "Not Lord Radnor, but his brother George."

"Hmm." Smithe looked dubious, but let it go and continued, "It seems those plans he had apparently ran amuck and he's been awaiting his chance to get at her again. It was just happenstance that Mrs. Morgan got involved. He was at the brothel the night before the incident that led to her being locked up there. Morgan happened to mention she was expecting the girl to tea the next day. I gather Findlay immediately pounced on that, then paid her scads of money to drug the girl, prepare her for him and present her for his pleasure. Said he was going to marry her . . . after." He shrugged. "Mrs. Morgan swears that's the only reason she agreed to it. The girl would be married all good and proper to a fine, respected lord and no harm done," he finished dryly.

Robert sat back with a curse. He'd suspected one of the men currying favor with Lisa might be the suitor, but he'd suspected Pembroke, not Findlay. It was Pembroke's pastries that had made her ill and forced her to stay home the night she was attacked. And it was at Pembroke's outing where the second attack had occurred. Of course, that had helped to push the suspicion Pembroke's way and he supposed a smart man would want the suspicion elsewhere. It had left Findlay free to court Lisa without interference. It had also knocked out his only strong competition when Robert had suggested Lisa stay away from Pembroke.

"Damn," he muttered.

Smithe nodded and pointed out, "There's little that can be done about Lord Findlay legally without tarnishing Miss Madison's reputation." He allowed a moment to pass and then added, "And even if you were willing to risk that, without Mrs. Morgan here as a witness to his involvement, it would be difficult to prove anything. But you did say to let the woman go if she gave us the name and so that's what we did."

Robert grunted at these words. He'd already realized all of that before he'd even known who the suitor was. He had no intention of going through legal channels to handle the man. He intended on hunting the bastard down and personally beating the hell out of him for putting Lisa through all of this, and for what he would have put her through had she not escaped Mrs. Morgan's that day.

"Of course, there are other, less legal ways to deal with a man like that," Smithe continued as if reading Robert's mind. "I don't usually encourage that sort of thing, but in this case it does seem the only way to keep the young lady safe . . . short of her marrying someone else and being removed as temptation. Is there any chance she will marry soon?"

"A very good chance indeed," Robert assured him grimly. His talk with Richard the night before had cleared his mind on certain issues and he had been trying to tell Lisa that when Smithe arrived. The minute the man was gone he would return to the parlor and tell her of the epiphany he'd had. How he'd realized that what he'd thought was true about his childhood and his mother wasn't true at all. That he'd come to see that his father was a bitter old woman hater who had infected him with his poison, but she was the antidote. He would tell her that he realized now how irrational and stupid his thoughts on marriage and wives had become, and that he did trust her, with all his heart.

Of course, Robert acknowledged that he would have the occasional habitual doubt enter his mind that he would have to fight off and deal with, but he would do his damnedest to ensure he did not take them out on Lisa. He would not drive her away as his father had done with his mother. He would cherish her and keep her close all the days they had together.

"Well, that ensures her safety at least. Findlay can hardly marry a married woman," Smithe said with satisfaction. "As for the other, there is a risk he might still try to get her alone to have his way with her, but I suspect a stern talking to and a fist or two to the man's face would be enough to discourage him from taking that tack."

"Undoubtedly," Robert agreed dryly.

"Just let me know if you want a couple of my boys to give him that talk and I'll see to it," Smithe said, standing up.

"I think I would prefer to handle that myself," Robert said silkily, getting to his feet as well.

"I thought you might," Smithe said with a grin as Robert walked him to the office door. "It's what I would do."

Robert didn't comment, but ushered him out into the hall and toward the front door. His fists were itching to plant themselves in Findlay's face.

"I shall send you my bill, my lord," Smithe said, pausing at the front door. Glancing back he raised one eyebrow. "To your proper address and not here, I imagine?"

"Yes. Please," Robert said, opening the door for him.

"Very good." Smithe nodded and then turned to step outside. Robert watched him go to his carriage, then closed the door and turned to head up the hall.

The parlor door was \still closed, and he paused to take a breath and sort out what he would say before opening it. He had a distinct sense of déjà vu when he finally pulled the door open and found himself staring in at an empty parlor.

"Handers!" he bellowed, wheeling toward the kitchens.

Lisa stared at Charles with shock and horror as his words played through her head. *"That Langley has bedded you?"*

"Forgive me for being so blunt," Charles said gently. "But it is rather obvious that's what has happened."

"How?" she asked with dismay.

Charles hesitated and then sighed. "Well, the way he looks at you has never been anything like filial. At first he watched you with a hunger only another man would recognize. But today, and the last time I saw you . . ." He paused briefly and said, "The day we had our picnic you were studiously ignoring him, but he could not take his eyes off you. His gaze roamed over you with the knowledge of a lover. And then, of course, I suspected something had happened the night you asked me to kiss you punishingly. You said he had kissed you as punishment, but it was more than a kiss, was it not?"

"Yes, but not — it was the next night that he — we — I —" She grimaced, and shook her head. "You may retract your proposal, my lord. I understand completely that you couldn't possibly want me now that you know."

"And yet I do," he said wryly, and smiled at her startled expression. "Lisa, you are a very attractive woman. I had heard of you before I met you, but once I met you . . ." He shrugged. "I have wanted you ever since first seeing you that night at the Landons' ball two seasons ago."

When she shook her head and tried to sit back, he kept hold of her hands and said, "It's true. I simply could not get you out of my head. All other women were faded pastels next to the vibrant crimson of your image in my memory. And I have spent a good portion of these last two years wishing I had snatched you up and run off to Gretna Green with you right there and then."

When her eyes widened incredulously, he shrugged. "I wish it even more now that I know that Langley took advantage of you. At least I could have saved you from that."

Lisa frowned. Robert hadn't taken advantage of her. She'd gone to his room fully intending to seduce and trap him into marriage. Of course, she hadn't had to try very hard, but he hadn't taken advantage of her at all.

"I do want you," Charles said firmly. "But, unlike Langley, my intentions are honorable and I would marry you first." He leaned closer, his expression gentle. "Say yes and I will have the driver head for Gretna Green right now. You can put Langley and everything that has happened firmly behind you and be Lady Findlay. We can live quietly in the country, reading our books, paddling on the water and exploring each other's bodies at night."

Charles brushed a hand down her cheek as he said the last, and Lisa was hard-pressed to keep from flinching. Her reaction was as much at the thought of their exploring each other's bodies as anything else. The idea held no appeal for her at all. She couldn't find it in her to want to explore him. She couldn't even imagine anyone's body but Robert's beside her in bed, Lisa acknowledged, and that is when she realized just how stupid she had been to think she could marry anyone else.

This was not like switching one dress for another. This was a husband. A man who would expect her to do with him all those intimate things she'd done with Robert.

339

Who would have the right to strip her, and touch her in places and ways that were . . . She shuddered at the very thought of marrying this man or anyone who was not Robert and letting him caress or suckle her, or bury his body in hers. If Robert could not see his way clear to believing she could be faithful, she would just rather be an old maid and single for the rest of her life.

"Lisa?"

Sighing, she raised her head and offered an apologetic smile. "I am sorry, my lord. I am touched, but I could not." When he released her hands and sat back in his seat, she bit her lip and tried to soften her rejection by pointing out, "I might be carrying his child, my lord. Surely you wouldn't want to raise his child as your own. You'd resent it, and me." She shook her head. "I like you too much to saddle you with another man's child. Besides, I would probably make you miserable. I really have loved Robert my whole life. I can't imagine that would ever change. I would be married to you and forever pining after him. I —"

"It is unfortunate you are such a romantic, my dear," Charles interrupted coldly. "A little practicality in that addlepated head of yours would have gone a long way toward making this easier."

Lisa gasped at the insult, shocked by the sudden change in his behavior. It seemed that since she was going to refuse him, he was taking off the kid gloves and showing his true thoughts of her. Addlepated? Because she loved another?

"Of course, it is not entirely your fault," Charles said. "Had Mrs. Morgan not allowed you to escape, we would have married the day after you arrived in London and Langley never would have got the chance to deflower you. He would already be nothing more than a faded memory next to the exquisite sensation I made you feel."

Lisa blinked at him several times as her mind struggled to make sense of what she'd heard. *Mrs. Morgan?*

"You are the suitor," she said slowly, wondering that she wasn't more shocked by the realization.

"Yes, I am. And you will marry me," he said calmly. "It has been the plan for years now and I am not losing out on that delicious body of yours because you have some romantic notion that you love Robert Langley, a man who doesn't even want you," he added dryly.

Lisa stared at him silently as very old puzzle pieces began fitting together with new ones in her head.

"You were the second man in cahoots with Dicky, I mean George," she murmured faintly as the past crashed with the present in her head. Two years ago she and Suzette had come to London to chase down their father and find out why he had not returned to the country estate and why he was not replying to any of their letters. They'd arrived to find him in his cups, bemoaning the fact that he'd gambled them to the edge of ruin.

In a panic, they had gone to Christiana, hoping that she could help them with a mad plan to find Suzette a husband who would be willing to pay off their father's debt in exchange for marrying Suzette and gaining the rather exorbitant dower their grandfather had left her. One he'd left to each of the girls.

However, they'd arrived at Christiana's home to find that all was not well with her marriage. The man who had wooed her with such vigor and charm a year earlier had become a cruel, controlling tyrant. That being the case, it had been more than a relief when the man had accommodatingly cocked up his toes and died the day of their arrival. At least it had been until they'd realized that his death would mean going into mourning and losing the chance to find

Suzette a husband.

In the end, the three sisters had done the only thing they could do; they'd hidden the death of Christiana's husband and set out to attend balls and such to find Suzette a husband who met their requirements. Imagine their amazement when Christiana's dead husband had come sauntering into the Landons' ball on the first night of the season.

It had turned out that the man Christiana had married wasn't Richard Fairgrave, the Earl of Radnor at all, but his twin brother, George, who had hired men to kill Richard so that he might take his place. However, George's hired assassins had reneged on their end of the deal, leaving Richard alive and well in America. And it was he who showed up at the ball that night, seeking justice and his life back, and scaring the three sisters silly.

They soon found out that fratricide and fraud weren't George's only sins. The man had found out about the large dowers the girls had been left by their maternal grandfather. That was the reason he'd married Christiana. And he'd been in cahoots with two other men to marry all three of the sisters and then see them dead in one grand accident that would have left the men rich widowers. The identity of Suzette's would-be husband and murderer had been discovered during the unraveling of who had killed George. But they had never sorted out who was supposed to marry Lisa. Until now.

"Yes, I was the third man in the plot to marry and kill off you and your sisters," Charles admitted, unabashed. "In truth, I wasn't all that interested when George suggested his plot to me. I like to gamble, but not as much as he does, and I have a very healthy estate that furnishes me with all the money I need to fund my play." He shrugged. "However, after seeing you at the Landons' ball . . ." He smiled wryly. "All that pale, perfect, lily-white skin and that golden glory crowning your head."

His gaze moved over her slowly, taking in every inch of the skin he spoke of so lovingly, and then up to caress her golden hair. "Well, I was sold on the plan then. I could not wait to get my hands on you and see how much more lovely your skin would look when mottled with a rainbow of bruises and welts. Or how that beautiful singsong voice of yours would sound when you moaned with pleasured pain."

Charles paused and leaned forward to push Lisa's chin up, closing her gaping mouth. She shrank back in her seat the moment he touched her, however, a shudder running down her back at the image he'd painted.

"Sadly," he continued, seeming unconcerned by her reaction, "Fate intervened and made attaining you rather difficult in the end. First George's plan went awry when he foolishly got himself murdered. Which was probably for the best. I'm sure we would have had a falling-out when I refused to let him kill you. However, then you and your father left town, making it virtually impossible to even try to woo or seduce you into marrying me." He scowled at her with displeasure. "And you stayed away for two damned years, languishing in the country, where I had no excuse to see you to woo you."

Findlay shook his head with disgust. "I had pretty much given up on having you when Mrs. Morgan happened to mention that you were in town and coming to tea." He shook his head with a laugh. "Well, it seemed too perfect to be true. I could have you, drag you off to Gretna Green and marry you, and then enjoy you at my leisure, forever. Imagine it, Lisa, years and years of exquisite play, exploring how much pain the body can take, and how much pleasure we can get from it," he said it as if she should be pleased that he planned to torture her for the next forty years or so, and then his mouth twisted with displeasure.

"Unfortunately, that old cow allowed you to escape, and I was forced to change my plans. I returned to the original plan of wooing and seducing you, but took the opportunities where I found them to try to claim you more quickly as well. However, it soon became obvious that you were interested in Robert, and no man had a chance at wooing you." His mouth twisted with displeasure, and then he added, "Even so, I stayed close in the hopes of keeping tabs on you and where you would be so that should the opportunity arise again, I could claim you and carry you off."

And she'd given him the perfect opportunity by hopping happily into his carriage today, Lisa realized grimly, but said, "You were behind the attack in my room the night I wasn't feeling well?"

He nodded.

Lisa frowned. "But how did you know I would be home? I didn't even know until I got sick from eating Pembroke's sweets. I planned to attend the ball that night."

"I knew because it wasn't Pembroke's sweets that made you sick," he said with mild amusement.

Lisa sat back slightly, her eyes narrowing. "It wasn't?"

Charles shook his head. "I slipped an emetic into your tea while Tibald was telling you all about the runner he'd hired. You were so busy chattering away, you didn't drink the tea until everyone got up to leave." He smiled wryly. "From the way you grimaced as you downed it, I thought for sure you would jump up and say there was something in your tea, but you didn't."

"It was cold and nasty but I thought it was just because I'd let it sit so long," she said quietly, recalling the sickly sweet taste.

"Ahh." Charles nodded, and then commented, "The emetic was supposed to be fast acting. I imagine you probably barely got upstairs before the vomiting started."

"I made it all the way to my room first," she informed him coldly.

"Hmm." He shrugged. "Not as fast acting as claimed then. Ah well, it's for the best, I suppose. Seeing other people get ill tends to turn my own stomach so it wouldn't have done for you to vomit on me."

Lisa was starting to think it was a shame she hadn't. She also thought she would definitely keep that tidbit handy for future reference. If she didn't escape, she would vomit on the man at every opportunity.

"And the attack during Pembroke's outing?" she asked, pushing away the possibility of not escaping.

Findlay shrugged with amusement. "He refrained from inviting me to it. Or Tibald for that matter. Cutting out the competition. Most unsporting of him, really," he said with a tsk, and then shrugged. "It didn't matter though, I knew what he'd arranged and bribed the boat captain to tell me where the planned stop for the picnic was so that I could send my man ahead to lay in wait."

He considered her for a moment and then admitted, "In truth, I didn't expect there to be much hope of grabbing you there. I expected you to stick close to the others, or for Langley to be keeping such a close eye that there would be no chance to snatch you. But you decided to walk along the beach, and while Robert followed, he then turned to leave you there."

"You were there?" Lisa asked with surprise.

"Good Lord, no. I was at my club, establishing my alibi so no one would come looking when I disappeared for a couple days to drag you to Gretna Green."

"Oh," she muttered.

"No, I sent my man. Sadly, from what he's told me, he tried to grab you too soon. He should have waited for Robert to return to the others. He said afterward that he was worried Langley would merely move away a bit and then turn to watch you from a distance, so he took the chance." Findlay shook his head at what he obviously thought had been a foolhardy decision. "The idiot earned himself a nasty knot on the head for his trouble too. But I gather he got in a good jab with his knife on Langley before that? At least he claimed he did."

"Not such a good jab. Robert managed to deflower me the next night despite the trifling wound," she said spitefully.

Charles's mouth tightened. "That is most disappointing."

"Good," Lisa said grimly. "I hope you choke on that knowledge."

Now he smiled. "So the kitten does have claws. Delightful. I like fight with my fun."

"I don't know about fun, but you'll certainly get a lot of fight from me, my lord," she assured him, and reached for the handle to the carriage door. But, as if he'd been waiting for just that, Charles caught her wrist at once and twisted viciously as he dragged it away from the door.

Lisa cried out and fell back on the bench

seat as he released her. Cupping the injured arm with her good hand, she stared at him as a pleased little smile claimed his lips.

"Does it hurt very much?" Charles asked solicitously.

Sensing that he would enjoy knowing he'd hurt her, Lisa removed her good hand from the wounded wrist and shrugged. "Not very, my lord."

As she'd expected, his mouth twisted slightly with disappointment at her words.

Suspecting he would try to hurt her again as punishment, Lisa quickly said, "I gather we are not on the way back to Radnor house?"

Charles blinked and then seemed to relax again and smile. "You are right, of course. We are on the way to my townhouse. I will continue my routine here in town for the next week or so to ensure suspicion is not cast my way, then retreat to the country, heartbroken at what I think is your defection after accepting my proposal."

"That's why you acted as if we were engaged with Robert," she said with realization. "I thought you were just trying to protect my reputation after getting caught kissing me."

He grinned. "Your reputation was already shot, my dear. Langley had bedded you, remember? I did suspect as much even then," he assured her and then added, "No, I claimed we were engaged so that I could play the wounded and bewildered swain when you come up missing. I can go to Radnor and demand to know what is being done to find you. As your fiancé, they will keep me apprised of everything and in a week or so . . ." He shrugged.

"You retreat to the country with your broken heart," Lisa repeated his words dryly.

"Exactly. At least that is what they will think. Instead I will be headed to Gretna Green with you."

"You cannot really think I will marry you?" she asked with amazement. "You cannot force me to say the words in front of the blacksmith."

"My dear Lisa," he said with cocky amusement. "After a week with me you will do whatever I wish you to."

The words sent a chill down the back of Lisa's neck.

"Ah, we're here," Charles announced, peering out the window as the carriage slowed.

Lisa stiffened. If she was going to escape, this was the time to do it. She had no idea where Charles lived, but it would be in an elite area with people everywhere. All she had to do was scream and make a break for it the minute she was out of the carriage and someone would help, Lisa thought, and then glanced to Findlay sharply when he suddenly snickered.

"It always amuses me when this point comes. You women all think alike, you know. Every one of you starts scheming, hope rising in your breast like a wave. You will get away now. This is your chance. Scream and run, or just run, or some such thing, you all think." He shook his head at her folly and said derisively, "As if I have not been taking unwilling women into my home for years and learned how best to do it with the minimum of risk and fuss."

The words were like a splash of cold water in Lisa's face. He had been taking unwilling women into his home for years? What for? And what had happened to those women? Certainly, he hadn't married them as he claimed he intended to do with her, she thought, and then glanced nervously from Charles to the door as the carriage stopped. Her body was tightening, preparing to flee despite his words, the blood pumping through her body in a rush.

Lisa was so tightly strung that when the carriage door opened, she actually gave a little start. She was hoping to see what lay beyond, but a large man filled the opening. Big beefy arms reached in, and before she quite knew what was happening, one sweaty hand was mashing her lips against her teeth and the other was yanking her out the door. She instinctively began to kick and thrash, but it was like doing battle with a wall. Her arms were pinned uselessly to her sides and her feet slammed into what could have been tree trunks, having as much impact as a child's weak blows.

Lisa was carted no more than four feet from the carriage to an open door. It was just long enough to see that they hadn't stopped in front of a house on a busy street, but in a high-walled courtyard at what was obviously the back of the house. No wonder Charles had been amused at her hopes of escape. She hadn't had a chance, she realized.

"Take her to the room, Max," Charles's voice ordered as they entered a large, hot kitchen. "I shall be along shortly."

Lisa glanced wildly around, peering over the large hand covering her mouth and lower face. The hand wasn't just covering her mouth, but her nose as well and she couldn't get any air. She began to struggle more desperately, afraid she was going to be smothered to death, but it had little effect and her vision was dimming by the time she was carted through a kitchen, down a narrow set of steps, and across an open area to a door with a small barred window in it.

Her captor kicked at the base of the door, sending it swinging open. He then walked in and dropped her.

Lisa grunted in pain as she landed on something hard, and then simply lay still for a moment, desperately gasping air into her starved lungs. After a moment, however, she began to feel better and found the energy to raise herself up to a sitting position and peer about. The only light was that coming from the barred window. It was just enough to see that she was in a tiny room with nothing but the narrow bed she had been dumped on. The mattress was hard and appeared to be stuffed with matted straw. The floor of the room was nothing more than hard-packed dirt. A basement then.

Pushing herself up from the bed, Lisa stumbled to the door and searched for a doorknob, but there was none, at least not on the inside, so she grabbed and pulled then pushed on the bars but that did nothing. The door didn't budge at all. Teeth grinding together, she peered through the bars into the room beyond and stared in horror at the scene. It looked like an ancient torture chamber with shackles everywhere: hanging from the ceiling, affixed to the walls at intervals, and even fitted on each corner of a table in the center of the open area. But it was the various whips and straps also hanging from the walls that made her blood run cold. She swore the ends of some of the items were painted with dried blood.

Swallowing, Lisa backed away and returned to sit shakily on the bed. Mrs. Morgan had understated things when she'd said that the suitor liked it a bit rough. Charles Findlay was obviously one of those twisted individuals who enjoyed inflicting pain, and in many and varied ways. Well, she wasn't going to sit about awaiting the fate he had planned for her. She would escape, Lisa decided, standing up. She just had to figure out how.

"Findlay?" Richard repeated the name with a frown.

"Yes," Robert said grimly, pacing to the parlor window and peering out at the street for the umpteenth time since finding Lisa missing.

"Bastard," Daniel muttered. "I've heard some gossip about him abusing prostitutes, but I didn't think he'd go after a woman of the gentry."

"Hmm," Robert muttered, staring at the empty street in front of the house and willing the hack Lisa had left in to roll up and for her to step lightly out, healthy, happy and well. It didn't happen of course, but then it hadn't happened any of the other times he'd willed it either.

"And Lisa has been gone all afternoon?" Daniel asked.

"Yes," Robert growled. "She had Harry hire a hack to take her out to hire a runner."

"What?" Richard asked with surprise. "Why is she hiring a runner?"

Robert ground his teeth together and then reluctantly admitted, "Bet says she wanted to hire a runner to guard her so that I didn't have to."

There was silence for a minute and then Daniel asked, "And she went by herself? She didn't even take Bet?"

"Apparently she was supposed to take Bet and a footman, but she ran off without either of them."

"Are we sure she went willingly and wasn't taken?" Richard asked grimly.

Robert sighed and rubbed his forehead. "Handers saw her leave. He said she ran out of the parlor and charged out the front door straight into the hack. He said she seemed upset."

"Why would she be upset?" Richard asked solemnly.

Robert shrugged. "We were talking just before that, but were interrupted. I said we would finish the talk when I was done."

"And she ran off to avoid that," Daniel guessed dryly, and walked over to slap him on the back. "You do seem to have a way with Lisa."

"Your sarcasm is not appreciated," Robert growled. "I was trying to tell her that I had come to the realization that my fears about her being unfaithful were ungrounded, a result of my father's woman-hating paranoia."

"I knew you'd come around eventually," Richard said quietly. "What did it?"

"Our talk last night," Robert admitted without glancing around. "You were right, Richard. My father was a bitter, woman-hating idiot." He sighed and shook his head. "Once I recognized that, it made me look at everything a little more objectively."

"Hmmm," Daniel grunted. "You say you were trying to tell Lisa that. Was she not listening?"

"She didn't get much of a chance to listen. I didn't get far before Handers announced that Smithe was here and I had to leave."

"And then *she* left," Daniel murmured and stepped up beside Robert to peer out the window. "She has been gone more than two hours then."

"I know. I didn't worry at first, travel can be slow this time of day, and the appointment may have taken as much as an hour. Still, just before you two returned, I sent Harry to check and be sure the hack driver isn't back without her or something. He's to come tell me what he learns when he returns." Robert had barely finished speaking the words when an uproar in the hall made him turn to peer at the door curiously. Richard was just moving toward the door to check on it when it burst open and Harry appeared, dragging a coachman by a hard grip on his upper arm.

"Sorry to burst in, my lord," the stable master muttered with a nod to his master. "But I'm thinking you'll want to hear what this 'gentleman' has to say about what he did to Miss Lisa."

"I didn't do nothing," the man protested, jerking wildly at his arm in an effort to try to get free of Harry's iron hold. "Didn't do a thing. Never hurt anyone in my life and didn't hurt her none either."

"Tell him what you told me," Harry

barked, giving him a shake, and then before he could speak, turned to Robert. "He let Miss Lisa out in the worst part of the city and then scarpered off, leaving her without protection or nothing," Harry announced with disgust. "Tried to tell me that she insisted he go and leave her, but Miss Lisa wouldn't do that, so I got a little persuasive-like with my crop. He finally admitted that just before Miss Lisa came out of the house, a feller what looked like a lord approached him, offering him a bag of coins if he left her wherever she was having him take her." Harry scowled at the wincing driver and growled, "And he took it, he did. Abandoned her there like some poor, homeless waif."

"Where?" Robert growled, crossing the room to glare down at the man. It was all he had to do, the driver babbled the address at once and Robert's head snapped back with shock. It was possibly the worst part of the city. No woman would be safe there, let alone a beautiful, unprotected woman like Lisa.

He started for the door without even thinking about it, but stopped abruptly when Richard caught his arm. "She won't be there anymore, Robert. He left her there more than two hours ago."

Robert stopped abruptly at those words and turned back with a frown.

"If Findlay had him leave her there, it was for a reason," Richard pointed out quietly. "No doubt he showed up to save the day when she was stranded."

"Yes," Daniel said dryly. "And she would have been so relieved to see a friendly face in that neighborhood that she would have climbed right into his carriage like a lamb to the slaughter."

Robert winced at the description, and said, "Then I shall go to Findlay's."

"He could already be dragging her off to Gretna Green," Daniel pointed out. "Mrs. Morgan said he planned to marry her."

"After he ravished her," Richard reminded him quietly.

Robert whirled toward the door again, but Richard caught him back once more. "Think, man. You can't just go rushing off to Findlay's place. He could be taking her away right now. Plans change."

"You're right," Robert said with a frown, recognizing the wisdom in his words. "We need to plan and cover all possibilities. And we could use some help. Smithe and his men would be useful."

"Now you're thinking," Richard said, sounding relieved. He then suggested,

"Send a message to Smithe to come here. We will sort out the various possibilities and decide who should check what. With enough men we can cover all of them and hopefully rescue Lisa before he has a chance to harm her or force her to marry him."

"If he forces her to marry him, she will be a widow by nightfall," Robert promised grimly.

Chapter Sixteen

The sound of footsteps descending the wooden stairs made Lisa stiffen. She then sat up a little straighter when what she really wanted to do was shrink back into a corner and disappear. Findlay had said he would come down after he'd ordered his man to put her in here. She had no doubt it was he approaching now, and had absolutely no desire to see him. However, she would not cower. The heroines in the books she read did not survive trials like this by being weak and silly females. They were bold and brave, and fate rewarded them for it. She would be bold and brave too . . . if it killed her.

That last bit was a truly unfortunate thought, Lisa decided as it rang through her head. Really, she could have phrased it better.

"Ah. I see you are settling in nicely."

Lisa glanced to the door at those words and raised her chin rebelliously when she saw Findlay peering in at her through the bars. He was eyeing her with interest, as if she were a caged animal on display.

"Come to gloat, my lord?" she asked coldly. "Really, it makes you very unattractive."

"Good. You've got fire," Charles said with amusement. "I knew you would."

"So happy to please you," Lisa sneered with disdain.

"No you aren't," he said on a laugh. "But you will be."

"I very much doubt that, my lord."

"Oh, you will," Charles assured her. "And I shall enjoy teaching you to be. I knew that from the first moment I laid eyes on you."

Lisa remained silent this time and merely peered at him with feigned indifference. He hadn't made a move to unlock the door and enter, which she could only think was a good thing. So she waited to see what he was about.

"It makes me wish I could start right away," he commented when she didn't respond. "Sadly, we shall have to refrain from enjoying each other for now. I must go to the Brewsters' ball tonight and act disappointed that you, my fiancée, have not made an appearance, and then shocked and horrified that you are missing. I may even shed a tear."

Lisa nearly sagged with relief at the news that he would leave her alone for now, but knew instinctively that it might be a bad idea to show her relief. It might move him to dally a bit before the ball, so she covered with a dry, "Do not strain yourself with the effort to squeeze that tear out, my lord. I doubt many shall be impressed by it anyway."

"Oh, I don't know. I can be a very good actor when I wish," he commented idly, looking amused.

"Yes, you can. After all you had me believing you were a gentleman," she said dryly. "And many others believing you are human."

"Oh, I do like your fire, Lisa. I can hardly wait to douse it," he crooned with a smile. "This night will seem to stretch on interminably until I can get back here to you."

"Don't rush on my account, my lord," she said sweetly. "Have fun, dance with all the pretty girls and drink a lot."

"Oh no, I shall remain clearheaded and save all my energy for you," he assured her with a laugh and then shook his head. "Did Langley realize what he had in you? Did he see the passion beneath all that happy chatter and romantic drivel?" His smile died abruptly. "Did you show it to him?"

Lisa hesitated. There was something almost angry in the last words. A tone that was almost jealous and possessive. It seemed it did bother him after all that Robert had been there first. Unsure how to respond, she remained silent and after a moment, Findlay sighed.

"Well, I suppose I should head to the ball now. Those carriage lines can be very long and I would not wish to miss any of the excitement. Of course, I doubt your sisters and their husbands will be there. I am sure they are searching madly for you this very moment. I shall have to hear the news that you are missing through a third party and then make my way to Radnor in a tizzy." He took a moment to fuss and straighten himself, and then glanced back through the bars to say, "You should sleep. It will be better for you if you're well rested when I return."

Charles turned away and moved out of sight then. Lisa waited a heartbeat to be sure he would not return and then let her breath out and sank slowly back to lean against the wall as she listened to his fading footsteps. Things definitely weren't looking good at this point. She had checked the door carefully and saw no way to get it open from inside, and there wasn't a window or other escape route to be had where she was.

So, escaping was out. That left fighting, which she had every intention of doing, but a weapon would be helpful. Taking a deep breath to bolster herself, Lisa pushed herself to her feet and then turned in a slow circle, surveying every inch of the cell she was in. It wasn't very encouraging. The bed, the mattress, the dirt floor . . .

Lisa hesitated for a moment and then returned her attention to the bed. It was a wood frame, cheap and rickety. She knelt in front of it and bent to look at it more closely. She then felt each leg, grasping it and giving a tug. Two of the legs were a bit loose, one more than the other.

Mouth tightening, Lisa set to work on the loosest of them and began to shift it slowly back and forth.

"There he goes," Richard murmured and Robert nodded as they watched the Findlay carriage ride out of the courtyard and head up the street.

"Smart," Daniel muttered. "Act natural, attend the night's ball and stick to his routine. Like you said, less likely to draw suspicion than his suddenly disappearing."

Robert nodded again, but didn't comment. He was using all his concentration to keep from leaping out of the hired hack they'd rented and charge the house shouting Lisa's name.

"Well, Findlay is a clever man, I'll give him that."

This time Robert managed to tear his eyes from the house across the street and glance to the speaker. Mr. Smithe was at the open window in the door behind them.

"What the hell are you doing here?" Robert growled, leaning to open the door and urge the man inside. "You're supposed to be on your way to Gretna Green to be sure they weren't headed there."

"I sent two of my men instead. A wasted trip as it turns out, since Findlay is still here. No doubt the girl is too," Smithe said calmly as he closed the door and settled on the bench seat beside Richard. Robert himself was kneeling on the floor to look out the window, while Daniel sat on the bench opposite Richard.

Robert scowled, but didn't point out that it might have been otherwise.

"Besides, I was about to leave when I recalled a certain light skirt who caters to men of Findlay's ilk. She don't mind it rough. Knows how to handle herself and them," he explained. "I thought it might be helpful if I asked her a couple questions. Turns out it was a good instinct. I got some information that might be useful."

"Tell me," Robert ordered.

"She says not to bother with the upper floors if you go in looking for the girl. All is kept normal as any other Lord's house in London on the main floor and the one above. She says it's the basement where he'll have the girl if she's here."

"The basement," Robert muttered, glancing back to the house.

"Yes, my lord," Mr. Smithe said solemnly. "It seems he has himself a right little torture chamber in his basement. Likes to lock the girls up in a room down there where they can see all his toys. She said he'd most likely leave her there and attend whatever ball or event was taking place tonight. As he obviously has," Smithe added dryly, glancing in the direction the carriage had taken. He turned back and added, "She says it allows the girls to get a real good scare growing in their belly at what's to come when he returns. And he likes them scared."

Robert's mouth tightened at the idea of Lisa being locked in somewhere, staring at Findlay's choice of torture tools, terrified and dreading what would come when the ball ended and he returned.

"She also said, don't expect no help from the servants or anyone else you encounter inside. They all know what's what and either turn a blind eye, or actively participate."

"Participate?" Robert asked sharply.

Smithe nodded. "Findlay lets some of his pet servants have a go at the girls on occasion. Either whipping them or . . . well, the other. Sometimes both."

A low growl slid from Robert's lips at this news and he turned a glowering look on the house. He would kill the bastard and his servants if any of them had laid a hand on her. Hell, he thought he would probably kill Findlay anyway on principle alone. The man was an animal.

"Did she say anything about what kind of locks we might encounter, or the best route to take to get to the basement?" Richard asked into the silence.

"Back door, she said," Smithe answered. "Through the courtyard and around the house. The door to the basement is in the kitchens. But she said the kitchens are always busy. It won't be easy to slip in."

"We'll need a distraction then," Daniel said grimly.

"Yes we will, and I have an idea about that," Smithe responded.

All three men turned to him at that comment. It was Robert who asked, "What idea is that?"

Smithe hesitated and then said, "Well, now, I'm thinking you men won't like it none. But I'm deuced sure it will work."

"What will work?" Robert asked impatiently.

Smithe pursed his lips and then said, "It seems to me the only thing that goes in and out of that basement is women."

"Women?" Daniel asked blankly.

"Yes sir. On a regular basis too. That gal I told you about said that Findlay not only sometimes shares women with his men, but that sometimes he surprises them with a couple just for them. Keeps them happy and less likely to go squawking to anyone about what Lord Findlay gets up to," Smithe said dryly. "And I'm thinking with a lady in there, he might send his men a couple of gals to keep them from getting any ideas about playing with his new toy before he does."

"Miss Madison is not a toy," Robert said with cold fury.

"Beggin' your pardon, my lord. But she is to Findlay."

"Are you suggesting we hire a couple of prostitutes to distract Findlay's men so

Robert, Daniel and I can slip in and get Lisa out?" Richard asked slowly.

"We could do that," Smithe said. "But you risk one of them speaking up later and raising a scandal for Miss Madison and the rest of you. It might be easier and safer all around just to enlist the aid of your wives."

"Our wives could never play prostitutes," Richard said firmly. "Besides, we sent them on to the ball and said we would meet them there later. They do not even know that Lisa is missing. We told them she and Robert were out discussing their future."

"Hmm." Smithe nodded. "And yet there they sit in the Radnor carriage not two carriage lengths behind you, watching the house as steady and grim as you three."

"What?" Richard asked with shock.

"Didn't notice them, huh?" Smithe asked mildly. "Well, don't feel bad. You were no doubt focusing on the house. Besides I'm trained to notice the little things, like great huge coaches with noble crests."

Daniel cursed and was out of the hired coach in a heartbeat with Richard right behind him.

"May as well follow them," Smithe suggested easily to Robert. "Bigger coach anyway and we need the women's help."

Nodding, Robert followed the other two

men with Smithe on his heels.

"What the devil are you doing here?" Richard was asking when Robert stepped up into the coach and claimed the bit of space remaining on the bench beside the couple.

"She is our sister, Richard," Christiana reminded him quietly. "Where else would we be?"

"But how did you even know —"

"How do you think we knew?" Suzette asked with exasperation from the opposite bench. "Bet was worried sick and listened at the door when Harry brought the hack driver back to the house. She heard everything and told us."

"Of course," Daniel muttered.

"Yes, of course. She is a loyal girl who doesn't try to keep secrets. So *of course* she told us *what our husbands should have,*" Suzette stressed accusingly.

"It wasn't my secret to tell," Daniel said quickly, and Suzette's eyes narrowed.

"Now where have I heard that old song before?" she asked dryly.

"We didn't want to worry you," he amended. "We planned to get Lisa back and then tell you so you wouldn't fret."

"Or try to be involved," she guessed dryly.

"Well, as to that," Smithe put in, drawing

everyone's eyes to where he had settled on the bench with Suzette and Daniel. "I was just saying to the men that we need your ladies' help to get Lisa out."

"Anything," Christiana said at once.

"They are not dressing up as light skirts and distracting the men," Richard said firmly. "We shall have to think of another distraction."

"Light skirts?" Christiana and Suzette asked together with interest.

CHAPTER SEVENTEEN

Lisa shifted uncomfortably on the small cot with the lumpy mattress. Lumpy because she'd removed some of the straw and done a hurried and ineffective job of redistributing what remained in the filthy skin. She had no intention of taking the time to better fix it, but it was damned uncomfortable, she acknowledged and shifted onto her side facing the wall. Her hand tightened on the bed leg she held, and she moved it close to her body. She'd tucked it under her skirts by her leg while on her back. It was just as well hidden now, she hoped.

With nothing else to do, Lisa had decided she should try to rest and relax a bit to garner some energy for when Findlay returned. She would need all her strength and energy then, but not for what Findlay intended. Lisa wanted to be strong and ready to bash him viciously about the head with her weapon. He thought himself so clever. She would wipe that smug smirk off his face.

The sound of a door clicking shut reached her ears, faint and far away by her guess. It might even be upstairs. She had already noted that something about the stone walls and open area seemed to distort sound somewhat. A couple of times, she'd thought someone was moving around in the open area, only to find it empty and realize that the footsteps or movement must have been upstairs, echoing down to her somehow.

When no sound followed the soft click, Lisa forced herself to relax. He was not back yet.

A moment later a sudden high trilling laugh drifted to her through the bars. Lisa stilled in the bed again, her ears straining. It had sounded like a woman, and now she could hear footsteps, several sets of feet tapping down the wooden stairs in the open area, she guessed. Another peal of laughter and the murmur of voices, both men's and women's sounded, verifying that, and Lisa gripped her bed leg nervously, not sure what was happening.

Had Findlay returned, bringing more victims? She bit her lip and listened, frowning at the sudden violent sounds that erupted. Thuds, flesh hitting flesh and then gasps and a stifled female squeal of alarm and then a hushed silence.

Lisa was listening so hard for further sounds from the other room to try to sort out what was happening that she almost missed the quiet sounds at her cell door. She had just become conscious of them when the door opened with a faint squeal of rusty metal.

Lisa's heart immediately leapt into her throat. Charles Findlay was back and coming for her. Her hand tightened on her bed leg, nails digging into the wood, but she waited, listening tensely to the soft sound of footsteps moving toward the bed. Lisa didn't move until she felt a hand on her shoulder. Whirling then, she swung her weapon with all her might for where she expected Findlay's head to be.

The bed leg with its nasty nails was already swinging up when she recognized Robert. Crying out with alarm she tried to stop her blow, but the best she could do was change the angle enough that she didn't plant the leg with its nails in his eye as she'd intended. Instead it glanced off the side of his head, making him leap back with a pained shout.

"Robert," she gasped, dropping the make-shift weapon and leaping off the bed to hurry to him as he dropped to his knees. "Oh God, I'm sorry! I thought you were Findlay. Are you all right?"

The answer was a groan, and Lisa frowned as she knelt beside him and tried to get a look at his head. However, his hand was covering the wound, and while she wanted to know how badly she'd injured him, she could only think that her not being able to see it was a good thing. While she was worried about the damage she'd done, she did have a tendency to go faint when presented with blood. It was probably better she didn't actually see the wound until they were safely away.

"What happened?"

Lisa glanced up from Robert to see Daniel standing in the open cell door, a frown on his face as he took in the situation. Apparently Robert hadn't come alone to rescue her, she realized. Although she hadn't a clue how they'd even known where to look for her. Putting that aside for now, she said unhappily, "I thought he was Findlay and hit him with the bed leg."

"The bed leg?" Daniel asked, his eyes sliding to the bed against the wall.

"I stuffed my petticoats with straw from the mattress and jammed it under the bed to take the place of the leg I removed," she explained wearily.

"Clever," Daniel commented, glancing over his shoulder to the room behind him and then back. "Can you walk, Robert? We should get out of here. There is a house full of servants upstairs. If one of them comes down for any reason, they could bring all of them down on us."

Robert grunted and struggled to get up. Lisa immediately moved to help, dragging his arm across her shoulders to help support his weight. When they staggered to the door, Daniel backed out to allow them to pass. His gaze dropped over her as he did and he asked quietly, "Are you all right, Lisa? Findlay didn't . . ."

"I'm fine," she assured him when he hesitated. "Findlay intended to start his fun after the ball tonight. The plan was for him to attend the ball, act the distraught fiancé, and then return to make me distraught," she said dryly.

Daniel's mouth tightened at the words and then he smiled crookedly. "Well, from the looks of it, he would have had a surprise waiting. It's almost a shame we weren't late enough for you to have koshed him a time or two first."

"While I would be delighted to kosh him a time or two. I am grateful to be getting out of here," Lisa assured him as she helped Robert across the open area. Her gaze slid around the room as she went, noting Richard and two light skirts standing by the stairs, watching over the unconscious bodies of a couple of Findlay's men.

"Lisa!" the dark-haired one cried in a loud whisper.

Lisa came to a halt, forcing Robert to one as well and watched wide-eyed as the dark-haired light skirt spotted her and rushed toward them. Her eyes widened incredulously when the woman hugged her, nearly knocking Robert to the ground in her eagerness. Lisa glanced to Daniel with bewilderment, silently asking who the hell the woman was.

"Suzette looks magnificent, doesn't she?" Daniel asked with a grin and she turned her gaze sharply to the woman, but all she could see was the side of her head from her embrace. And then her gaze slid to the blonde approaching at a more dignified walk with Richard following, trying to drape his jacket over her, and Lisa's eyes nearly fell out of her head as she recognized Christiana.

"Dear God," she muttered, amazed at just how well her sisters could pass for prostitutes. Good Lord, it was rather shocking really. It made her think that if they took a light skirt off the street and dressed her proper, she could pass for a lady. The concept was one she had never contemplated. Lisa had always thought there was something different about such women, that they would be recognized for what they were no matter their dress or surroundings. But if Suzette and Christiana could pass for light skirts so easily . . . well, perhaps there wasn't really that much difference between ladies and light skirts except for circumstance.

"Thank God you are all right," Christiana murmured, hugging both her and Suzette at once.

"Why are you dressed like this?" Lisa asked uncertainly, and then paused to glance worriedly at Robert as he groaned and leaned more heavily against her.

"What the devil is taking you people so long?" a deep voice hissed.

Lisa glanced toward the top of the stairs to see a tall fellow with salt-and-pepper hair glaring down at them from the open door. He looked vaguely familiar, but it took her a moment to recognize him as the man Robert had met with several days ago.

"We are coming now, Mr. Smithe," Richard assured him quietly and then caught

Christiana and Suzette's arms and urged them toward the stairs, before turning to Lisa. "Why do you not let Daniel and I help Robert up the stairs? It will go faster."

She hesitated, but then gave up her position under Robert's arm and stepped away to allow the two men to take up position on either side of the injured man. Once assured they had him, she turned to follow Christiana and Suzette past the unconscious men on the floor. Lisa managed to keep walking and refrain from stopping to kick the big beefy one she recognized as the fellow who had dragged her out of the carriage and nearly smothered her to death before dumping her in the cell. If looks could kill, however, she doubted he'd be waking up from his enforced sleep.

Lisa hurried quickly and quietly up the stairs behind her sisters, with the men bringing up the rear. At the top, they stepped into the kitchens she'd been dragged through on arriving.

An aproned woman sat at the table, apparently asleep. Or perhaps unconscious. The tall thin man who had urged them to hurry was there as well, and stood by a door leading to the rest of the house. He glanced around at their arrival and waved them on toward the outer door, then continued his vigil in presumably watching for approaching servants. Now that they were off the narrow stairs, Christiana and Suzette each grabbed one of Lisa's arms and scampered out of the house, pulling her with them as if afraid she might dally.

Not bloody likely, Lisa thought grimly. She couldn't get out of there quickly enough for her liking.

A hired hack sat waiting in the courtyard behind the house when they hurried outside and her sisters led her to it, urging her in first before following. Lisa settled on one of the narrow benches, but sat forward anxiously to watch for Robert as her sisters climbed in. Suzette and Christiana both claimed the opposite bench seat, leaving just enough room beside Lisa for Robert to be set beside her once the men reached it.

"What about you men?" Lisa heard Christiana ask with concern as she leaned forward to peer into Robert's dazed face. Apparently, she had really nailed him with the bed leg. It was a darned good thing that she'd recognized him and offset her blow or he might be dead. A shame it hadn't been Findlay though, she thought, as Richard assured her sister that they would follow in the Radnor carriage.

He then slammed the carriage door. Both

Suzette and Christiana peered anxiously out the window at their husbands as the vehicle began to move. A moment later, Suzette sagged back against the squabs with a sigh and announced, "They got to the carriage without anyone stopping them. So did Mr. Smithe."

"Good," Lisa murmured, assuming Mr. Smithe was the tall man with salt-and-pepper hair. She glanced to Christiana as her older sister relaxed as well, and managed a smile for the two women before glancing to Robert again.

His eyes were closed. He appeared asleep and his hand was no longer covering his head, but fortunately, his head was pressed against her shoulder, hiding the wound and the blood that was no doubt there. Letting out her breath, she glanced back to her sisters and took in their outfits. "Why are you dressed like that?"

"We had to distract Findlay's servants so the men could slip into the house," Suzette said with a grin.

"Distract them? Really?" Lisa asked with amazement, wondering what that had consisted of. Although she supposed so much cleavage on display would have been distracting on its own with most men.

"Yes, and gad, it was fun," Suzette said on

a laugh, and then wrinkled her nose. "Well, mostly it was. Wasn't too keen when the one fellow pinched me as we were heading down the stairs."

"Daniel didn't appreciate it much either," Christiana said dryly. "I swear he put a little more vigor into knocking out the fellow than was strictly necessary once we got downstairs where he and Richard were waiting."

Suzette grinned again. "And he kicked him something fierce between the legs as he went down too," she said on a laugh.

Christiana shook her head and glanced to Lisa. "She always was the more violent-natured of the three of us."

Lisa smiled faintly, but then said, "Thank you . . . for helping save me."

Christiana got all misty-eyed at once and leaned forward to squeeze her hand. "We could do nothing else. And you would have done the same for us."

"Aye," she said simply and turned her hand over to squeeze her back. "How did you sort out where I was?"

Christiana quickly explained the events that had led to her rescue. Lisa listened silently, and when she finished, asked, "What will they do about Findlay?"

Suzette and Christiana exchanged a

glance. It was Suzette who sighed and said, "I am not sure they can do anything, Lisa. At least not without dragging you into scandal."

"So he just gets away with everything?" she asked with a scowl.

"I don't know," Christiana said unhappily. "I hope not, but we shall have to wait and see what the men come up with to handle him. I doubt they will just let him get away with it unless absolutely necessary. They have to think of you too, Lisa."

She grimaced with displeasure at this, but then the carriage slowed and stopped and she glanced out the window to see they were home. Lisa was just wondering how they were to get the unconscious Robert inside, when the carriage door opened and Richard peered in. The Radnor carriage had obviously followed very closely, or had overtaken them at some point and arrived first for him to be there that quickly.

Lisa and her sisters got out and waited at the side of the carriage while Daniel got in to hand Robert down to Richard. The women then followed as the men carried him into the house. They took him straight to his room upstairs, but when Lisa started to move to the bed once he was laid out on it, Suzette caught her arm and urged her away.

"Blood," she said simply for explanation when Lisa frowned at her.

Lisa shoulders immediately drooped with defeat and she allowed herself to be urged to the window of Robert's room while Christiana tended to him. She stared silently out the window as she waited for him to be cleaned up enough that she could see him without fainting.

She and Suzette were silent as they waited, each of them casting the occasional glance toward the trio crowded around Robert's bed as Christiana cleaned the wound and did whatever else needed doing. It seemed to take a long time, but Lisa suspected that was because she was waiting, and then Christiana straightened and said something to the men before moving to join them by the window.

"How is he?" Lisa asked with concern.

"He's got a cut and a bit of a knot on the side of his head, but I think he'll be all right," Christiana said quietly.

Lisa stared at her silently, recognizing the worry in her eyes. "He's unconscious."

"Yes," she said with a sigh. "And that's worrisome. But I really do think he'll be okay, Lisa. I doubt he has eaten anything all day, and he was under a great deal of stress fretting over you. That may have just exacerbated the situation and weakened him. I'm sure he'll wake up soon." Christiana hesitated and then said, "Why do you not go lie down for a bit? You had a long rough day as well. I will come get you when he regains consciousness."

Lisa hesitated, but then nodded and turned to head for the door. It *had* been a long day. Very stressful, really. First the hack driver had abandoned her to the mercies of the men on the street, and then Findlay had shown his true colors and taken delight in scaring her silly about his plans for her. She was very tired, Lisa acknowledged to herself as she slipped from Robert's room and crossed the hall to her own.

It was only as she reached for the door to her room that Lisa wondered where Bet was. According to her sisters it was the maid who had revealed what the men were keeping from them, that Findlay had paid the hack driver to abandon her and the men suspected it had been so that he could take her away. She would have expected the maid to be waiting anxiously to see if Lisa was rescued. However, there had been no sign of the girl since their return.

Releasing the doorknob, Lisa turned and

headed up the hall instead of entering her room. She then hurried lightly down to the ground floor and moved quickly up the hall to the door to the kitchen. She found Cook and a couple of other servants seated at a table there, chattering quietly. They all paused and glanced her way as she opened the door, and each offered a relieved smile and a comment regarding being glad to see her there healthy and well. Lisa wasn't surprised. She had no doubt they knew what had happened, or at least a good portion of it. It was simply impossible to keep secrets from servants.

She murmured a quiet thank-you and then asked after Bet, only to be told she'd gone up to Lisa's room to await her return. If she hadn't made an appearance yet, she'd probably fallen asleep waiting, was the overriding belief. Smiling, Lisa nodded and thanked them, then left them to their relaxation. She entered her room a couple moments later and glanced around as she closed the door behind her, expecting to find Bet nodding off in a chair there . . . and she did find Bet in a chair. She wasn't asleep, however. She was wide awake, wide-eyed, and bound and gagged in the chair she sat in.

Lisa stilled at once, and then following

the direction of her maid's glance, whirled instinctively back to the door. Findlay stood, leaning against the wall beside the door, arms and ankles crossed in a relaxed pose and smiling widely.

"You are lucky I am a patient man, Lisa, else I would surely punish you for making me wait so long for your return," he commented with a smile. Then he straightened and moved toward her, saying, "Of course, I suppose I can hardly blame you. The men appear to have taken their time in bringing you back. Dare I hope they ran into trouble with my men? I did notice that Langley had to be carried in."

Lisa opened her mouth to scream for help, but Findlay was fast. Before a sound could slip from her lips, he was on her, covering her mouth with one hand, and pulling her tight up against his chest with the other at the back of her neck. Lisa grabbed at his arms to keep her balance in the awkward position and had to hold on to stay on her feet.

"I spotted the Radnor carriage sitting on my street as I headed out for the ball. It seemed obvious to me that I hadn't been as clever as I'd thought and help was on the way," he whispered, urging her backward. "I debated what to do. Return to the house and warn the servants to prepare for all-out battle? Or flee for the Continent?

"However, then it occurred to me that there was no real need to flee for the Continent. They weren't likely to call in the authorities. After all, that would damage your reputation. It made me realize I had another option. I could come here. They would rescue you, bring you back here and relax a bit thinking you were safe in the bosom of your family, and then I could take you away right from under their noses. It would mean at least one whole night's head start to drag you to Gretna Green and force you into marriage before they even knew you were missing."

Lisa glared at him over the hand he had over her mouth.

"I know, I know," he said with a shake of the head. "It means having to bypass all those lovely little pleasures I'd thought we might enjoy tonight. But we can still enjoy them after the wedding."

Lisa felt the window ledge press against the backs of her legs and tried to glance around, but he was holding her head still with the hand over her mouth. Pinning her against the window ledge with his hips, he removed the arm from around her and dragged something out of his pocket. In the next moment he'd shoved a balled-up cloth of some sort into her mouth. Lisa instinctively lifted her hands to remove it, but found her wrists immediately clasped in his hands and dragged behind her back. Holding them there with one hand, he then retrieved another strip of cloth from his pocket and quickly bound her wrists.

While he was distracted with tying her hands, Lisa tried to work the gag out of her mouth. All it would take was one good shout and help would be there in an instant. She almost managed it, but just as Lisa was about to spit the last of it out and give that shout, Charles finished with her hands and returned his attention to her gag, pushing it back into her mouth to the point where she thought she might choke on it. He then produced another strip of cloth and placed it over her mouth, forcing it between her lips and then tying it around behind her head.

"Now," he said pleasantly once he'd finished. "This is going to be tricky, but we are going out the window and down the tree. You, of course, don't have your hands to help you so will have to depend on me to keep you from falling. I will keep you safe . . . unless you try to escape. If you try to escape, I will let you fall. Do we understand each other?"

When Lisa hesitated, he squeezed her bound wrists together painfully. "Do we understand each other?"

She nodded abruptly.

"Good." Charles smiled.

Lisa eyed him warily, and then gasped into her gag when he suddenly turned her to face the window.

"Here we go," he murmured by her ear.

CHAPTER EIGHTEEN

It was the constant, unbearable pounding in his head that roused Robert. Groaning, he opened his eyes and blinked when he found himself peering into Lisa's blurry face, her hair a golden halo around her head. He didn't even think, just reached for her and began to drag her down, intent on kissing her silly in his relief that she was all right.

"Robert, if you don't unhand my wife I will be very annoyed. I may even forget you are suffering a head wound, and give you another."

"Richard?" he said uncertainly, freezing at the words even as he recognized the voice. Releasing who he realized must be Christiana, Robert glanced about and immediately spotted the man approaching the bed from the general direction of the window where Daniel now stood next to Suzette, grinning with amusement.

Sighing, he glanced back to Christiana,

able to see her more clearly as his vision improved.

"Sorry, Chrissy," he muttered with chagrin. "I thought you were —"

"Lisa," she finished for him with an amused smile. "I sorted that out pretty quickly."

Grunting, he glanced around the room again, but Lisa didn't suddenly appear and rush forward to apologize for knocking him silly when all he'd been doing was rescuing her.

"I sent her to lie down," Christiana said quietly, guessing who he was looking for. "She had a stressful day. Besides, you know how she reacts to the sight of blood."

"Oh, yes," Robert said with a grimace. Lisa probably would have fainted and then would have been lying in bed next to him. Not such a bad outcome, he thought wryly. At least that way he wouldn't have to go look for her.

"Oh, Robert, just lie still and rest," Christiana admonished when he sat up with a wince and swung his legs off the bed. "You took a good hit. Rest and recover."

"I have to talk to her," he said quietly, relieved to find that sitting up didn't make his head hurt any worse. It even seemed to ease it somewhat and clear his thoughts and vision quite a bit. Strange.

"But —" Christiana began, pausing when Richard caught her hand.

"Let him go. It's best if they sort this out," he said solemnly.

Sighing, she nodded and made no further protests. She merely watched worriedly as he stood up.

Robert didn't know who was more relieved when he didn't sway on his feet, him or Christiana, but he offered the woman a reassuring smile. "I think I'm well enough. Other than the headache I feel okay. Lisa has one hell of swing though," he added wryly.

"That could come in handy what with the way she gets herself into trouble," Daniel said with amusement, leading Suzette closer to the bed.

Robert smiled at the words and headed for the door, moving a little slowly at first just to be sure he wasn't suddenly taken dizzy and made to fall flat on his face.

"Good luck with her," Daniel said and then teased, "Shout if she takes another swing at you . . . I wouldn't want to miss that."

"Ha ha," Robert muttered, but he was smiling. He knew Lisa hadn't deliberately hit him. He supposed he should have spoken up before touching her shoulder. It would have saved him a headache.

Robert almost shook his head at his own thoughts, but caught himself before he did. The pain in his head was easing a little with every step, but he suspected shaking it about might bring the aching on again.

Robert crossed the hall to Lisa's door and then paused briefly, unsure what he was going to say. There was a lot to tell her, but he wanted to get it out right. This was important. After aligning his thoughts in his head, he took a deep breath and tapped lightly at the door.

No one had said how long ago it was that Lisa had come to lie down. It hadn't even occurred to him that she might already be sleeping, but the silence that met his knock made him frown and consider that she was. Robert hesitated, shifting his feet briefly, and then turned reluctantly away. If she was sleeping, he supposed he'd have to wait until tomorrow. He'd rather not, but she would hardly be receptive to anything he had to say if she was grumpy from being woken up, he supposed. However, he'd only taken one step away from the door when a crash sounded in the room behind him.

Whirling, Robert didn't even hesitate, but opened the door and rushed in, then paused and stared in amazement at Bet, who lay on her side on the floor, apparently tied to a chair. That had been the crash, he realized as he rushed to help her. She'd toppled her chair with herself in it, probably to get whoever had knocked to come in.

"Findlay," Bet gasped the moment Robert knelt and removed the gag from her mouth. She jerked her head toward the window, gasping, "He took her."

Robert glanced to the window as he straightened, but didn't even run to it to check and see how far Findlay had got with Lisa. He'd made that mistake the night she was attacked in here, trying to climb quickly down after her attacker, who'd had a head start. This time he would be smarter.

Turning on his heel, he charged out of the room, nearly knocking down Daniel who had stepped into the hall with Suzette.

"Help Bet," Robert shouted as he charged up the hall to the landing. He didn't wait to see if Daniel listened, but hurried downstairs and yanked open the front door. It had been the right choice. He hurried out the front door and rushed to the corner in time to see Findlay come around the back of the house with Lisa over his shoulder, her head hanging down his back and his arm across the backs of her thighs, just below her bottom. Both men froze at once, eyeing each other warily.

"Let her go, Findlay," Robert said grimly.

"Robert?" Lisa rose up on Findlay's shoulder, trying to peer behind her to where he stood, and Robert saw that a dislodged gag hung around her neck and her hands were bound behind her back. She was using only her stomach muscles to raise herself and twist but it wasn't enough and she sagged back down his back. Her voice was strong and nattering though when she said, "You shouldn't be out of bed. Go get Richard or Daniel and let them handle this."

Robert rolled his eyes at the order. The woman was bound and being carried off and thought he should run and get someone else to handle this? Madness, he thought with a shake of the head.

"I suggest you get out of my way, Langley," Charles said pleasantly, drawing his attention back to the man to see that he'd withdrawn a pistol from somewhere on his person and was holding it pointed at him. "Otherwise this could get messy."

Robert eyed the gun, his body tightening for action, but raised his hands and backed up several feet.

Findlay immediately started forward with his burden.

"I really have to insist that you release my sister-in-law, Findlay. Or things will get messier than you planned."

Robert and Charles both glanced to the side to see that Richard had followed and now stood to the side, a gun of his own in hand and aimed at the man presently holding Lisa.

"You wouldn't shoot me, you might hit Lisa," Findlay said confidently.

"Shoot him! I don't care if you hit me. He's just going to torture me anyway." Lisa cried, and then added fretfully, "Just try not to hit me in the bottom, please Richard. The leg would be better for sitting and lying down while I recover."

Robert rolled his eyes, and then started forward. He was not allowing Findlay to get away with her, nor was he allowing Lisa to get shot.

"Back, Langley," Charles said, his hand tightening on the pistol as he lost some of his aplomb for the first time during this encounter. "I *will* shoot."

"I wouldn't suggest you do, Findlay," Daniel growled from behind him as he came around the house.

Charles turned sideways to glance to him while trying to keep Richard and Robert in his view too. He hesitated for a moment and then cursed and suddenly charged toward Robert. Just when Robert thought the man was going to try to charge right over him, Findlay suddenly hefted Lisa off his shoulder and threw her at him like a sack of potatoes.

Robert instinctively lunged to catch Lisa, barely noticing that Findlay had dodged around him and was running for the road.

"Are you all right?" Robert asked, easing Lisa to her feet and peering at her worriedly. He waited long enough to see her nod, and then urged her toward an approaching Daniel and turned to charge after Findlay.

The man was almost to the road when Robert set out. Furious at the thought that the bastard would get away, he bellowed his name. It was enough to make Findlay look over his shoulder as he ran, a deadly mistake. He was just feet in front of his carriage, and stumbled as he glanced back. It made him stagger and then fall directly in front of his own horses. That might not have been much of a problem had he not been carrying his pistol. The weapon went off as he hit the ground and the stray bullet hit one of his horses. Both of the beasts whinnied in terror and reared, hooves pawing the air wildly before they came slamming down . . . on Findlay.

Robert winced and slowed to a stop as the terrified animals trampled the man and then charged forward, running him down despite the coachman's shouts and efforts to control them.

"Do you think the horse is all right?" Lisa asked, drawing his attention to the fact that she, Daniel and Richard had reached him.

Robert gave a short laugh at the question. He supposed it said exactly what Lisa thought of Findlay that she was more concerned for the horse racing off down the street with the other horse and the carriage than she was with the man lying bleeding in the street.

"I'll check Findlay," Richard said quietly, moving past Robert to head for the man's twisted body.

The comment seemed to draw Lisa's attention to Charles and she glanced to him now, apparently for the first time. At least that's what Robert decided when she suddenly paled at the sight of the blood quickly pooling around the man.

"Oh dear," she murmured and began to sway, and then her legs seemed to give out and she started to sink to the ground. Robert caught her before she fell, scooping her into his arms with a grunt.

"Take her in. We'll see to Findlay," Daniel

401

said quietly.

"Nothing to see to," Richard announced grimly, straightening from kneeling to examine the body. "He won't be bothering anyone anymore."

"Good," Robert muttered. "Where is Smithe?"

"We sent him home in the Radnor carriage when we got here," Daniel answered. "I'll send for him. He can handle matters here."

Robert nodded and turned to carry Lisa into the house. Christiana and Suzette were rushing down the stairs with Bet on their heels when he entered and he took a moment to reassure them that Lisa was fine, that she'd just fainted after seeing the blood from Findlay's body staining the street. He then assured them that Richard and Daniel were fine as well and were outside. Leaving the women to hurry outside to see for themselves, he then carried Lisa upstairs. Robert had intended to take her to her room, but aware that Bet was following and determined to get a few moments alone with Lisa when she woke up so that he could tell her about the epiphany he'd had and ask her to marry him, he turned into his room instead and kicked the door closed behind him. It was a silent but effective message. At least, Bet didn't knock at the door or otherwise try to interfere.

Glad she didn't, Robert carried Lisa to the bed and set her on it. He then peered down at her silently for a moment before turning to pace to the window and peer out while he waited for her to stir.

CHAPTER NINETEEN

Lisa woke up slowly to find herself lying in a strange bed. It only took a moment to recognize that she was in Robert's room. A heartbeat later she spotted the man himself standing at the window, peering out into the darkness. He looked so heartbreakingly beautiful standing there in silhouette that for a minute she simply lay staring at him.

The man had saved her four times now, risking himself and taking damage three of the four times. Only this last time had he escaped uninjured, and that was pure luck. Charles could easily have shot him as not, out there in the yard. Robert had been chasing her around for days, trying to keep her safe, and got hurt doing it. He loved her, she was sure of it. Perhaps he thought he loved her only as a friend or a little sister, but the passion he poured over her when they were together was not that of a friend or a big brother. And what was love if not friendship, passion and trust?

Trust was the missing ingredient. But she also knew he wouldn't be able to give that trust to another woman either. Perhaps two out of three of the ingredients was good enough to start, she thought solemnly. Perhaps he would learn to trust her with time. Lisa hoped so, because she very much feared she was going to marry the stupid man anyway. She just couldn't help it. She liked him, she loved him, she wanted him and she trusted him . . . with her life. She would marry him without having gained his trust if necessary, but couldn't resist making one more attempt to gain it.

"Robert."

Robert glanced around. Spotting Lisa sitting up in bed, he smiled and crossed the room toward her. Settling on the side of the bed, he brushed the hair back from her face and asked, "How are you feeling?"

"I feel fine. I am not the problem," she informed him grimly. "You are."

"I am?" he asked with amusement, thinking she looked adorable with the militant expression that presently graced her face.

"Yes, Robert, you are," she said firmly. "Whether you will admit it or not, you love me. I was made for you. And while you are apparently too stubborn and stupid to see that, I can see it, and I am —"

"I love you," he interrupted quietly, and Lisa paused and blinked in surprise.

"You do?" she asked uncertainly and the question brought an amused quirk to his lips.

"Lisa, in the last few days I've completely given up my own life to protect yours. I've twisted my ankle and been stabbed trying to protect you, not to mention knocked out by you in my efforts. If that's not love, I don't know what the hell it is."

"Oh," Lisa breathed, eyes wide, and then she frowned. "But what about trust, Robert? Love includes trust and —"

"I trust you," Robert said solemnly, which brought a dubious expression to her face. Sighing, he took her hands in his and squeezed them briefly before saying, "I was trying to tell you this earlier today before Smithe's arrival interrupted us. Richard and I had a talk last night. He made me realize that my father was nothing more than a bitter woman hater. That he distrusted and suspected, accused and even punished my mother unjustly for adulterous behavior for years before she even looked at another man. In effect, I think he drove her into the comforting arms of another man with his cruel and hateful behavior.

"But she only started up with one man, Gower, and she only did that after her marriage to my father was as good as dead. If it weren't for the scandal I think she would have divorced my father. As it was, they were living apart, leading separate lives, when she took up with Gower. It made me wonder if the same thing didn't happen with my grandfather and his father before him," he admitted solemnly and then grimaced.

"Once I looked at the situation, I realized that the Langley men aren't so much cursed with adulterous wives as cursed with a sour and suspicious disposition that may have driven their women from them." He let that sink in for a moment and then added, "And were it not for my friendship with you and your sisters I may very well have grown up just as suspicious and hateful toward women."

Robert squeezed her hands again. He admitted, "Even with the three of you to show me that all women are not lying, cheating adulteresses, I may still have been as paranoid and hateful to a wife — to you," he added solemnly, "as my father was to my mother . . . and I would have carried on this mythical Langley-men curse. But I was most fortunate," he said with a small smile.

"I had you and Suzette and Christiana in my life. The three of you are the cream of the crop when it comes to women, Lisa, and you are the best of the bunch in my eyes."

"I am?" she asked with wonder.

Robert nodded firmly, and then pointed out, "We enjoy each other's company, like reading together, have lively grand debates, prefer the same foods, love to dance, share the same values. And no other woman in my life has ever stirred the passion in me that you do.

"I do love you, Lisa Madison. I love your dreamy-eyed romanticism, your undaunted loyalty, your quirky sense of humor, your courage, your passion, your intelligence, and even your occasional naivety. I trust you with my heart, my name, and my very life. And while I can't promise that I will never have a single doubt, or that my father's ravings might not someday rise up to instill worry and fear in me, I can promise I shall try to nip it in the bud if and when that does happen, and that I definitely will not take it out on you."

"Oh," Lisa breathed.

Robert turned her hands over in his, contemplating them briefly and then met her gaze and added, "I hope that that promise is enough to encourage you to be my wife, Lisa. Because I do not think I could bear — no," he corrected himself grimly, "I *know* I could not bear a life without you in it as my friend, lover, wife and partner."

"Oh," Lisa repeated shakily and then suddenly snatched her hands away, leapt up and rushed from the room.

Robert stared after her nonplussed. He waited for a moment, and waited, his shock turning to confusion and then despair and finally anger. He had just poured his heart out to the woman and what had she done? Run off. What the hell?

Standing angrily, he hurried across the room and out into the hall. He'd expected to find her door closed and locked or something, but it was wide open. He suspected that meant she'd run downstairs, but glanced into the room anyway, just in case. He relaxed a bit when he spotted her seated at the small table in her room, writing quickly in a notebook, but not fully.

"Lisa," he began irritably.

"One moment, Robert. I am almost done," she murmured, continuing her writing.

Robert frowned and shifted his feet. He then asked impatiently, "Done what?"

Rather than answer, she glanced around

to ask, "What did you say after the part about loving my quirky sense of humor? Was it courage or passion?"

Robert's mouth dropped, and then he asked with amazement, "Are you writing down everything I said?"

"I am trying to, but I can't remember what came after my sense of humor," she said, sounding vexed.

He stared at her silently, the last of his tension slipping away. She hadn't run off because she was unwilling to marry him. She'd run off to write down what he'd said. He had no idea why she was writing it down, but that was more encouraging than just running away. Trying to remain patient, he said, "Lisa, I just bared my heart to you and asked you to be my wife. An answer would have been the more appropriate response."

"Oh." She blinked once, glanced back to her notebook and then stood to move in front of him and take his face in her hands. "Of course I shall marry you, Robert."

Relief rushing through him, he slid his arms around her waist and drew her forward into his embrace, but just as he started to lower his head intending to kiss her, she added, "Now that you have come to your senses and realize what a catch I am and that we were meant to be together, there is no reason not to."

Robert stilled, and then grimaced and said dryly, "Thank you."

"You're welcome," she said brightly and slipped from his arms to hurry back to her notebook. "Now what came after 'humor'?" Robert was scowling when she added, "I want to write it down so I never forget what you said." He was just relaxing, a smile curving his lips when she added, "I have long wanted to try my hand at writing and what you said was beautiful. I should like the hero in my tale to say exactly that to the heroine at the end."

"Dear God," Robert muttered, and gave up his patience to stride across the room, catch her by the hand and drag her out of her seat.

"Robert, I want to get down what you said," she protested as he dragged her to the bed. "I shall forget the last of it entirely if I do not write it down at once, and really it was the most touching and beautiful speech a girl could ask for."

"I am glad it pleased you," he said wryly, pausing beside the bed and bringing her in front of him and then turning her so her back was to him. Quickly undoing her gown, he added, "However, I cannot recall what it is exactly I said."

"You can't?" she asked with obvious disappointment as he finished with the gown and pushed it off her shoulders. The material drifted down like a feather to pool on the floor.

"Not precisely, no," he said, setting to work on her chemise next. "However, never fear, there is a lifetime of speeches like that in your future, my love."

"Oh, that's lovely too," she murmured, her words coming muffled under the material of her chemise as he lifted it up and off over her head. "Pray, try to remember that one for later, my lord. I would write it down as well."

"As you wish," he said with amusement, tossing the chemise aside. Lisa immediately turned to face him.

"You really do love me, don't you Robert?" she said with a shy smile.

"I really do," he assured her, slipping his arms around her and drawing her against his chest. "But you knew that, didn't you?"

"I thought so," she said quietly, and then admitted, "but there were times when I was sure I had been mistaken."

"You were not mistaken," he assured her, bending to press a kiss to her forehead. "You were absolutely right and I was just too stubborn and . . . er . . ."

"Stupid," she offered to aid his memory.

"Yes, that," he muttered. "I didn't see it."

"I'm glad your eyes are open now," she said with a happy smile.

"So am I, my love. So am I," he assured her, allowing those open eyes to roam all the lovely flesh he'd revealed. Then he bent to kiss her as his hands followed the same path his eyes had blazed. Lisa responded at once, pressing closer and slipping her arms around his neck with a little moan, and Robert saw something else with his open eyes; he saw a long, happy life with a marriage full of friendship, love, passion, children and trust. He was quite sure the Langley curse had finally been broken.

"Ah hem."

Robert stilled and then broke their kiss to glance around at that very loud and obvious throat clearing. Richard and Christiana stood in the door with Daniel and Suzette behind, he saw with confusion, and then glanced back to Lisa with surprise when she squealed and dropped to her haunches, trying to cover her nakedness.

Scowling at the embarrassing intrusion, Robert quickly grabbed his robe off the bed and knelt to help her into it. Once he had her properly covered up, he straightened and turned to scowl at the two couples. "What is the meaning of this?"

Four pairs of eyebrows shot up at the question and Robert was just realizing that his outrage may have been misplaced when Richard asked, "Shall I have the carriage readied for a trip to Gretna Green?"

"The alternate course is that you head back to your house and visit Lisa with someone present until we can arrange a wedding here in town," Christiana pointed out gently.

"She could be carrying your child even now," Suzette pointed out. "A quick trip to Scotland might be best."

"Besides, why break with a family tradition now," Daniel asked dryly. "We all made hasty trips to Gretna Green."

"We were married at Radnor," Christiana reminded Daniel quickly.

"Only by luck. The plan was for Gretna Green," Suzette pointed out at once.

"True," Christiana acknowledged.

All four people then turned back to peer at him in question.

Gretna Green or a long wait to be wed properly, Robert thought. And no doubt with the four of them ensuring that he and Lisa had absolutely no time alone together. The preferred option was obvious.

414

"You four get packing. I shall arrange the carriage," Robert said dryly.

"No need," Richard said with amusement. "We knew you'd come to your senses eventually. We have been packed for days."

"Christiana and I will help Lisa pack though, while you boys have the carriages readied and loaded," Suzette announced, bustling into the room to urge Lisa to her feet. She then glanced back to add, "We will need three, of course, for everyone. We cannot go without our maids."

"Damn," Robert muttered, mentally calculating how long it would take them to crawl to Gretna Green with three carriages stuffed full of them, their servants, and their luggage. It would be a couple days before he got to finish what he'd just tried to start with Lisa.

"Cheer up," Daniel said, slapping him on the back with amusement. "You're about to join the ranks of the soldiers in matrimonial hell."

Robert smiled wryly. "There is that."

"Welcome to the family," Richard said, as he and Daniel urged him toward the door. "It's official now. Instead of being a pseudo brother to Suzette and Christiana you will be a brother-in-law to them . . . but not to Lisa," he pointed out.

"No, never to Lisa," Robert agreed solemnly as they stepped out of the room.

CHAPTER TWENTY

"I am going up there," Robert said grimly, heading for the parlor door.

"I would not suggest it," Richard said quietly, standing to place his son against his shoulder and rub the crying three-month-old's back soothingly. "The women will not welcome you, and Lisa will not be happy to see you."

"Hmm," Daniel said with amusement. "Do you not recall what happened when Richard went up while Christiana was in labor?"

The words made Robert pause. He did recall. Christiana had cursed her husband, and thrown the first thing she could find at him, ranting about putting her through "this hell" before screaming in agony as another contraction had hit her. Richard had come away with a bloody nose from being hit in the face with the book Christiana had wheeled at him.

"About now Lisa is probably cursing all men to hell, but most especially you for getting her into this predicament," Richard pointed out in almost a whisper as his son, Richard Junior, began to nod off to sleep.

"Well, I hardly did it alone. She participated," Robert muttered, but turned back and resumed his pacing of the small parlor at Madison Manor.

Daniel chuckled at his disgruntled expression and walked to the front window to peer out. Probably checking on his two-year-old son, Christopher, Robert supposed, knowing the child's nurse had taken the boy out front for some fresh air. Daniel did dote on his son. As much as Richard doted on his own and they all doted on their wives. But then they were women well worth doting on, Robert thought, marveling over the fact that he actually felt that way about a wife. His Lisa. It was all due to her. Any other woman would have run off with Pembroke or Tibald or one of the other suitors who had tried to claim her attention when he was acting a complete idiot and refusing to acknowledge his feelings for her. Not Lisa though. She had heart, tenacity and was fiercely loyal.

That was so obvious now, that nearly three years on, he couldn't believe he'd been so stupid. This time with Lisa had been the happiest of his life to date. Oh, they had the occasional spat, the odd falling-out, and Lisa could try his patience at times as much as he tried hers, but all in all, life was good. Better than good. The Langley curse had well and truly been broken.

While Robert had suffered one or two bouts of jealousy and worry when other men had paid more attention to his wife than he liked, Lisa had always seemed to sense his feelings and had found some way to reassure him that she loved him as much today as she always had, and those moments had passed. He doubted any other woman would have been quite as sensitive and understanding, but Lisa knew him better than anyone else. Sometimes she even seemed to understand him better than he knew himself, Robert thought wryly. He was a lucky man indeed.

"My lord?"

Robert glanced around at Bet's voice, worry claiming him as he raised his eyebrows in question. "Yes?"

"You can go up now," Bet said and then quickly hurried away before he could ask if Lisa was all right or if it was a boy or girl.

Swallowing, he headed for the door at once, aware that Richard and Daniel were on his heels.

"What's happening?" Lord Madison asked, appearing at his office door as the men passed.

Robert didn't even slow, merely saying, "We can go up now," on his way past. He wasn't surprised when Lisa's father immediately joined the small parade.

Lisa was sitting up in bed with a small bundle caught protectively to her chest. She looked absolutely exhausted but beautiful when Robert hurried into the room with the other men. He spared barely a glance for Suzette and Christiana, who stood on either side of the bed like bookends. His eyes went directly to Lisa's face and stayed there with concern when he saw the worry on her expression.

"Are you all right?" he asked, dropping to sit on the side of the bed, and hard-pressed not to take her hands in his. He couldn't, however, without dislodging the baby she held, so he touched her hip instead, wanting the contact to reassure himself despite her nod.

"Don't you want to see your child?" she asked when he continued to just stare at her. She seemed nervous, he noted with a frown.

"Of course he does," Suzette said, bending to unwrap the blanket a bit so the baby was more easily viewed. "My lord, your daughter, Lady Sara Maitland."

"I thought it would be nice to name her after my mother," Lisa babbled quickly. "I hope you don't mind."

"No, of course not," he murmured, glancing to the small red-faced child. She was absolutely beautiful, of course. But how could she not be, with Lisa for a mother, he thought. Reaching out, Robert brushed one finger against the baby's soft cheek, smiling when one waving hand shot up and grasped it, trying to draw it to its mouth.

"The first girl in the family," Richard murmured, moving closer to get a better look.

"Hmmm. She shall be spoiled rotten by her doting uncles," Daniel promised with a grin.

"And terrorized by her male cousins," Christiana said with amusement.

"No doubt," Lisa murmured.

"Can I hold her?" Lord Madison asked, moving up between Christiana and Richard.

Lisa nodded and held the baby up and the old man took her as carefully as if she were made of spun glass.

"Little Sara," he cooed, rocking the child

slightly as he walked a little away from the bed. "You shall grow up to be as lovely as your grandmother was. I shall tell you all about what a wonderful woman she was."

Robert smiled faintly at the words and then glanced back to Lisa as the others followed the old man and baby like they were rats following the siren song of the pied piper. But seeing the concern still on Lisa's face, he frowned.

"What is it, my love?" he asked, taking her hands in his now that they were free. "Is something wrong? You are okay, aren't you?"

"Yes, of course," she assured him quickly. "I just — are you very disappointed?"

Robert frowned with confusion. "Disappointed with what?"

"Well, I know most men want a boy rather than a girl, and . . ." Her words died as he chuckled softly.

Shaking his head, he squeezed her hands gently. "My love, I am happy to have a girl. The Langleys have produced only boys for centuries. 'Tis time a little girl joined the ranks and I am proud to provide her." He bent to kiss her gently, and then sat up and added, "I guess this means the curse definitely is ended. I can hardly raise a daughter to be a woman hater."

"You are not a woman hater, my lord,"

Lisa said, smiling and relaxing now that she knew he was pleased to have a daughter.

"No I am definitely a lover of women," he agreed, leaning his forehead against hers and adding, "And you are the one who taught me how to be one."

"Oh, I do love you, Robert," she whispered, slipping her arms around his shoulders.

"And I you, Lisa," he assured her. "Thank you for my daughter. And for being patient enough to let me learn that I loved and trusted you."

Lisa responded by kissing him. He suspected she had intended it to be a light brushing of lips, but as always he couldn't resist deepening the kiss. When she pulled away with a groan, he rubbed his nose against hers and whispered, "How long until we can begin working on a little sister for Sara?"

"Well I would really rather wait a year or so to recover from this birth, my lord, before having another," she said dryly. "But we can begin practicing soon I'm sure."

"Practice is good," Robert said with a grin, and kissed her again, but this time keeping his passion in check. They had a lifetime to practice. He was looking forward to it.

The employees of Thorndike Press hope you have enjoyed this Large Print book. All our Thorndike, Wheeler, and Kennebec Large Print titles are designed for easy reading, and all our books are made to last. Other Thorndike Press Large Print books are available at your library, through selected bookstores, or directly from us.

For information about titles, please call:
  (800) 223-1244

or visit our Web site at:
  http://gale.cengage.com/thorndike

To share your comments, please write:
  Publisher
  Thorndike Press
  10 Water St., Suite 310
  Waterville, ME 04901